Monday Starts on Saturday

Monday Starts on Saturday

ARKADY and BORIS STRUGATSKY

Translated by Andrew Bromfield
Illustrations by Yevgeniy Migunov

CHICAGO
REVIEW
PRESS

Published by Chicago Review Press Incorporated
814 North Franklin Street
Chicago, IL 60610
ISBN 978-1-61373-923-5

Library of Congress Cataloging-in-Publication Data
Names: Strugatskiĭ, Arkadiĭ, 1925–1991, author. | Strugatskiĭ, Boris,
   1933–2012, author. | Bromfield, Andrew, translator. | Migunov, E.,
   illustrator.
Title: Monday starts on Saturday / Arkady and Boris Strugatsky ; translated
   by Andrew Bromfield ; illustrations by Yevgeniy Migunov.
Other titles: Ponedel'nik nachinaetsiā v subbotu. English (Bromfield)
Description: Chicago : Chicago Review Press Incorporated, 2017. |
   Description based on print version record and CIP data provided by
   publisher; resource not viewed.
Identifiers: LCCN 2017018448 (print) | LCCN 2017020595 (ebook) |
   ISBN 9781613739242 (PDF edition) | ISBN 9781613739266 (EPUB
   edition) | ISBN 9781613739259 (Kindle edition) | ISBN 9781613739235
   (pbk. edition)
Classification: LCC PG3476.S78835 (ebook) | LCC PG3476.S78835 P6613 2017
   (print) | DDC 891.73/44—dc23
LC record available at https://lccn.loc.gov/2017018448

Cover design: Sarah Olson
Cover image: iStock.com/kevinruss
Typesetting: Nord Compo

Printed in the United States of America
5 4 3 2

Contents

Foreword

by Adam Roberts

Every now and then one chances upon a novel, little known in the West, that deserves to sell more copies than cookbooks. *Monday Starts on Saturday* is one such novel.

As to why it is so little known in Anglophone territories, I'm not sure I can understand. It is probably true that the Strugatsky brothers are best known in the West for their great science fiction novel *Roadside Picnic* (1972), made into the almost unbearably powerful film *Stalker* (1979) by Russian director Andrei Tarkovsky. That film has perhaps overlaid Western perceptions of the sort of books the Strugatskys wrote. In fact the original *Roadside Picnic* novel is considerably more varied and perky than Tarkovsky's cinematic masterpiece; in fact, that's true of all the novels written by these two giants of Russian science fiction. Their output was large and varied, but they were always inventive, charming, thought-provoking, and wonderful writers. And *Monday Starts on Saturday* is not just an ingenious and gripping read but simply a delight from start to finish. Some novels provoke admiration, some a cooler and more distanced respect. This is a novel with which to fall in love.

Sasha is a young computer programmer from Soviet-era Leningrad, driving north to meet up with friends for a tour of the unspoiled nature of Karelia, the region of Russia that borders on Finland. The novel was written in the mid-1960s, when computers were brand new and the size of a small house. So Sasha's job is rather more cutting edge and high tech than is implied by the term nowadays. He picks up two hitchhikers, who persuade him to take a job with their employer, the National Institute for the Technology of Witchcraft and Thaumaturgy, or NITWiT. (There's a similar joke in the original Russian: the name Nauchno-Issledovatelskiy Institut Charodeystva i Volshebstva is abbreviated to "NIIChaVo," which sounds like *nichevo*, Russian for "It doesn't matter!" or "Don't mention it!") After initial reluctance, Sasha agrees. He goes on to have a series of brilliant, wrong-footed, and often hilarious adventures.

The Institute utilizes and researches magic, treated here as a peculiar and unpredictable branch of science. Much of the humor depends on the way the Strugatsky brothers combine a well-observed portrayal of a typical academic community with the sort of magical characters and artifacts found in myth and Russian folklore.

The brothers knew whereof they spoke. When they were writing *Monday Starts on Saturday*, Boris was still working as an academic astronomer and computer engineer (he became a full-time writer in 1966), and Arkady's linguistic training meant he had a great deal of experience working for large Soviet-era organizations. However colorful and inventive the magical elements of this story, what makes the novel so vivid is its authors' profound understanding of how these sorts of human organizations function. *Function* isn't really the right word, actually. The Institute is gloriously, colorfully, and perfectly believably *dys*functional. The scholars of the Department of Absolute Knowledge, for instance, devote themselves to the study of the infinite. Since the proper study of such a thing would require infinite time, it doesn't matter whether they work or don't work, except that working would have the side effect of increasing the entropy of the cosmos. So they do no productive work. Most universities today follow a similar, if unacknowledged, logic.

Readers sometimes draw comparison between this novel and the Harry Potter books. The parallels are certainly clear: both are comically inventive accounts of a group of people studying magic at an official establishment located in the north. I suppose it is possible J. K. Rowling was aware of the Strugatskys' tale and drew some inspiration from it, but it must be acknowledged that the *flavor* of this novel is quite different from that of the Potter series. For Rowling's characters, magic is a coherent system, complex but graspable and taken very seriously by those who study it. For the Strugatskys magic is far stranger and more random, although equally delightful. The gigantic talking pike that grants wishes, the mermaid in the tree, the cat who can remember only the beginning of stories, the magic coin that returns to your pocket when you spend it (but not if you accidentally drop it), the sofa that can translate dreams, the motorcycle that can zoom its rider into the imagined futures of science fiction—it's all superbly inventive and charming and imaginative. But it is also written in a way that deliberately confounds the reader's expectations, more P. K. Dick than J. K. Rowling. Portions of the novel remind me a little of Terry Pratchett, for the Strugatskys' many colorful wizards, vampires, and officers, pompous or officious or simply strange, read rather like Discworld characters. But, again, Pratchett is in the business of providing coherent story lines and an identifiable ethical throughline in his novels. The Strugatskys don't really see the world that way, and their novel is more morally open ended, more episodic. In short, *Monday Starts on Saturday* is profoundly, beautifully left field. It's so left field it pretty much passes out of the field altogether and reemerges, unexpectedly, *right*.

The Institute attempts to investigate magic scientifically; but it is in the nature of magic, as this novel conceives it, to resist all modes of systematization. Accordingly we might want to read the book as a satire on scientific hubris, or more specifically on science as it was practiced in the Soviet Union. One major character in the novel, Ambrosius Ambroisovich Vybegallo, is based loosely on the infamous Soviet "scientist" Trofim Lysenko, and Vybegallo's grandiose and disastrous experiments are hilariously described here. But calling the novel "a satire on science" makes it sound much drier and less palatable than it actually is. I prefer to read it as an exploration of the place of magic in humanity's myths and stories.

It's hard to deny that magic is the default mode of human storytelling. All the old myths and poems contain transcendent magical powers and transitions; medieval romances and epics are full of fantastical and miraculous things. It wasn't until the eighteenth and nineteenth centuries that a mode of storytelling arose in which nothing magical happened and verisimilitude became the watchword. We sometimes call it realism. I have nothing against realist novels, as it happens; I just think we need to acknowledge that they are the aberration in the larger context of humanity's appetite for stories.

For the moment, however, this rejection of the power of miracles extends even to our stories about the miraculous. One feature that Rowling's and Pratchett's series share with pretty much all other narratives predicated upon "magic" is that the magic *has rules*. This is because "magical thinking" has rules—psychological rules, that is. Magical thinking is that near-ubiquitous human state of mind at work in superstition, ritual, prayer, and religion, as well as obsessive-compulsive behaviors—the belief that there is a causal relationship between human actions and beliefs and cosmic eventuality. I wonder what it would be like to write a fantasy novel in which the magic has *no rules at all*. That would be bracing, and might bring out this buried truth: millions who think they love fantasy because of the magic actually love it because of the rules.

Monday Starts on Saturday isn't quite that book, but it comes closer than any other I can think of. The Strugatskys understand that, for most people, science and magic are not opposite terms, since for most people "science" is now so complex and specialized, so incomprehensible, so apt to being translated into mere technological marvelousness, that it is in effect a form of magic. Not one person in a hundred million *really* understands what goes on inside his or her iPhone. The scientific publications of the Institute might as well be alchemical gobbledygook, or indeed fairy stories, as far as the average, reasonable woman or man is concerned.

This in turn has a strange consequence, something this marvelous novel understands on a deep level. We talk about "real magic" to distinguish it from "stage magic"—which, as illusion, is of course not magic at all. It's a "false magic." But the irony here is that real magic is *the kind of magic that can't actually be done*, whereas the "unreal" stage magic is the kind that can actually be performed. This is a nice irony, but it's more than that. It's symptomatic of the way performance—whether on stage, on screen, in a book, or in song—upends the logic of actuality. This curious paradox is at the heart of this superlative novel. If magic were "real," it would insert itself into the logic of the stage, of performance and theatrical companies, or of people bickering and scheming and looking for the main chance. But if magic is unreal, not a part of the real world, then it retreats to the logic of dreams, wish-fulfillment, and psychological fantasy. And where else does this exercise in imaginative creation take us?

Monday Starts on Saturday

But what is strangest and most incomprehensible of all, is how authors can choose such subjects. I confess I find this totally incomprehensible, it is as if. . . no, no, I don't understand it at all.

—Nikolai Gogol

The Commotion over the Sofa

1

TEACHER: *Children, write down the sentence "The fish sat on the tree."*
PUPIL: *But do fish really sit on trees?*
TEACHER: *Well . . . this fish was crazy.*

—A school joke

I was nearing my destination. On both sides the green forest pressed right up against the road, giving way now and then to clearings overgrown with yellow sedge. The sun had been trying in vain to set for hours and still hung low over the horizon. As the car trundled along the crunching gravel surface of the narrow road, I steered the wheels over the large stones, and every time the empty gas cans in the trunk clanged and clattered.

Two figures emerged from the forest on the right, stepped out onto the edge of the road, and halted, looking in my direction. One of them raised his hand. I eased off the accelerator as I examined them. They looked to me like hunters, young men, perhaps a little older than me. I liked the look of their faces, and I stopped. The one who had raised his hand stuck his swarthy, hook-nosed face into the car and asked with a smile, "Could you give us a lift to Solovets?"

The other one, who had a ginger beard but no mustache, peeped over his shoulder, also smiling. They were definitely nice people.

"Get in," I said. "One in the front and the other in the back—the backseat's pretty cluttered."

"Our guardian angel!" the hook-nosed one exclaimed delightedly, slipping his gun off his shoulder and getting into the seat beside me.

The one with the beard glanced in uncertainly through the rear door and said, "Do you mind if I just . . . ?"

3

I leaned over the back of my seat and helped him clear the space that was occupied by the sleeping bag and folded tent. He sat down cautiously, setting his hunting gun between his knees. "Make sure you close the door properly," I said.

So far everything seemed normal. I drove on. The young man with the hooked nose turned to face the back and started talking boisterously about how much nicer it was to ride in a car than to walk. The young man with the beard mumbled his agreement and kept trying to slam the door shut.

"Pull in your raincoat," I advised him, looking through the rear-view mirror. "Your coat's jamming it."

Five minutes later everything was all sorted out. "About ten kilometers to Solovets, isn't it?" I asked.

"Yes," replied the hook-nosed one. "Or maybe a bit more. Only the road's not so good, of course—it's just for trucks."

"The road's just fine," I retorted. "I was told I wouldn't be able to get through at all."

"You can get down this road even in autumn."

"Here, maybe, but from Korobets on it's a dirt track."

"It's a dry summer this year—everything's dried out a bit."

"They say there's rain up around Zaton," remarked the bearded young man in the backseat.

"Who says?" asked the hook-nosed one.

"Merlin says." And for some reason they laughed.

I took out my cigarettes, lit up, and passed them around.

"The Clara Zetkin Plant," said the hook-nosed one, eyeing the pack. "Are you from Leningrad?"

"Yes."

"Doing a bit of traveling?"

"Yes," I said. "Are you local?"

"Born and bred," said the hook-nosed one.

"I'm from Murmansk," declared the bearded one.

"I suppose from Leningrad there's no difference between Solovets and Murmansk—it's all the North," said the hook-nosed one.

"No, not at all," I said politely.

"Will you be staying in Solovets?" asked the hook-nosed one.

"Certainly," I said, "Solovets is where I'm headed."

"Have you got family or friends there?"

"No," I said, "I'm just going to wait for some guys. They're hiking along the coast, and we arranged to meet up in Solovets."

I spotted a large patch of rocks ahead, braked, and said, "Hold on tight." The car started shuddering and shaking. The young man in the front hit his hooked nose against the barrel of his gun. The motor roared and stones smashed against the bottom of the car.

"Your poor car," said the hook-nosed one.

"Can't be helped," I replied.

"Not everyone would drive down a road like this in their own car."

"I would," I said.

The patch of large rocks came to an end. "So, it's not your car then," the hook-nosed one deduced.

"Where would I get a car from? It's rented."

"I see," said the hook-nosed young man, and I thought he sounded disappointed.

I was stung, so I answered, "What's the point of buying a car for driving around on asphalt? The places covered in asphalt aren't interesting, and in the interesting places there isn't any asphalt."

"Yes, of course," Hook-Nose agreed politely.

"I think it's stupid to turn a car into a fetish," I declared.

"It is," said the bearded one, "but not everybody thinks that way."

We talked a bit about cars and came to the conclusion that if you were going to buy anything, then it should be a GAZ-69 all-terrain model, but unfortunately they weren't for sale.

The hook-nosed one asked, "Where do you work?"

I answered the question.

"Tremendous!" he exclaimed. "A programmer. A programmer's just what we need. Listen, why don't you leave your institute and come to work for us?"

"And what have you got?"

"What have we got?" asked the one with the hooked nose, turning around to the back.

"An Aldan-3," said the one with the beard.

"A very versatile machine," I said. "And does it run OK?"

"Well, how can I put it . . . ?"

"I get it," I said.

"Actually, they haven't debugged it yet," said the bearded one. "If you stayed with us you could debug it."

"We could arrange the transfer in no time at all," added the hook-nosed one.

"What's your line of work?" I asked.

"Like all science," said the hook-nosed one, "our work deals with human happiness."

"I see," I said. "Something to do with space?"

"Yes, space too," said Hook-Nose.

"I'm happy enough where I am," I said.

"A capital city and good pay," the bearded passenger muttered in a low voice, but I heard him.

"That's not the point," I said. "You can't measure everything in money."

"I was only joking," said the bearded one.

"It's just his sense of humor," said the hook-nosed one. "You won't find any place more interesting than here with us, though."

"What makes you think so?"

"I'm certain of it."

"But I'm not."

The hook-nosed one laughed. "We'll come back to that later," he said. "Are you going to be in Solovets for long?"

"Two days at the most."

"Then we'll talk about it the day after tomorrow."

The bearded passenger declared, "Personally I see the finger of fate in this—there we are strolling through the forest and we run into a programmer. I think it's your destiny."

"Do you really need a programmer that badly?" I asked.

"We need a programmer desperately."

"I'll have a word with the guys," I promised. "I know a few who aren't too happy."

"We don't need just any old programmer," said the young man with the hooked nose. "Programmers are in short supply; they've gotten spoiled, but we need an unspoiled one."

"Yes, that's a bit more difficult," I said.

The hook-nosed passenger started bending down his fingers as he counted: "We need a programmer who is (a) not spoiled; (b) keen and willing; (c) who'll agree to live in a hostel . . ."

"And (d)," put in the bearded one, "for 120 rubles a month."

"Perhaps you'd like one with wings?" I asked. "Or maybe with a halo around his head? That's one in a thousand!"

"We only need one," said Hook-Nose.

"And what if there are only nine hundred?"

"We'll make do with nine-tenths."

The forest opened up in front of us. We drove across a bridge and trundled on between fields of potatoes.

"It's nine o'clock," said the hook-nosed one. "Where are you planning to spend the night?"

"I'll sleep in the car. How late do your shops open here?"

"Our shops are already closed," said the hook-nosed one.

"You can stay in the hostel," said the bearded one. "I've got a spare bed in my room."

"You can't drive up to the hostel," the hook-nosed one said pensively.

"I suppose not," said the bearded one, and for some reason he laughed.

"You could park the car by the police station," said the hook-nosed one.

"This is just plain stupid," said the bearded one. "I'm talking drivel and you're no better. How will he get into the hostel?"

"Yeah, damn it," said the hook-nosed one. "You're right, take one day off work and you clean forget all these little wrinkles."

"Maybe we could transgress him?"

"Oh, sure," said the hook-nosed one. "He's no sofa. And you're no Cristóbal Junta, and neither am I . . ."

"Don't worry about it," I said. "I'll sleep in the car. I've done it before." But I suddenly felt a terrible longing to sleep between sheets. I'd already spent four nights in a sleeping bag.

"I know," said the hook-nosed one. "Oho! The Lohuchil!"

"Right!" exclaimed the bearded one. "We'll take him to the curving seashore!"

"Honestly, I can sleep in the car," I said.

"You're going to sleep in a house," said the hook-nosed one, "in more or less clean sheets. We have to thank you somehow."

"We can't just slip you fifty kopecks," said the bearded one.

We drove into the town, with its lines of sturdy old fences and massive timber houses built out of gigantic blackened logs, with carved lintels around the narrow windows and wooden cockerels on their roofs. We passed a few dirty brick buildings with metal doors, and at the sight of them my memory threw up the half-forgotten word "emporium." The street was straight and wide and it was called Peace Prospect. Ahead of us, closer to the center of town, we could see two-story cinder block buildings with small open yards.

"The next side street on the right," said the hook-nosed one.

I signaled, braked, and turned right. The roadway here was overgrown with grass, but there was a brand-new Zaporozhets car nestling against one gate. The numbers of the houses hung above the gateways, the figures barely discernible on the rusty tin-plate signs. The alley bore the elegant name of Curving Seashore Street, but its narrow passage was squeezed in between massive old fences that had probably been erected in the days when Swedish and Norwegian pirates roamed these parts.

"Stop," said the hook-nosed passenger. I braked sharply and he banged his nose against the barrel of his gun again. "All right," he said, rubbing his nose. "You wait for me while I go and arrange everything."

"Really, there's no need," I said one last time.

"No arguments. Volodya, you keep a close eye on him."

The young man with the hooked nose got out of the car, hunched over, and wedged himself through a low wicket gate. I couldn't see the house behind the towering gray fence. The main gates were absolutely immense, like the gates of a railway depot, with rusty iron hinges that must have weighed sixteen kilograms apiece. I was astonished when I read the signs, of which there were three. On the left-hand gate there was a respectable-looking blue sign with silver letters glinting behind thick glass:

N I T W i T
The Log Hut on Chicken Legs
A historical monument of old Solovets

Hanging on the right-hand gate was a rusty tin plate with the legend 13 CURVING SEASHORE STREET, N. K. GORYNYCH, and below it was a quaint piece of plywood with a crooked, sprawling inscription in ink:

CAT NOT WORKING
Management

"What CAT's that?" I asked. "The Committee for Advanced Technology?"

The young man with the beard chuckled. "Don't you worry about a thing," he said. "This is a funny old place, but everything will be just fine."

I got out of the car and started wiping the windshield. Suddenly I heard a commotion above my head. I glanced up. Settling down on the gate, trying to make himself comfortable, was a gigantic cat— I'd never seen one like it—a black and gray tabby. When he finally settled down, he peered at me with his well-fed, indifferent yellow eyes. *"Puss-puss-puss,"* I said automatically. The cat opened its

sharp-toothed jaws with polite indifference, emitted a hoarse, throaty sound, then turned and began looking back into the yard, beyond the fence, from where I heard my hook-nosed passenger's voice say, "Vasily, my friend, I'm sorry to trouble you."

The bolt squeaked. The cat stood up and vanished into the yard without a sound. The gates swayed ponderously, creaking and groaning in a quite terrifying manner, and the left-hand gate slowly swung open to reveal the young man with the hooked nose, red faced from the effort.

"Guardian angel!" he called to me. "Please drive in!"

I got back into the car and drove slowly into the spacious yard. Standing at the back of it was a house built of thick logs, and standing in front of that was a low, handsome oak tree with an immensely thick trunk and a broad, dense crown that hid the roof of the house from view. Running from the gates to the house, skirting the oak tree, was a path of flagstones. To the right of the path was a vegetable garden, and to the left, rising up in the middle of a plot of grass, stood a wooden well with a windlass, its logs all black with age and covered with moss.

I parked the car off to the side, turned off the engine, and climbed out. Bearded Volodya also climbed out, set his gun against the side of the car, and began settling his rucksack on his shoulders. "So now you're home," he said.

The young man with the hooked nose closed the gates with a creak and a groan. I looked around, feeling rather awkward and not knowing what to do.

"And here's the lady of the house!" Volodya exclaimed. "Good health to you, Naina Kievna!"

My hostess must have been over a hundred years old. She walked slowly toward us, leaning on a knotty stick, shuffling along on feet clad in felt boots with rubber galoshes. Her face was dark brown; from the center of a solid mass of wrinkles her nose protruded out and down, as crooked and sharp as a Turkish dagger, and her eyes were pale and dull, as if they were covered by cataracts.

"Welcome, welcome, little grandson," she said in a surprisingly resonant bass. "So he's going to be the new programmer? Welcome, dear guest, welcome indeed!" I bowed, realizing that I should keep quiet. Over the fluffy black shawl knotted under her chin, the old granny's head was covered by a cheerful nylon scarf with brightly colored pictures of the Atomium and an inscription in several languages: BRUSSELS INTERNATIONAL EXHIBITION. Her chin and upper lip had a sparse covering of coarse, gray stubble. She was wearing a sleeveless padded vest and a black woollen dress.

"It's like this, Naina Kievna!" said the young man with the hooked nose, brushing the rust off his hands as he walked toward her. "We have to put our new colleague up for two nights. Allow me to introduce . . . *mmm* . . ."

"Don't bother," said the old woman, looking me over closely. "I can see for myself." And she ran through the answers to the standard employment questionnaire: "Alexander Ivanovich Privalov, born 1938, male, Russian, member of the Leninist Komsomol, none, no, never joined, never has, none—but you, my treasure, shall travel a distant road and do business in a public place, and you should beware, my precious, of a wicked man with red hair, come, cross my palm with gold, my darling one . . ."

"*Hm-hmm!*" the hook-nosed young man said loudly, and the old woman stopped short. An awkward silence set in.

"You can call me Sasha," I said, forcing out the phrase I'd prepared in advance.

"And where am I going to put him?" the old granny inquired.

"In the storeroom, of course," said the hook-nosed young man, slightly annoyed.

"And who's going to take responsibility?"

"Naina Kievna!" the hook-nosed young man bellowed in the thunderous tones of a provincial tragedian, grabbing the old woman by the arm and dragging her toward the house. I could hear them arguing: "But we agreed!" "But what if he pinches something?" "Keep your voice down! He's a programmer, don't you understand? A Komsomol member! A scientist!" "And what if he sucks on his teeth?"

I turned in embarrassment toward Volodya. Volodya was giggling.

"I feel kind of awkward about this," I said.

"Don't worry about it—everything will be just fine."

He was about to say something else, but then the old granny roared out, "And what about the sofa, the sofa!"

I shuddered and said, "You know, I think I'd better go . . ."

"Quite out of the question!" Volodya said firmly. "We'll sort everything out. It's just that the old woman's looking for a bribe, but Roman and I don't have any cash with us."

"I'll pay," I said. By this time I really wanted to leave; I can't stand these so-called domestic altercations.

Volodya shook his head. "Certainly not. Here he comes now. Everything's OK."

Hook-nosed Roman came up to us, took me by the arm, and said, "Right, that's all settled. Let's go."

"Listen, I feel kind of awkward," I said. "After all, she's not obliged—"

But we were already walking toward the house. "Yes she is, yes she is," Roman intoned.

Rounding the oak tree, we came to the back porch. Roman pushed open the leatherette-upholstered door, and we found ourselves in a hallway that was spacious and clean but poorly lit. The old woman was waiting for us, with her hands clasped over her belly and her lips pursed. At the sight of us she boomed out vindictively, "I demand a receipt this instant! All right and proper: received, such-and-such and such-and-such from so-and-so, who has leased out the aforementioned to the undersigned . . ."

Roman let out a low howl, and we went through into the lodging assigned to me. It was a cold room with a single window covered by a short chintz curtain. Roman said in a tense voice, "Please, make yourself at home."

The old woman immediately inquired malevolently from the hallway, "Are you sure as the gentleman doesn't suck on his teeth?"

Without turning around, Roman snapped, "No, he doesn't! I told you—the gentleman doesn't have any teeth."

"Then let's go and write out the receipt."

Roman raised his eyebrows, rolled his eyes upward, bared his teeth, and shook his head violently, but he went out anyway. I looked around. There wasn't much furniture in the room. Standing by the window was a solid table covered with a threadbare gray tablecloth with a fringe, and in front of the table was a rickety stool. There was a spacious sofa set against a bare log wall, and on the opposite wall, which was covered with an assortment of wallpapers, was a set of hooks with various pieces of junk hanging on them (padded jackets, mangy fur coats, tattered cloth caps, and fur hats with earflaps). Jutting out into one corner of the room was a large Russian brick oven, gleaming with fresh whitewash, and hanging in the opposite corner was a large, cloudy mirror in a frame with peeling varnish. The floor had been scraped clean and covered with striped mats.

I could hear two voices muttering on the other side of the wall, the old woman booming away on a single bass note and Roman's voice repeatedly rising and falling. "One tablecloth, inventory number 245 . . ."

"Why not put in all the floorboards while you're at it!"

"One dining table . . ."

"Are you going to put the oven in too?"

"Rules are rules. One sofa . . ."

I went over to the window and pulled back the curtain. The window looked out at the oak tree, and I couldn't see anything else. I started looking at the tree. It was obviously very ancient. Its bark was gray and somehow lifeless looking, and the monstrous roots that had crept up out of the ground were covered with red and white lichen.

"Why not put in the oak tree as well?" said Roman on the other side of the wall.

There was a plump, well-thumbed book lying on the windowsill. I leafed through it idly, then walked away from the window and sat down on the sofa. And immediately I felt sleepy. I thought of how I'd driven for fourteen hours that day but probably needn't have been in such a hurry, how my back ached and everything was getting muddled up in my head and when it really came down to it I couldn't give a damn about this tedious old woman, and how I wished it would all be over soon so I could lie down and go to sleep . . .

"Right, then," said Roman, appearing in the doorway. "The formalities are concluded." He brandished one hand in the air, its splayed fingers stained with ink. "Our little fingers are exhausted; we've been writing and writing . . . You go to bed. We're leaving. You just relax and go to bed. What are you doing tomorrow?"

"Waiting," I replied listlessly.

"Where?"

"Here. And outside the post office."

"You probably won't be leaving tomorrow, then?"

"Probably not. Most likely the day after."

"Then we shall meet again. Our love is yet to come." He smiled, waved, and went out. I thought sluggishly that I ought to have seen him off and said good-bye to Volodya, then I lay down. That very moment the old woman came in. I got up. The old woman stared at me intently for a while.

"I fear, dear guest, as you might start a-sucking on your teeth," she said anxiously.

"I'm not going to suck on my teeth," I said wearily. "I'm going to go to sleep."

"Lie down, then, and sleep . . . Pay your money and go to sleep . . ."

I reached into my back pocket for my wallet. "How much?"

The old woman raised her eyes to the ceiling. "Let's say a ruble for the room . . . Fifty kopecks for the bedsheets—they're mine, not state property. For two nights that makes three rubles . . . And whatever you want to throw in out of the kindness of your heart—for the inconvenience, that is—that's up to you . . ."

I held out a five-ruble note. "For a start it's one ruble out of the kindness of my heart," I said. "We'll see how things go."

The old woman grabbed the money avidly and left the room, muttering something about change. She was gone for quite a long time, and I was on the point of giving up hope of any change or any sheets when she came back and laid out a handful of dirty coppers on the table.

"There's your change, dear guest," she said. "One ruble exactly—you don't need to count it."

"I'm not going to count it," I said. "What about the sheets?"

"I'll make up the bed straightaway. You go out and have a stroll in the yard, and I'll make up the bed."

I went out, tugging my cigarettes out of my pocket on the way. The sun had finally set and the white night had begun. Somewhere dogs were barking. I sat on a little bench sunk into the ground under the oak, lit up, and began staring at the pale, starless sky. The cat appeared soundlessly out of nowhere, glanced at me with his fluorescent eyes, scrambled rapidly up the oak, and disappeared into the dark foliage. I immediately forgot about him, and I was startled when he began rustling about above me and debris came showering down onto my head. "Why you . . ." I said, and started brushing myself off. I felt exceedingly sleepy. The old woman came out of the house without noticing me and wandered across to the well. I took this to mean that the bed was ready and went back into the room.

The spiteful old woman had made up my bed on the floor. Oh no, I thought, closed the door on the latch, heaved the bedding up onto the sofa, and started getting undressed. A dim twilight came in at the window; the cat rustled about noisily in the oak tree. I started shaking my head around to get the detritus out of my hair. It was strange detritus, unexpected: large, dry fish scales. That's going to feel prickly in the night, I thought, then collapsed onto the pillow and instantly fell asleep.

2

The deserted house has been transformed into the lair of foxes and raccoon dogs, and therefore strange werewolves and phantoms may appear here.

—Ueda Akinari

I woke up in the middle of the night, because someone was talking in the room. There were two voices, speaking in a barely audible whisper. The voices were very similar, but one was a little muffled and hoarse, while the other betrayed extreme irritation.

"Don't wheeze," whispered the irritated voice. "Can you manage that, not wheezing?"

"Yes," replied the muffled voice, and started clearing its throat.

"Keep it down," hissed the irritated voice.

"My throat tickles," explained the muffled voice. "It's a smoker's cough." It started clearing its throat again.

"You get out of here," said the irritated voice.

"It doesn't matter, he's asleep."

"Who is he? Where did he appear from?"

"How should I know?"

"It's annoying . . . It's such incredibly bad luck."

The neighbors can't sleep again, I thought, only half awake. I imagined I was at home. I shared a flat with two brothers, physicists, and they just loved working at night. Round about two o'clock in the morning they ran out of cigarettes, then they crept into my room and started groping around, clattering the furniture around and squabbling with each other.

I grabbed the pillow and flung it into space. Something tumbled onto the floor with an almighty racket and everything went quiet.

18

"Give back the pillow," I said, "and get out. The cigarettes are on the table."

The sound of my own voice finally woke me completely. I sat up. The dogs were barking despondently and the old woman was snoring menacingly on the other side of the wall. I finally remembered where I was. There was no one else in the room. In the dim twilight I made out my pillow lying on the floor, with the junk that had fallen off the hooks. The old granny will have my guts for garters, I thought, and leaped out of bed. The floor felt cold and I stepped onto the mats. The old woman stopped snoring. I froze. The floorboards creaked; something crackled and rustled in the corners. The old woman gave a deafening whistle and started snoring again. I picked up the pillow and tossed it onto the sofa. The old clothes smelled of dogs. The set of hooks had slipped off one of its nails and was hanging askew. I set it straight and began picking up the junk. The moment I hung up the last shapeless old woman's coat, the hooks came loose again and went scraping down the wallpaper to end up hanging on one nail. The old granny stopped snoring and I broke into a cold sweat. Somewhere nearby a cock started screeching. You're for the soup, I thought vindictively. The old woman next door began tossing and turning, her bedsprings creaking and clanking. I waited, poised on one leg. Outside someone said softly, "It's time to go to sleep, we've sat up late today." It was a young voice, a woman's.

"I suppose it is," a different voice responded. I heard a protracted yawn.

"Aren't you going to take another dip today?"

"It's a bit chilly. Let's go bye-byes."

Everything went quiet. The old granny began snarling and muttering, and I walked carefully back to the sofa. I could get up early in the morning and fix everything properly . . .

I lay down on my right side, pulled the blanket up over my ear, closed my eyes, and suddenly realized I didn't feel sleepy at all—I felt hungry. Oh, hell, I thought. Urgent measures had to be taken, and I took them.

Let's take, for instance, a system of two integral equations, such as stellar statistics equations; both unknown functions are under the integral. Naturally, the only way to determine them is numerically—say, on a BESM. I remembered our BESM, the cream-colored control panel . . .

Zhenya puts down a bundle wrapped in newspaper on the panel and unwraps it without hurrying. "What have you got?"

"I've got cheese and sausage." Lightly smoked Polish sausage, in round slices.

"You ought to get married! I've got rissoles, with garlic, homemade. And a pickle." No, two pickles . . . Four rissoles and, to balance the figures, four crunchy pickles. And four pieces of bread and butter . . .

I threw off the blanket and sat up. Maybe there was something left in the car? No, I'd eaten everything. There was nothing left but the cookbook for Valka's mother, who lived in Lezhnev. How did it go? . . . Piquant sauce. Half a glass of vinegar, two onions . . . and pepper. Serve with meat dishes . . . I can just picture it now—with small beefsteaks. The words surfaced from somewhere in the depths of my subconscious: *He was served the dishes usual at inns, namely: sour cabbage soup, brains with peas, pickles* . . . I gulped. *And the ubiquitous sweet layered cake* . . . I've got to distract myself, I thought, and picked up the book from the windowsill.

It was Alexei Tolstoy's *Bleak Morning*. I opened it at random. "Makhno, having broken the key off the sardine can, took a mother-of-pearl knife with fifty blades out of his pocket and carried on working with that, opening cans of pineapple"—this is not good, I thought—"French pâté, and lobster, which filled the room with a pungent smell."

I carefully replaced the book and sat down on the stool at the table. There was suddenly a delicious, pungent smell in the room—it must have been the smell of lobsters. I began wondering why I had never even tried lobster. Or oysters, for instance. In Dickens everybody eats oysters, working away with their folding knives, carving thick slices of bread and spreading them with butter . . . I began nervously smoothing out the tablecloth. I could see the old stains on it that hadn't washed out. A lot of tasty food had been eaten on that tablecloth. Lobsters and brains with peas had been eaten on it. Small beefsteaks with piquant sauce had been eaten on it. Large and medium-sized beefsteaks too. People had stuffed themselves to bursting and sucked on their teeth in satisfaction . . . I had nothing to stuff myself with, but I started sucking my teeth.

My sucking must have sounded loud and hungry, because the old woman's bed next door began creaking, she started muttering angrily and clattering about, and suddenly she came into my room. She was wearing a long gray shirt and carrying a plate, and the room was instantly filled with a smell of food that was real, not imaginary. The old woman was smiling.

She set the plate down right in front of me and boomed out in honeyed tones, "Eat, dear guest, Alexander Ivanovich. Eat what God has given, what he has sent with me."

"Oh no, Naina Kievna," I mumbled, "you shouldn't have gone to so much trouble."

But out of nowhere a fork with an ivory handle had already appeared in my hand and I began eating, with the old granny standing beside me, nodding and intoning, "Eat, dear guest, eat to your heart's content."

I ate it all. It was hot potatoes with clarified butter . . .

"Naina Kievna," I said fervently, "I'd have starved to death without you."

"Had enough?" asked Naina Kievna, suddenly sounding rather unfriendly.

"That was magnificent. Thank you very, very much! You have no idea—"

"I don't need any of your ideas," she interrupted, seriously annoyed. "I asked if you'd had enough. Give me your plate here . . . I said, give me your plate!"

"By . . . by all means," I said.

"'By all means, by all means' . . . And that's all I get for feeding you . . ."

"I can pay," I said, beginning to get angry.

"'Pay, pay' . . ." She went to the door. "And what if it's something as can't be paid for? And why did you have to go and lie?"

"What do you mean, lie?"

"Just that, lie! You said you wouldn't go sucking on your teeth." She stopped speaking and went out.

What's wrong with her? I thought. A strange sort of old granny . . . Maybe she'd noticed the clothes hooks? I could hear the springs creaking as she squirmed about on her bed, muttering irritably. Then she started singing in a low voice, a strange, barbaric kind of song: "Oh, I'll go strolling and I'll go rolling, when I've eaten young Ivan's tasty flesh." Suddenly I felt a cold draft from the window. I shivered and stood up to go back to the sofa—then it struck me that I'd locked the door before I went to sleep. Bewildered, I walked over to the door and reached out a hand to check the latch, but the moment my fingers touched the cold metal, everything went hazy and I found myself lying on the sofa with my face buried in the pillow and my fingers groping at a cold log in the wall.

I lay there for a while in a half swoon before I realized that the old woman was snoring somewhere close at hand and there was someone talking in the room. A quiet voice was intoning solemnly and didactically, "The elephant is the largest of all animals that live on land. On the front of his face he has a large lump of flesh that is called a trunk, it being hollow and elongated like a pipe. He can extend it and flex it in all sorts of ways and use it instead of a hand . . ."

Chilled but curious, I cautiously turned over onto my right side. The room was as empty as ever. The voice continued even more didactically: "Consumed in moderate amounts, wine is highly beneficial for the stomach, but when too much is drunk, it produces vapors that degrade man to the level of mindless cattle. You have sometimes seen drunks and still remember the just revulsion that you felt for them . . ."

I jerked upright on the sofa and lowered my feet to the floor. The voice stopped. I got the feeling it had been speaking on the far side of the wall. Everything in the room was back the way it had been; I was surprised to see that even the set of hooks was hanging as it ought to be. And to my amazement, I felt very hungry again.

"Ex vitro tincture of antimony," the voice suddenly declared. I shuddered. "*Magifterium antimon angeli salae. Bafilii oleum vitri antimonii alexiterium antimoniale!*" I clearly heard giggling. "What a load of gibberish!" the voice said, and continued in a tone of lament, "Soon these eyes, as yet unopened, shall no longer behold the sun, but allow them not to close without the viscero-beatific message of my forgiveness and bliss . . . These are *The Spirit or Ethical Thoughts of the Glorious Jung, Abstracted from His Nocturnal Meditations.* On sale in Saint Petersburg and Riga in Sveshnikov's bookshops for two rubles in pasteboard." Someone sobbed. "More raving nonsense," the voice said, then declaimed with feeling:

> *All beauty, rank and affluence,*
> *All life's delights and opulence*
> *E'er slacken, fade, decline, depart.*
> *False happiness rots swift away,*
> *Morbidity devours the heart,*
> *Bright glory yields to dark decay.*

I had realized now where the voices were. The sound was coming from the corner where the cloudy mirror hung.

"And now," said the voice, "next: 'Everything is a single Self; this Self is the universal Self. The identification with ignorance that results from the eclipse of the light of the Self disappears with the development of spirituality.'"

"And where's that gibberish from?" I asked. I wasn't expecting an answer. I was certain I was asleep.

"Aphorisms from the Upanishads," the voice promptly replied.

"And what are the Upanishads?" I asked, no longer certain that I was asleep.

"I don't know," said the voice.

I got up and tiptoed over to the mirror. I couldn't see my reflection. The cloudy glass reflected the curtain, the corner of the brick oven, and all sorts of other things. But I wasn't there.

"What's the matter?" asked the voice. "Do you have questions?"

"Who's that speaking?" I asked, glancing behind the mirror. Behind the mirror there was a lot of dust and dead spiders. I pressed on my left eye with my forefinger. That was an ancient method for recognizing hallucinations that I'd read about in V. V. Bitner's fascinating book *What to Believe and What Not to Believe*. All you have to do is press on your eyeball with your finger, and all the real objects—as distinct from the hallucinations—go fuzzy. The mirror went fuzzy, and my reflection appeared in it—a drowsy, anxious image. I could feel a draft on my feet. Curling up my toes, I went across to the window and looked out. There was no one outside, and there was no oak tree either. I rubbed my eyes and took another look. In front of me I could clearly see the mossy well with its windlass, the gates, and my car standing beside them. I am asleep, I thought in relief. My gaze fell on the windowsill and the tattered book. In my previous dream it had been the third volume of Alexei Tolstoy's *Road to Calvary*. Now I read on the cover "P. I. Karpov. *The Creative Work of the Mentally Ill and Its Influence on the Development of Science, Art, and Technology*." Shuddering, with my teeth chattering, I leafed through the book, looking at the colored inserts. Then I read poem number 2:

> *Soaring through the clouds on high,*
> *Black wings fluttering apace,*
> *A solitary of the sky,*
> *See the fleeting sparrow race.*
> *Flying by the moon's pale glow*
> *In the deepest dead of night,*
> *His spirit unoppressed by fright,*
> *He views the world spread out below.*
> *Haughty, frenzied bird of prey,*
> *He revels in his shady flight,*
> *His eyes ablaze, as bright as day.*

The floor suddenly tilted beneath my feet. There was a long, earsplitting creak and then, like the rumbling of a distant earthquake, I heard a thunderous *"Cluuuck, cluuck . . ."* The hut started pitching to and fro like a boat on choppy water. The yard outside the window shifted sideways and a gigantic chicken leg emerged from below the window and thrust its talons into the earth, making deep furrows in the grass before disappearing from sight again. The floor keeled over sharply, and feeling myself falling, I grabbed hold of something soft with both hands, banged my side and my head against something hard and tumbled off the sofa. I lay there on the mats, clutching the pillow that had fallen with me. It was quite light in the room. Outside the window someone cleared his throat thoroughly.

"Very well, then . . ." said a well-trained male voice. "In a kingdom long ago, in a certain state I know, there lived a king called . . . *mmmeh* . . . well, it doesn't really matter that much. Let us say . . . *mmmeh* . . . Polyeuctus . . . And he had three princely sons. The first . . . *mmmeh* . . . The third prince was a fool, but what was the first?"

Crouching down like a soldier under fire, I crept over to the window and peeped out. The oak was back in its proper place. Standing on his hind paws with his back to the tree, lost in thought, was the cat Vasily. He had a water lily clenched between his teeth. The cat looked down at his feet and drawled: *"Mmmeh-eh . . ."* Then he shook his head hard, put his front paws behind his back, and, stooping slightly like the university professor Dubino-Knyazhitsky giving a lecture, strode smoothly away from the oak tree.

"All right . . ." the cat muttered to himself. "Once upon a time there were a king and a queen. This king and this queen had one son . . . *Mmmeh*. A fool, of course . . ."

The cat spat out the flower in annoyance, pulled a wry face, and rubbed his forehead.

"This is getting desperate," he said. "I do remember something, though! 'Ha-ha-ha! Such tasty viands there'll be to savor:

the steed for dinner, the youth for supper . . .' Now where would
that be from? Anyway, Ivan—he's a fool, you know—answers,
'The more fool you, vile monster, to devour the snow-white
swan before she's caught!' And then, of course, there's the red-
hot arrow, and off with all three heads. Ivan takes out the three
hearts and brings them home to Mother, the cretin . . . What a
charming present!" The cat gave a sardonic laugh, then heaved
a sigh and declared, "It's a sickness, that's what it is—arteriosclerotic dementia."

He sighed again, turned back toward the oak, and started to sing:
"Quack-quack my little children! Quack-quack, my little darlings!
I . . . *mmmeh* . . . I have fattened you on my tears . . . fed you, that
is . . ." he sighed for a third time and carried on walking for a while
without speaking. Drawing level with the oak tree, he suddenly bellowed tunelessly, "I have left you the daintiest morsel!" Suddenly he
was holding an immense psaltery in his paws—I didn't see where he
got it from. He struck it despairingly with one paw and, plucking
at the strings with his claws, started bellowing even louder, as if he
were trying to drown out the music:

> *Dass im Tannwald finster ist,*
> *Das macht das Holz,*
> *Das . . . mmmeh . . . mein Schatz . . . or Katz?*

He stopped bellowing and strode about for while, banging on the strings without speaking. Then he started singing in a low, uncertain voice:

Of my stay in that wee garden
I'll tell true, by your sweet pardon.
This is how they dig and hoe
To make the crimson poppies grow . . .

He went back to the oak tree, leaned the psaltery against it, and scratched himself behind one ear with his back paw.

"All work, work, work," he said. "Nothing but work!"

He put his front paws behind him again and walked away from the oak tree to the left, muttering, "I have heard, oh great and mighty king, that once in the glorious city of Baghdad there dwelt a tailor, by the name of . . ." He went down on all fours, arched his back and hissed viciously. "Oh, how I loathe all these repulsive names! Abu . . . Ali . . . Some Ibn somebody or other . . . All right, then, let's call him Polyeuctus. Polyeuctus Ibn . . . *mmmeh* . . . Polyeuctovich . . . But anyway, I don't remember what happened to the tailor. To hell with him, let's start a different one . . ."

I lay there with my belly on the windowsill, fascinated to watch the unfortunate Vasily wandering around the oak tree, first to the left and then to the right, muttering, clearing his throat, whining, groaning, dropping down on all fours when the strain was too much for him—in short, suffering quite inexpressibly. The extent of his knowledge was vast. He didn't know a single story or song more than halfway through, but there were Russian, Ukrainian, Western Slavic, German, and even, I think, Japanese, Chinese, and African fairy tales, legends, fables, ballads, songs, romances, jingles, and rhymes. His inability to remember drove him into a fury; several times he threw himself at the trunk of the oak tree and shredded the bark with his claws, hissing and spitting, and when he did this his eyes blazed with the fires of hell and his tail, fluffed out as thick as a log, stood vertically erect or twitched convulsively or lashed at his sides. But the only song he sang right through was the Russian rhyme about the little bird, "Chizhik-Pyzhik," and the only story he told coherently was *The House That Jack Built* in Marshak's Russian translation, and even then with several abridgements. Gradually—evidently as he became exhausted—the feline accent of his speech became more and more distinct. "And in the field, the *fiaowld*," he sang, "the *pli-aow* runs of itself, and *mmmeh* . . . *mmmeow*, and following that *pli-aow* . . . *mmeow* . . . Our Lord himself does walk . . . or stalk?"

Eventually, when he was totally exhausted, he sat down on his tail and stayed there for a while, hanging his head. Then he gave a final quiet, desolate meow, picked up the psaltery under one front leg, and hobbled off slowly on the other three across the dewy grass.

As I got down off the windowsill I dropped the book. I remembered quite clearly that last time it had been *The Creative Work of the Mentally Ill*, and I was certain that was the book that had fallen on the floor. But what I picked up and put on the windowsill was *Crime Detection* by A. Svensson and O. Wendel. I opened it, feeling rather stupid, ran my eye over several paragraphs at random, and instantly got a strange feeling that there was a hanged man dangling from the oak tree. I looked up warily. Hanging from the lowest branch of the oak tree was a wet, silver-green shark's tail. The tail was swaying heavily in the gusty morning breeze.

I started back and banged my head against something hard. A telephone began ringing loudly. I looked around. I was lying sprawled diagonally across the sofa, the blanket had slipped off me onto the floor, and the morning sun was shining through the leaves of the oak tree and in at the window.

3

It occurred to me that instead of the usual interview with the devil or a magician, an ingenious use of scientific patter might with advantage be substituted.

—H. G. Wells

The telephone was ringing. I rubbed my eyes and looked out the window (the oak tree was there, all right), looked at the set of hooks (it was in the right place, too). The telephone kept ringing. There was no sound from the old woman's room on the other side of the wall. I hopped down onto the floor, opened the door (the latch had been on), and went out into the hallway. The telephone was still ringing. It was standing on a little shelf above a large water tub—a very modern piece of equipment in white plastic, like the ones I'd seen in movies and in our director's office. I picked up the receiver.

"Hello . . ."

"Who's that?" asked a piercing woman's voice.

"Who do you want?"

"Is that Lohuchil?"

"What?"

"I said, is that the Log Hut on Chicken Legs or not? Who is this?"

"Yes," I said, "this is the hut. Who do you want?"

"Oh, damnation," said the woman's voice. "I have a telephonogram for you."

"All right."

"Write it down."

"Just a moment," I said. "I'll get a pencil and paper."

"Oh, damnation," the woman's voice repeated.

I came back with a notepad and a pencil. "I'm listening."

"Telephonogram number 206," said the woman's voice. 'To citizeness Naina Kievna Gorynych . . .'"

"Not so fast . . . Kievna Gorynych . . . OK, what's next?"

"'You are hereby . . . invited to attend . . . today the twenty-seventh . . . of July . . . at midnight . . . for the annual . . . republican rally . . .' Have you got that?"

"Yes, I have."

"'The first meeting . . . will take place . . . on Bald Mountain. The dress code is formal . . . Mechanical transport is available . . . at your own expense. Signed . . . Head of Chancellery . . . C. M. Viy.'"

"Who?"

"Viy! C. M. Viy."

"I don't understand."

"Viy! Chronos Monadovich Viy! You mean you don't know the head of the chancellery?"

"No, I don't," I said. "Spell it out for me."

"Damnation! All right, I'll spell it out: Vampire, Incubus, Yeti. Have you got that?"

"I think so," I said. "I've got 'Viy.'"

"Who?"

"Viy."

"Have you got adenoids or something? I don't understand!"

"Vile, Inconceivable, Yucky!"

"Right. Read back the telephonogram."

I read it back.

"Correct. Transmitted by Onuchkina. Who received it?"

"Privalov."

"Cheers, Privalov! Been in harness long?"

"Horses wear harness," I said angrily. "I do a job."

"You get on with your job then. See you at the rally."

The phone started beeping. I hung up and went back into the room. It was a cool morning. I rushed through my exercises and got dressed. It seemed to me that something extremely curious was going on. The telephonogram was somehow associated in my mind with the events of the night, although I didn't have a clue exactly how. But I was beginning to get a few ideas, and my imagination had been stimulated.

There was nothing in what I had witnessed that was entirely unfamiliar to me. I'd read something about similar cases somewhere, and now I remembered that the behavior of people who found themselves in similar circumstances had always seemed to me extremely exasperating and quite absurd. Instead of taking full advantage of the attractive prospects that their good fortune presented to them, they took fright and tried to get back to ordinary, everyday reality. There was even one hero who adjured his readers to keep as far away as possible from the veil that divides our world from the unknown, threatening them with mental and physical impairment. I still did not know how events would unfold, but I was already prepared to take the plunge enthusiastically.

As I wandered around the room in search of a scoop or a mug, I continued with my deliberations. Those timid people, I thought, were like certain experimental scientists, very tenacious and very industrious but absolutely devoid of all imagination and therefore ultracautious. Having produced a nontrivial result, they shy away from it, hastily attempting to explain it away by experimental contamination and effectively rejecting the new because they have grown too accustomed to the old that is so comfortably expounded in authoritative orthodox theory . . . I was already mulling over several experiments with the whimsical book (it was still lying there on the windowsill, but now it was Aldridge's *The Last Exile*), with the talking mirror, and with sucking my teeth. I had several questions to ask the cat Vasily, and the mermaid who lived in the oak tree was an especially interesting prospect. Although there were moments when I thought I must have dreamed her after all. I've got nothing against mermaids, I just can't imagine how they can clamber around in trees . . . but then, what about those scales?

I found a dipper on the tub under the telephone, but there was no water in the tub, so I set out for the well. The sun had already risen quite high. There were cars droning along somewhere in the distance, I could hear a militiaman's whistle, and a helicopter drifted across the sky with a sedate rumbling. Walking up to the well, I was delighted to discover a battered tin bucket on the chain, and I began winding out the rope with the windlass. The bucket sank down into the black depths, clattering against the sides of the well shaft. There was a splash and the chain went taut.

As I turned the windlass I looked at my Moskvich. The car had a tired, dusty look; the windshield was plastered with midges that had been flattened against it. I'll have to put some water in the radiator, I thought. And all those other jobs . . .

The bucket seemed very heavy. When I stood it on the wall of the wooden well, a huge pike stuck its green, mossy-looking head up out of the water. I jumped back.

"Are you going to drag me off to the market again?" the pike asked in a strong northern accent. I was too flabbergasted to say anything. "Why can't you just leave me alone, you pest? How many more times? I'm just getting settled, just snuggling down for a bit of a rest and a doze—and out she pulls me! I'm not a fit young thing any longer; I must be older than you are . . . and my gills are giving me trouble too . . ."

It was strange to watch the way she spoke, exactly like a pike in the puppet theater—the way the opening and closing of her sharp-toothed jaws coincided with the sounds she pronounced was very disconcerting. She pronounced that final phrase with her jaws clamped shut.

"And the air is bad for me," she went on. "What are you going to do if I die? It's all because of your stupid, peasant meanness . . . always saving, but you have no idea what you're saving up for . . . Got your fingers badly burned at the last reform, didn't you. Oh yes! And what about those old hundred-ruble notes you used to paper the inside of your trunks! And the Kerensky rubles! You used the Kerensky notes to light the oven . . ."

"Well, you see . . ." I said, recovering my wits slightly.

"Ooh, who's that?" the pike said in fright.

"I . . . I'm here by accident, really . . . I was just going to wash up a little."

"Wash up! And I thought it was the old woman again. I can't see too well; I'm old. They tell me the index of refraction in air is quite different. I ordered myself some air goggles once, but then I lost them and I can't find them again . . . But who are you, then?"

"A tourist," I said tersely.

"Ah, a tourist . . . And I thought it was the old granny again. The things she does to me, you wouldn't believe! If she catches me she drags me off to the market and sells me. For chowder, so she says. So what else can I do? Naturally, I tell the buyer: It's like this, you let me go back to my dear little children—only what little children could I have at my age? Those that are still alive are all grandparents by now. You let me go, I say, and I'll grant you a wish: you just have to say, 'By the pike's true command, at my urgent demand.' And they let me go. Some out of fear, some out of kindness, and some out of sheer greed . . . So there I go, swimming back along the river, swimming along, and it's cold and I've got rheumatism, until finally I get back into the well, and there's the old woman again with her bucket . . ."

The pike ducked under the water, gurgled a bit, releasing a few bubbles, and stuck her head out again. "So what are you going to ask for, my fine soldier boy? Only keep it simple—folks keep asking for televisions and transistor radios and what have you . . . One fellow went absolutely crazy: 'Fulfill my annual quota at the sawmill,' he says. But I can't go sawing wood at my age."

"Aha," I said. "But you could manage a television, then?"

"No," the pike confessed honestly. "I can't manage a television. And I can't do that . . . music center thing with a record player either. Keep it nice and simple. Something like a nice pair of seven-league boots, or a cap of darkness . . . Eh?"

My hopes of getting out of changing the oil in the Moskvich wilted and died. "Don't worry about it," I said. "There isn't anything I need, really. I'll just let you go."

"Good," said the pike calmly. "I like people like that. There was one not all that long ago . . . He bought me at the market, so I promised him a king's daughter. There I was, swimming along the river, feeling so ashamed I didn't know what to do with myself. I couldn't see where I was going and I swam into these nets. So they pull me out and I'm thinking, now I'll have to start lying all over again. But what does the man do? He grabs me around the jaws so I can't open my mouth. That's it, I thought, they'll boil me for soup. But no. He clips something on my fin and tosses me back in the river. Look!" The pike rose up out of the bucket and held out a fin with a metal tag clipped around its base. On the tag it said, "This specimen released in the Solova

River in 1854. Return to His Imperial Majesty's Academy of Sciences, Saint Petersburg."

"Don't tell the old woman about it," the pike warned me. "She'll rip my fin off to get it. She's so mean and greedy."

What could I ask her for? I thought frantically. "How do you work your miracles?"

"What miracles are those?"

"You know . . . granting wishes . . ."

"Oh, that! How do I do it? I was trained when I was little, so I just do it. How should I know how I do it? The Golden Fish used to do it even better, but she still died all the same. You can't cheat fate." I thought I heard the pike sigh.

"From old age?" I asked.

"What d'you mean, old age? She was still young and full of life . . . They got her with a depth charge, my soldier boy. Turned her belly up, and sank some submarine that happened to be there as well. She'd have bought them off, but they didn't bother to ask—the moment they saw her, they just dropped the bomb . . . That's the way it goes sometimes." She paused for a moment. "So, are you letting me go or not? It's feeling a bit close; there's going to be a storm."

"Of course, of course," I said with a start. "Should I throw you in, or use the bucket?"

"Throw me in, my fine boy, throw me in."

I carefully lowered my hands into the bucket and lifted out the pike—she weighed at least eight kilograms. She muttered, "Right, then, and if you should happen to fancy a magic tablecloth or a flying carpet, you know where I am . . . I'll see you all right."

"Good-bye," I said, and released my grip. There was a loud splash.

I stood there for a while, gazing at the green stains on my hands. I felt rather strange. Every now and again I was visited, like a gust of wind, by the realization that I was sitting on the sofa in the room, but I only had to shake my head and there I was back beside the well. Then it passed. I washed up in the fine icy water, filled the car radiator, and had a shave. The old woman still hadn't put in an appearance. I was hungry, and I had to go into town to the post office, where the guys might already be waiting for me. I locked the car and went out through the gate.

I walked slowly along Curving Seashore Street, with my hands stuck in the pockets of my gray bomber jacket from the GDR, looking down at my feet. The old woman's copper coins jangled in the back pocket of my favorite jeans, crisscrossed all over with zippers. I thought things over. The thick pamphlets of the "Knowledge" Society had accustomed me to believe that animals were not capable of speech. Ever since I was a child folktales had assured me of the opposite. Naturally, I had agreed with the pamphlets, because I'd never seen any talking animals, not once. Not even parrots. I had known one parrot who could growl like a tiger, but he couldn't talk like a human being. And now I had the pike, the cat Vasily, and even a mirror. But, then, inanimate objects talked all the time. That was an idea that could never have occurred to my great-granddad, for instance. From his point of view, a talking cat would be nowhere near as fantastic as a shiny wooden box that wheezes, howls, plays music, and speaks all kinds of languages. As far as the cat was concerned, the situation seemed more or less clear. But how did the pike manage to speak? A pike doesn't have any lungs. That's certain. True, it must have an air bladder, the function of which, as far as I'm aware, is still not entirely clear to ichthyologists. One ichthyologist I know, Zhenka Skoromakhov, even believes that this function is in fact entirely unclear, and when I try to argue, using the evidence from my "Knowledge" Society pamphlets, Zhenka starts growling and spitting and entirely loses the power of human speech . . . I have the impression that we still know very little about what animals are capable of. Only recently it was discovered that fish and marine mammals exchange signals underwater. What they write about dolphins is very interesting.

Or take the monkey Raphael, for instance. I've seen for myself. True, he can't actually talk, but he did develop a reflex response: green for a banana, red for an electric shock. And everything was just fine until they switched on the red light and the green light at the same time. Then Raphael started behaving the same way as Zhenka does. He got terribly worked up, started squealing and growling, made a dash at the little window where the experimenter was sitting, and started spitting at it. And then there's that joke—one monkey says to another, "Do you know what a conditioned reflex is? It's when the bell rings and all those pseudo-monkeys in white coats come running across with bananas and sweets." It's all highly complicated, of course. The terminology hasn't been developed yet. In such circumstances, you feel absolutely helpless when you try to answer questions about the psychology and potential abilities of animals. But then, on the other hand, it doesn't make you feel any better when they give you, say, that stellar statistics–type system of integral equations with unknown functions under the integral. The important thing is to think. As Pascal said, "Let us learn to think well—that is the fundamental principle of morality."

I emerged onto Peace Prospect and stopped, my attention claimed by an unusual sight. There was a man holding children's toy flags in his hands walking along the road. Creeping along slowly about ten steps behind him with its engine roaring came a large white MAZ truck towing a gigantic, silverish tank that was giving off smoke. The tank bore the words FIRE HAZARD, and creeping along just as slowly on the right and the left of it were two red-painted jeeps bristling with fire extinguishers. From time to time a different sound mingled with the even roar of the engine, sending an icy shower down my spine, and then yellow tongues of flame erupted from the hatches of the tank. The firemen's helmets were pulled down tight above their grimly courageous faces. A crowd of little kids swarmed around the cavalcade, screeching piercingly, "Swing him up and swing him down, they've brought the dragon into town!" Adult passersby apprehensively pressed themselves back against the fences on both sides, their faces clearly expressing the desire to protect their clothes from possible damage.

"They've brought my sweetheart," a familiar rasping voice boomed right in my ear.

I turned around. Standing behind me looking rather mournful was
Naina Kievna, with a mesh bag full of blue packets of sugar. "They've
brought him," she repeated. "Every Friday they bring him . . ."

"Where to?" I asked.

"Why, to the firing range, dear guest. They're always experimenting . . . They've got nothing better to do with their time."

"But who is it they've brought, Naina Kievna?"

"What do you mean, who? You can see for yourself, can't you?"

She turned and walked away, but I caught up with her. "Naina Kievna, there was a telephonogram for you."

"Who's it from?"

"C. M. Viy."

"And what's it about?"

"You've got some kind of rally today," I said, looking at her intently. "On Bald Mountain. Dress code formal."

The old woman was clearly delighted. "Really?" she said. "Goody-goody! Where's the telephonogram?"

"On the phone in the hall."

"Does it say anything about membership dues?" she asked, lowering her voice.

"What do you mean?"

"You know, outstanding dues owed must be paid as from seventeen hundred—" she stopped.

"No," I said, "It didn't say anything like that."

"That's all right, then. What about transport? Will they send a car or what?"

"Let me carry your bag for you," I offered. The old woman started back.

"What for?" she asked suspiciously. "You just stop that—I don't like it . . . Give him my bag! And him still so young; he must be an early starter . . ."

I don't like old women, I thought.

"So, what about the transport?" she asked again.

"At your own expense," I said with malicious delight.

"*Agh*, the misers!" the old woman groaned. "They took my broomstick and put it in a museum, they don't repair the flying mortar, they try to rob me of five rubles' membership dues, and say I've got to get to Bald Mountain at my own expense! That's some expense, dear guest of mine, and while the taxi's waiting . . ." Mumbling and coughing, she turned and walked away from me. I rubbed my hands together and also went on my way. My conjectures had been confirmed. The knot of remarkable events was being drawn ever tighter. I'm ashamed to admit it, but at that moment it seemed to me even more interesting than modeling a reflex arc.

Peace Prospect was by now almost deserted. There was a swarm of little kids scurrying about at the crossroads—I think they were playing tipcat. Catching sight of me, they abandoned their game and started moving in my direction. Sensing approaching hostility, I walked hurriedly past them and set off toward the center of town. I heard a muffled exclamation of delight behind me: "Dandy!" I started walking faster. "Dandy!" several voices immediately howled out together. I began almost running. Behind me they squealed, "Dandy! Skinny-legs! Fancy-pants!" Passersby were giving me looks of sympathy. In situations like this the best thing to do is to go to ground somewhere. I dived into the nearest shop, which turned out to be a grocery store, and walked along the counters, noting that they had sugar in stock and that the range of salami and sweets wasn't very extensive but the choice of so-called fish products exceeded all possible expectations. What wonderful salmon they had! I drank a glass of sparkling water and glanced out into the street. The little boys were gone, so I went out of the shop and continued on my way. Soon the "emporiums" and log-built fortress-huts came to an end and their place was taken by the modern two-story apartment blocks with little open yards, where little infants toddled and crawled about, middle-aged women knitted something warm, and middle-aged men played dominoes.

In the center of the town I found a wide square surrounded by two-story and three-story buildings. The surface of the square was covered with asphalt, and in the middle of it there was a little green garden. Rising up out of the greenery was a large red board with the inscription BOARD OF HONOR, and several smaller boards with maps and diagrams. I found the post office on the square too. I had agreed with the guys that the first to arrive would leave a note saying where he was. There was no note for me, so I left a letter giving my address and explaining how to get to the Log Hut on Chicken Legs. Then I decided to have some breakfast.

Walking around the square I came across the following: a theater that was showing the film *Kozara*; a bookshop that was closed for inventory; the town council building, with several dusty jeeps standing in front of it; the Icebound Sea Hotel, which, as usual, had no rooms available; two kiosks selling sparkling water and ice cream; shop number 2 (industrial goods) and shop number 18 (household goods); cafeteria number 11, which opened at twelve o'clock, and buffet number 3, which was closed with no explanation offered. Then I discovered the town militia station, and in front of its open doors I had a conversation with a very youthful militiaman holding the rank of sergeant, who explained to me where the gas station was and which was the road to Lezhnev.

"And where's your car?" the militiaman inquired, surveying the square.

"At my friends' place," I replied.

"Ah, at your friends' place . . ." the militiaman said with emphasis. I believe he made a mental note of me. I timidly said good-bye, feeling nervous.

Beside the huge three-story bulk of the Solovets Fish Suppliers, Processors, and Consumers Trust (as I deciphered the sign SOLFISUPPROCONSUMTRUST) I eventually found the tidy little tearoom number 16/27. It was very pleasant inside. There weren't many people and they really were drinking tea and speaking about things I could understand: how the bridge at Korobets had finally collapsed and now you had to ford the river; how it had been more than a week since the traffic police post on the fifteen-kilometer mark had been removed; how "it's sparking fit to kill an elephant, but it just won't turn over." The place smelled of gasoline and fried fish. Those who were not engaged in conversation inspected my jeans in great detail, and I felt glad that they had a working-man's stain at the back—fortunately I'd sat on a grease gun two days earlier.

I took a plate full of fried fish, three glasses of tea, and three sturgeon sandwiches, paid with a heap of the old woman's copper coins ("Been standing begging at the church door . . ." the woman at the counter growled), made myself comfortable in a secluded corner, and tucked in, observing with pleasure these manly men with voices hoarse from smoking cigarettes. It was a pleasure to see how tanned, independent, and robust they were, how well they knew life, how they enjoyed eating their food, smoking, and talking. They were squeezing every last drop out of their break before the long hours jolting down a dull road in the stuffy heat of the cabin, the dust, and the sun. If I weren't a programmer, I would have been a driver, and I wouldn't have been working in some pitiful little automobile, or even on a bus, but on some great monster of a truck so big you'd need a ladder to climb up into the cabin and a small crane to change a wheel.

The two young men sitting at the next table didn't look like truckers, so I paid no attention to them at first. And they paid no attention to me either. But just as I was finishing my second glass of tea, I heard the word "sofa." And then one of them said, "In that case, it's not clear why that Lohuchil exists at all . . ." and I started listening. Unfortunately they were talking softly and I was sitting with my back to them, so I couldn't hear very much. But the voices sounded familiar: "No theses . . . just the sofa . . ."; "That hairy one?"; "The sofa . . . sixteenth degree . . ."; "For transgression no higher than the fourteenth degree . . ."; "Easier to model the translator . . ."; "Well, who doesn't giggle at him!"; "I'll give him a razor . . ."; "We can't do it without the sofa . . ." Then one of them tried to clear his throat in such a familiar manner that I immediately remembered the night before and turned around, but they were already walking toward the door—two big young guys with massive shoulders and bodybuilders' necks. I saw them through the window for a while, too: they walked across the square, around the little garden, and disappeared behind the diagrams. I finished off my tea and my sandwich and went out. So they're concerned about the sofa, I thought. They're not bothered about the mermaid. They're not interested in the talking cat. But it seems they can't manage without the sofa . . . I tried to remember what the sofa in my room was like, but I couldn't recall anything unusual. Just an ordinary sofa. A good sofa. Comfortable. Only the reality you dreamed about on it was rather strange.

It would be a good idea now to go back there and get a firm grip on all this sofa business. Try experimenting a bit with the whimsical book, have a frank word with Vasily the cat, and see whether there was anything else interesting to be found in the Log Hut on Chicken Legs. But my Moskvich was waiting for me back there, and I needed to carry out a DM and a TS. I could just about live with the idea of a DM—that was only *daily maintenance*, shaking out the floor mats and washing the car down with a pressurized hose, which if necessary could be replaced by a garden watering can or a bucket. But that TS . . . On a hot day any man who likes to keep himself neat and tidy shudders at the very thought of a TS, because a TS is a *technical service*, and a technical service involves me lying under the car with a grease gun in my hands, gradually transferring the contents of the gun to the grease nipples and my own facial features. It's hot and stuffy under the car, and its bottom is crusted with a thick layer of dried-on mud . . . In other words, I didn't really feel like going back.

4

Who dares insult us with this blasphemous mockery? Seize him and unmask him—that we may know whom we have to hang at sunrise, from the battlements!

—Edgar Allan Poe

I bought the day before yesterday's *Pravda*, drank a glass of sparkling water, and settled down on a bench in the little garden, in the shade of the Board of Honor. It was eleven o'clock. I looked through the newspaper carefully. It took me seven minutes. Then I read an article about hydroponics, an exposé about bribe-takers in Kansk, and a long letter to the editor from the workers at a chemical plant. Maybe I should go to the movies, I thought. But I'd already seen *Kozara*—once in the theater and once on television. Then I decided to have another glass of water, folded up the newspaper, and stood up. I only had a five-kopeck piece left out of all the old woman's coppers. I'll drink it all away, I decided, downed a glass of sparkling water with syrup, received one kopeck change, and bought a box of matches with it at the next kiosk. Now there was absolutely nothing at all left for me to do in the center of town, so I just followed my nose—into the narrow street between shop number 2 and cafeteria number 11.

There was almost no one on the street. A big, dusty truck with a clattering trailer overtook me. The driver had his elbow and head stuck out of the window of his cab, drearily observing the cobbled road surface. The street ran downhill around a sharp turn to the right, and beside the pavement at the bend there was the cast-iron barrel of an old cannon sticking up out of the ground, its mouth choked with earth and cigarette butts. Soon after that the street ended at the sheer bank of the river. I sat on the steep edge, admiring

the view, then crossed to the other side of the street and started
making my way back.

I wonder where that truck went, I thought. There was no way
down that steep bank. I started looking around for gateways along
the street, and I came across a small but very strange building,
squeezed in between two gloomy brick "emporiums." The windows
on the ground floor of the building were protected by iron bars and
painted over halfway up with whitewash. There were no doors into
the house at all. I noticed that straightaway because here the sign
that is usually set beside the gates or over the entrance was hanging
between two windows. It read NITWiT AS USSR. I backed away to
the middle of the street: yes, two stories, each with ten windows,
and not a single door. And adjoining emporiums on the left and the
right. NITWiT of the Academy of Sciences of the USSR, I thought.
National Institute of TWiT, I suppose. And Lohuchil, the Log Hut
on Chicken Legs, I thought, is this NITWiT's museum. My traveling companions must be from here too. And those others in the
tearoom . . . A flock of crows rose into the air from the roof of a
building and circled, cawing, above the street. I turned and walked
back toward the square.

We are all naive materialists, I thought. And we are all rational-
ists. We demand an immediate rational explanation for everything;
we want everything reduced to a handful of known facts. And not
one of us has even an ounce of dialectics. It never occurs to anybody that the known facts and some new phenomenon might be
separated by an entire ocean of the unknown, so we declare the
new phenomenon supernatural and, therefore, impossible. What
kind of response, for instance, would Montesquieu have given to
the statement that a dead man had revived forty-five minutes after
his heart was known to have stopped? No doubt a hostile one. He
would have declared it obscurantism and superstitious nonsense.
That is, if he didn't simply dismiss such a claim out of hand. But
if it had happened in front of his very eyes, then he would have
found himself in an extremely difficult situation. As I did now, only
I was more used to it. He would have been obliged to regard the

resurrection as a fraud, or to deny the evidence of his own senses, or even to abandon materialism. Most likely he would have chosen to regard the resurrection as a fraud. But for the rest of his life the memory of that cunning trick would have irritated his mind, like a mote in his eye . . .

We, however, are children of a different age. We've seen all sorts of things: a live dog's head sewn to the back of another living dog, and an artificial kidney the size of a wardrobe, and a dead metal hand controlled by living nerves, and people who can remark casually in passing, "That was after I died the first time . . ." Yes, in our time Montesquieu's chances of remaining a materialist wouldn't have been too good. But we seem to manage it without too much bother.

It can be difficult at times, of course—when a chance breeze wafts the petals of mysterious plants across the ocean to us from the vast continents of the unknown. And what makes it difficult most often is when what you find is not what you were looking for. Soon the zoos and museums will be showing amazing animals, the first creatures from Mars or Venus. Yes, of course, we'll gape at them and slap our thighs, but we've been expecting these animals for a long time already, and we're well prepared for them to put in an appearance. We'd be far more amazed and disappointed if these animals proved not to exist at all, or to resemble our cats and dogs. As a rule, the science in which we believe (quite often blindly) prepares us long in advance for the miracles that lie ahead, and we only suffer psychological shock when we come up against the unforeseen, like some hole through into the fourth dimension, or biological radio communication, or a living planet . . . Or, say, a log hut on chicken legs . . . Volodya with the ginger beard was right when he said this was a funny old place they had here . . .

I reached the square and halted in front of the sparkling water kiosk. I remembered quite definitely that I had no change and I would have to break a note, and I was already preparing an ingratiating smile, because the kiosk women who sell sparkling water hate changing paper money, when I suddenly discovered a five-kopeck piece in the pocket of my jeans. I was amazed and delighted, but mostly delighted. I drank a glass of sparkling water with syrup, received a wet kopeck in change, and had a brief word with the kiosk attendant about the weather. Then I set off resolutely to walk home, to get the DM and TS over and done with as soon as possible and continue with my rational dialectical deliberations. As I stuck the kopeck in my pocket I stopped dead on discovering that there was another five-kopeck piece in there. I took it out and looked at it. The coin was slightly damp, and in the inscription "5 kopecks 1961" the "6" was obscured by a shallow dent. Perhaps even then I might not have paid any attention to this minor incident if it weren't for the familiar, fleeting feeling that at one and the same time I was standing here on Peace Prospect and sitting on the sofa, gazing stupidly at that set of hooks. And this time, too, when I shook my head, the feeling disappeared.

I walked on slowly for a while, absentmindedly tossing the five-kopeck piece up in the air and catching it (it always fell on my palm tails up) and trying to concentrate. Then I saw the grocery store where I'd taken refuge from the crowd of kids that morning. Holding the coin between my finger and thumb, I went straight back to the counter where they sold fruit juices and water and drank a glass of water without syrup, and without enjoying it one little bit. Then, clutching the change in my fist, I walked off to one side and checked my pocket.

It was one of those cases when there is no psychological shock. I would have been more surprised if the five-kopeck piece hadn't been there. But it was there—damp, dated 1961, with a dent over the digit "6." Someone gave me a shove and asked if I was asleep. Apparently I was standing in the line for the cash desk. I said I wasn't asleep and took a sales check for three boxes of matches. I was perfectly calm. After collecting my three boxes I went back out onto the square and began experimenting.

My experiment took about an hour. During that hour I made ten rounds of the square, until I was bloated with water and heavily burdened with boxes of matches and newspapers. I got to know

all the salesmen and saleswomen and reached a number of interesting conclusions. The coin came back if it was used to pay. If
you simply threw it away, dropped it, or lost it, then it would
stay where it was. The coin returned to the pocket at the moment
when the change passed from the seller's hands into the hands of
the buyer. If at that moment I held my hand in one pocket, the
coin appeared in the other. It never appeared in a pocket that
was closed with a zipper. If I kept both my hands in my pockets
and took my change with my elbow, the coin could appear anywhere at all on my body (in one case it turned up in my shoe).
The coin's disappearance from the saucer of coppers was quite
imperceptible; the five-kopeck piece immediately became invisible
among the other copper coins and no movement occurred in the
saucer at the moment when the five-kopeck piece moved back to
my pocket.

And so, what we were dealing with was a so-called "unchangeable" five-kopeck piece in action. In itself the fact of unchangeability
did not interest me very much. What astounded me most of all was
the possibility of extraspatial displacement of a physical body. It was
absolutely clear to me that the mysterious transference of the coin
from the seller to the buyer represented a clear case of the notori-
ous "zero-transport," well known to lovers of science fiction under
its various pseudonyms: hypertransit, repagular leap, Tarantoga's
phenomenon, etc. The possibilities in prospect were dazzling.

I had no scientific instruments. A basic laboratory thermometer
would have been very useful, but I didn't even have that. I was
obliged to restrict myself to purely visual, subjective observation. I
began my final round of the square with the following objective in
mind: *Placing the five-kopeck piece beside the saucer for small change and
as far as possible preventing the salesperson from putting it in with the other
money until he or she hands me my change, visually monitor the process
of the coin's displacement in space, while at the same time attempting to
determine, at least qualitatively, the change in temperature in the vicinity
of the presumptive trajectory of transit.* However, the experiment was
interrupted before it had even begun.

When I approached the sales assistant Manya, now an acquaintance of mine, the youthful militiaman with the rank of sergeant was already waiting for me. "All right, then," he said in his professional voice.

I gave him an inquiring look, feeling an uneasy presentiment.

"Your papers, if you don't mind, citizen," said the militiaman, saluting and looking straight past me.

"What's wrong?" I asked as I took out my passport.

"And the coin too, if you don't mind," the militiaman said as he took the passport. I handed him the five-kopeck piece without speaking. Manya watched me with angry eyes. The militiaman inspected the coin, said "Aha . . ." in a satisfied tone of voice, and opened my passport, which he studied the way a bibliophile studies a rare incunabulum. I waited in torment. A crowd was gathering around me, and some members of it were already expressing various opinions concerning my character.

"You'll have to come with me," the militiaman said eventually. I went with him. While we were on our way, the crowd that escorted us concocted several different versions of my troubled life history and proposed a large number of hypotheses concerning the reasons for the investigation that was beginning before their very eyes.

In the station the sergeant handed on the five-kopeck piece and the passport to a lieutenant, who inspected the five-kopeck piece and invited me to sit down. I sat down. The lieutenant said casually, "Hand over your small change," and then also immersed himself in the study of my passport. I raked the coppers out of my pocket. "Count it, Kovalyov," said the lieutenant, and setting aside the passport began looking into my eyes.

"Buy a lot, did you?" he asked.

"Yes," I replied.

"Hand that over too," said the lieutenant.

I set out on the table in front of him four copies of the day before yesterday's issue of *Pravda*, three issues of the local newspaper the *Fisherman*, two issues of the *Literary Gazette*, eight boxes of matches, six Golden Key toffees, and a reduced-price wire brush for cleaning Primus stoves.

"I can't hand over the water," I said dryly. "Five glasses with syrup and four without."

I was beginning to understand what the problem was, and the realization that I would have to justify my actions gave me an extremely awkward and unpleasant feeling.

"Seventy-four kopecks, comrade Lieutenant," the youthful Kovalyov reported.

The lieutenant contemplated the heap of newspapers and boxes of matches. "Just having fun were you, or what?" he asked me.

"What," I said morosely.

"Careless," said the lieutenant. "Very careless, citizen. Tell me about it."

I told him. At the end of my story I earnestly requested the lieutenant not to interpret my actions as an attempt to save up the money to buy a Zaporozhets car. My ears were burning. He laughed.

"Why shouldn't I?" he inquired. "Some people have managed it."

I shrugged. "I assure you, the idea could never even have entered my head . . . I mean it really never did!"

The lieutenant maintained a long pause. The youthful Kovalyov took my passport and began studying it again.

"I can't even imagine it . . ." I said in dismay. "An absolutely crazy idea . . . Saving up kopeck by kopeck . . ." I shrugged again. "You'd be better off standing out on the church porch . . ."

"We're waging a campaign against begging," the lieutenant said emphatically.

"Quite right, of course . . . I just don't understand what it's got to do with me, and—" I realized that I was shrugging my shoulders a lot and promised myself not to do it anymore.

The lieutenant maintained another excruciatingly long pause while he examined the five-kopeck piece. "We'll have to draw up a report," he said eventually.

I shrugged. "By all means . . . although . . ." But I didn't actually know "although" what.

The lieutenant carried on looking at me for a while, waiting for me to continue, but I was trying to work out which article of the criminal code my activities came under. Then he pulled across a sheet of paper and began writing.

The youthful Kovalyov returned to his post. The lieutenant scraped his pen across the paper, frequently dipping it into the inkwell with a bang. I sat there, idiotically examining the posters hanging on the walls and thinking vaguely that in my place Lomonosov, for instance, would have grabbed his passport and leaped out of the window. What is the essential point here? I thought. The essential thing is whether or not a person thinks of himself as guilty. In that sense I am not guilty. But guilt, it seems, may be either objective or subjective. And a fact is a fact: all those copper coins amounting to seventy-four kopecks are from a legal point of view the fruit of theft committed with the use of a technical device—to wit, one unchangeable five-kopeck piece . . .

"Read that and sign it," said the lieutenant.

I read it. It emerged from the report that I, the undersigned A. I. Privalov, had in a manner unknown to me come into possession of a working model of an unchangeable five-kopeck piece of type State Standard 718-62, of which I had made improper use; that I, the undersigned A. I. Privalov, asserted that I had acted in this way solely for purposes of scientific experimentation and entirely unmotivated by the pursuit of personal gain; that I was prepared to reimburse the state for the losses inflicted on it in the sum of one ruble and fifty-five kopecks; and finally, that I had, in accordance with Solovets Municipal Soviet decree of March 22, 1959, surrendered the aforesaid working model of an unchangeable five-kopeck piece to the duty officer at the local militia station, Lieutenant U. U. Sergienko, and received in exchange five kopecks in the valid currency of the Soviet Union. I signed it.

The lieutenant checked my signature against the signature in my passport, counted the copper coins carefully once again, phoned somewhere to confirm the cost of the toffees and the Primus stove brush, then wrote out a receipt and handed it to me together with five kopecks in valid currency. As he gave me back the newspapers, matches, sweets, and brush, he said, "On your own admission, you drank the water. So altogether you owe another eighty-one kopecks."

I settled my debt with a tremendous sense of relief. The lieutenant leafed carefully through my passport once again and handed it back to me.

"You can go, citizen Privalov," he said. "And take more care from now on. Are you going to be in Solovets long?"

"I'm leaving tomorrow," I said.

"Well, try to be more careful until tomorrow."

"Oh, I'll do my best," I said, putting away my passport. Then, on a sudden impulse, I asked him in a quiet voice, "But tell me, comrade Lieutenant, don't you find things a bit strange here in Solovets?"

The lieutenant was already looking through some papers. "I've been here a long time," he said absentmindedly. "I'm used to it."

5

"But do you yourself believe in ghosts?" one of the students asked the lecturer.

"No, of course not," the lecturer replied as he slowly dissolved into thin air.

—A true story

Until that evening I tried to be extremely careful. From the militia station I set off straight back home to Curving Seashore Street, and once there I climbed straight under the car. It was very hot. A menacing black cloud was slowly advancing from the west. While I was lying under the car covering myself with grease, old Naina Kievna, who had suddenly become very attentive and polite, came toadying up to me with a request to give her a lift to Bald Mountain. "They do say, dear guest, that it's bad for a car to be standing around idle," she cooed in her rasping voice, glancing in under the front bumper. "They say it's good for it to go driving about. And I'd pay you, you can be sure of that." I didn't want to drive to Bald Mountain. In the first place, the boys might turn up at any moment. In the second place, I found the old woman's unctuous persona even less endearing than her cantankerous one. And then it turned out that the journey to Bald Mountain was ninety versts in one direction, and when I asked the old granny how good the roads were, she declared happily that I needn't worry about that—the road was smooth and if there was a problem she'd push the car herself. "Don't you worry about me being old, dear guest, I'm still fit and strong," she said.

After her first unsuccessful sally the old woman beat a temporary retreat, withdrawing into the house. The cat Vasily came and joined me under the car. He watched my hands closely for about a minute and then pronounced in a low but clearly audible voice, "I

wouldn't advise it, citizen . . . *mmnaa* . . . I wouldn't advise it. They'll eat you up." Then he immediately left, twitching his tail. I was still trying to be very careful, so as soon as the old woman launched her second assault, I asked her for fifty rubles in order to put an end to the whole thing there and then. She retreated immediately, giving me a respectful look.

I carried out the DM and the TS, drove to the gas station with extreme caution to fill the tank, ate lunch in cafeteria number 11, and had my papers inspected once again by the vigilant Kovalyov. Just to make sure my conscience was clear, I asked him which was the road to Bald Mountain. The youthful sergeant gave me a very suspicious look and said, "Road? What are you talking about, citizen? What road? There isn't any road there." I drove back home in pouring rain.

The old woman had gone. The cat Vasily had disappeared. In the well two voices were singing a duet, and the effect was terrifying and dismal. The heavy rain was soon replaced by a dreary drizzle. It got dark.

I went into my room and tried to experiment with the whimsical book, but something in it had gotten jammed. Perhaps I was doing something wrong, or perhaps it was the influence of the weather, but no matter what I tried it stayed the way it was—F. F. Kuzmin's *Practical Exercises in Syntax and Punctuation*. Reading a book like that was absolutely out of the question, so I tried my luck with the mirror. But the mirror reflected anything and everything and said nothing. Then I just stretched out on the sofa and lay there. I was on the point of nodding off from the boredom and the sound of the rain when the telephone suddenly started ringing. I went out into the hall and picked up the receiver. "Hello . . ."

The only sound in the earpiece was crackling.

"Hello," I said, and blew into the mouthpiece. "Press the button." There was no reply.

"Give it a bang," I advised the silence. I blew into the phone again, tugged on the wire, and said. "Try calling again from a different phone."

Then a voice in the receiver suddenly inquired, "Is that Alexander?"

"Yes," I said, astonished.

"Why don't you answer?"

"I am answering. Who's this?"

"This is Petrovsky calling. Go down to the pickling shop and tell the foreman to give me a call."

"What foreman?"

"Well, who have you got in today?"

"I don't know . . ."

"What d'you mean, you don't know? Is that Alexander?"

"Listen, citizen," I said. "What number are you trying to call?"

"Seven two . . . Is that seven two?"

I didn't know. "Apparently not," I said.

"Then why did you say you were Alexander?"

"Because that's who I am!"

"*Pah!* . . . Is this the manufacturing plant?"

"No," I said. "This is the museum."

"Ah . . . Then I beg your pardon. You can't call the foreman, then . . ."

I hung up and went on standing there for a while, examining the hallway. There were five doors: the ones leading to my room, the yard, the old woman's room, and the bathroom, and one covered in metal sheeting with a huge padlock. Boring, I thought. Lonely. And the lamp's dim and dusty too . . . Shuffling my feet, I went back to my room and stopped in the doorway.

The sofa was gone.

Everything else was exactly the way it had been: the table, the brick oven, the mirror, the clothes hooks, and the stool. And the book was lying on the windowsill exactly where I'd left it. But where the sofa had been there was nothing now but a rectangle of thick dust on the floor, littered with rubbish. Then I saw the bedsheets lying neatly folded under the set of hooks.

"There was a sofa here a moment ago," I said out loud. "I was lying on it."

Something in the house had changed. The room was filled with an unintelligible hubbub—someone holding a conversation, music, people laughing, coughing, and shuffling their feet. For an instant a vague shadow obscured the light of the lamp, and the floorboards creaked loudly. Then suddenly I caught a medicinal smell like a drugstore and felt a puff of cold air in my face. I stepped back. And immediately I distinctly heard a sharp knock at the outside door.

The noises instantly disappeared. Casting a glance around at the spot where the sofa had been, I went out into the hallway and opened the door.

Standing in front of me in the drizzle was a short, elegant man wearing a spotlessly clean cream raincoat with the collar turned up. He raised his hat and spoke in a dignified manner: "I'm very sorry to bother you, Alexander Ivanovich, but could you possibly spare me five minutes of your time?"

"Of course," I said, confused. "Come in."

It was the first time I'd ever seen this man, and the thought crossed my mind that perhaps he might be connected with the local militia. The stranger stepped into the hallway and set off straight toward my room. I blocked his way. I don't know why I did it—probably because I didn't want to answer any questions about the dust and rubbish on the floor.

"I'm sorry," I babbled, "why don't we talk here? My room's a bit of a mess. And there's nowhere to sit."

The stranger jerked his head up sharply. "What do you mean?" he asked in a soft voice. "What about the sofa?"

We looked into each other's eyes without speaking for about a minute. "Mmm . . . Yes, what about the sofa?" I asked, for some reason speaking in a whisper.

The stranger hooded his eyes. "Ah, so that's the way it is!" he said slowly. "I understand. What a pity. Well, I'm sorry to have bothered you."

He nodded politely, put his hat on, and strode resolutely toward the door of the bathroom.

"Where are you going?" I called. "That's the wrong way." Without bothering to turn around, the stranger mumbled, "Oh, it makes no difference," and closed the door behind him. Without thinking, I switched the light on for him and stood there listening for a while, then suddenly jerked the door open. The bathroom was empty.

I gingerly took out a cigarette and lit up. The sofa, I thought. What does this have to do with the sofa? I'd never heard any fairy tales about sofas. There was a flying carpet. There was a magic tablecloth. There were caps of darkness, seven-league boots, and self-playing psalteries. There was a magic talking mirror. But there wasn't any magic sofa. People sat or lay on sofas; a sofa was a very solid object, very ordinary . . . Yes, really, what kind of fantasies could be inspired by a sofa?

Going back into my room, I immediately saw the Little Man. He was sitting on the brick oven up by the ceiling, doubled over into a very uncomfortable position. His wrinkled face was unshaven and his gray ears were hairy.

"Hello," I said wearily.

The Little Man twisted his long lips into a woeful grimace. "Good evening," he said. "I do beg your pardon, I'm not quite sure how I came to be up here . . . I've come about the sofa."

"Then you've come too late," I said, sitting down at the table.

"So I see," the Man said in a quiet voice, shifting awkwardly. Flakes of whitewash showered down.

I smoked and looked him over thoughtfully. The Little Man glanced down uncertainly.

"Would you like me to help?" I asked, making a move toward him.

"No thank you," the Man said despondently. "I'd better do it myself . . ."

He crept to the very edge of the sleeping platform, covering himself in white chalk, and launched himself awkwardly into the air, falling headfirst. My heart skipped a beat, but he stopped dead in midair and then began descending slowly, jerking his arms and legs outward. It wasn't very elegant, but it was amusing. He landed on all fours and immediately stood up and wiped his wet face on his sleeve.

"I'm getting old," he declared hoarsely. "A hundred years ago, or in Gonzast's time, they'd have stripped me of my diploma for a descent like that, no two ways about it, Alexander Ivanovich."

"Where did you graduate from?" I inquired, lighting up another cigarette.

He wasn't listening. He sat down on the stool opposite me and continued his lament: "There was a time when I used to levitate

like Zeks. But now I can't even get rid of this growth in my ears. It
looks so untidy . . . But what's to be done if you've got no talent?
The immense number of temptations there are all around, all sorts
of degrees and titles and prizes, but I've got no talent. Many of us get
rather hirsute as we grow old. Of course, that doesn't apply to the
grand masters. Gian Giacomo, Cristóbal Junta, Giuseppe Balsamo,
or comrade Fyodor Simeonovich Kivrin, for instance . . . Not a trace
of superfluous hair there!" He gave me a triumphant look. "Not a
trace! Such smooth skin, such elegance, such grace . . ."

   "I beg your pardon," I said, "You mentioned Giuseppe Balsamo . . . But he is the same person as Count Cagliostro! And
according to Alexei Tolstoy, the count was fat and very unpleasant-
looking."

   The Little Man looked at me pityingly and smiled condescendingly. "You're simply not aware of the facts, Alexander Ivanovich,"
he said. "Count Cagliostro is not at all the same as the great Balsamo. He is . . . how can I explain it to you . . . He is a rather unsuccessful copy of him. In his youth Balsamo made a matrix mold of
himself. He was quite exceptionally talented, but you know how it
is when you're young . . . Get it done quick, have a laugh, any old
way will do . . . Yes indeed . . . So don't you ever say that Balsamo
and Cagliostro are the same. You could end up feeling rather stupid."

   I felt rather stupid. "All right," I said, "of course, I'm no specialist, but . . . pardon my impertinence, but what's all this business with
the sofa about? Who's taken it?"

   The Little Man shuddered. "Such unpardonable conceit," he
said loudly, getting to his feet. "I made a mistake and I am prepared to admit it without the slightest reservation. When giants
like that . . . And there are those impudent boys too . . ." He started
bowing and pressing his pale little hands to his heart. "Please forgive my intrusion, Alexander Ivanovich, I have inconvenienced
you . . . Allow me to apologize unreservedly once again and take
my leave immediately." He moved closer to the oven and glanced
upward apprehensively. "It's my age, Alexander Ivanovich," he said
with a deep sigh. "My age . . ."

"Perhaps it would be more convenient if you went through the . . . *err* . . . There was another comrade here just before you and he used it."

"*Ahh*, my dear fellow, then that was Cristóbal Junta! Seeping ten leagues through the drains is no problem for him . . ." The Little Man gestured mournfully. "We're not up to that sort of thing . . . Did he take the sofa with him or transgress it?"

"I-I don't know," I said. "Well actually, he got here too late as well."

The Little Man plucked at the fur in his right ear in stupefaction. "Too late? Him? Incredible! But then, who are you and I to judge? Good-bye, Alexander Ivanovich. Please forgive me."

With a visible effort he walked through the wall and disappeared. I tossed my cigarette butt into the rubbish lying on the floor. This sofa was big news all right! Not your garden-variety talking cat. This was something more serious altogether . . . There was real drama here. Perhaps even a genuine drama of the intellect. There would probably be others arriving too late as well. There were bound to be. I glanced at the rubbish. Where was it I saw that twig broom?

The twig broom was standing beside the drinking water tub under the telephone. I started sweeping up the rubbish and suddenly something heavy snagged on the broom and rolled out into the center of the room. Glancing at it, I saw an elongated cylinder about the size of my index finger. I touched it with the broom. The cylinder swayed to and fro; there was a dry crackling sound and a sudden smell of ozone. I dropped the broom and picked up the cylinder. It was smooth, highly polished, and warm to the touch. I flicked a fingernail against it and it crackled again. I turned it around to look at its end and immediately felt the floor starting to slip away from under my feet. The world turned upside down before my eyes. I stubbed my toes painfully against something, then banged my shoulder and the top of my head. I dropped the cylinder and fell.

I was badly shaken, and it was a moment before I realized that I was lying in the narrow crevice between the oven and the wall. The lamp above my head was swaying, and looking up I was astonished to see the ribbed tracks of my shoes on the ceiling. Wheezing and groaning, I clambered out of the crevice and inspected my soles. They had whitewash on them.

"Well now," I thought out loud, "thank goodness I didn't end up seeping through the drains!"

I looked around to find the cylinder. It was standing with the circumference of its end surface touching the floor, in a position that couldn't possibly be balanced. I cautiously moved a bit closer and squatted down beside it. The cylinder crackled quietly and rocked to and fro. I looked at it for a long time, then stretched out my neck and blew on it. The cylinder began swaying faster and leaned over, and immediately I heard a hoarse screech and felt a puff of wind on my back. I glanced around and immediately sat down on the floor at the sight of a gigantic vulture with a naked neck and a menacingly curving beak sitting on the oven, carefully folding away its wings.

"Hello," I said. I was certain that the vulture could talk.

The vulture inclined its head and peered at me with one eye, which made it look like a chicken. I waved my hand in greeting. The vulture opened its beak slightly, but it didn't talk to me. It raised one wing and started searching for lice underneath it, clicking its beak. The cylinder carried on swaying and crackling. The vulture stopped, pulled its head back into its shoulders, and veiled its eyes with a yellow film. Trying not to turn my back to it, I finished cleaning up and tossed the rubbish outside into the rainy darkness. Then I went back into the room.

The vulture was sleeping and there was a smell of ozone in the air. I looked at the clock: it was twenty minutes past twelve. I stood looking down at the cylinder for a while, pondering the law of conservation of energy and matter. Vultures were unlikely to condense out of nothing. If this vulture had appeared here in Solovets, then a vulture (not necessarily this one) had disappeared in the Caucasus or wherever it was they lived. I made a rough estimate of the energy of translocation and cast a wary glance at the cylinder. Better not touch it, I thought. Better cover it with something and let it stand there. I brought the dipper in from the hallway, lined it up carefully, and, holding my breath, put it over the cylinder. Then I sat down on the stool, lit a cigarette, and started waiting for what would happen next. The vulture was sniffling audibly. In the light of the lamp its feathers glinted with a copper sheen and its massive claws were dug deep into the whitewash. It gave off a smell of decay that was gradually filling the room.

"You shouldn't have done that, Alexander Ivanovich," said a pleasant male voice.

"What exactly?" I asked, glancing around at the mirror.

"I meant the plywitsum . . ."

It wasn't the mirror talking. It was someone else. "I don't understand what you mean," I said. There was no one in the room, and that made me feel annoyed.

"I'm talking about the plywitsum," said the voice. "You really shouldn't have covered it with the iron dipper. A plywitsum, or as you call it, a magic wand, should be treated with extreme caution."

"That's why I covered it up . . . But do come in, comrade. This is a very inconvenient way to talk."

"Thank you," said the voice. A man unhurriedly condensed out of the air in front of me—pale, very respectable looking, wearing a supremely well-fitting gray suit. Inclining his head to one side, he inquired with quite exquisite politeness, "May I make bold to hope that I am not inconveniencing you too greatly?"

"Not in the slightest," I said, getting to my feet, "Please take a seat and make yourself at home. Would you like some tea?"

"Thank you," said the stranger, and sat down facing me, pulling up his trouser legs with an elegant gesture. "But as for tea, please excuse me, Alexander Ivanovich, I have only just finished supper."

He looked into my eyes for a while, smiling urbanely. I smiled back. "I suppose you are here about the sofa," I said. "I'm afraid the sofa is gone. I'm very sorry, I don't even know—"

The stranger fluttered his hands in the air. "Such petty trifles!" he said. "All that fuss over some nonsense—I beg your pardon—that nobody actually believes in anyway . . . Judge for yourself, Alexander Ivanovich, these petty squabbles and wild goose chases, like some movie, upsetting people over some mythical—I am not afraid to use the word—some mythical White Thesis . . . Every sober-minded individual regards the sofa as a universal translator, somewhat bulky, but extremely durable and reliable. The old ignoramuses with their idle talk about the White Thesis are just making fools of themselves . . . No, I do not wish to talk about the sofa."

"Just as you please," I said, concentrating all my urbanity in this one phrase. "Do let us talk about something else."

"Superstition . . . Prejudice . . ." the stranger said absentmindedly. "Mental sloth and envy, hirsute envy . . ." He interrupted himself. "Forgive me, Alexander Ivanovich, but I will after all be so bold as to request your permission to remove that dipper. Unfortunately iron is effectively opaque to the hyperfield, and a buildup of hyperfield tension in a confined space . . ."

I raised my arms in assent. "By all means, just as you wish! Remove the dipper . . . You may even remove that . . . erm . . . erm . . . that magic wand." At this point I stopped, amazed to see that the dipper was no longer there. The cylinder was standing in a puddle of liquid that looked like colored mercury. The liquid was rapidly evaporating.

"It is for the best, I assure you," said the stranger. "But as for your magnanimous suggestion that I remove the plywitsum, unfortunately I am unable to avail myself of it. It is a matter of morality and ethics—a question of honor, if you wish . . . Convention is such a powerful force. Permit me to suggest that you do not touch the plywitsum again! I see that you have hurt yourself, and as for this eagle . . . I think you can sense . . . eh-eh . . . a certain fragrance . . ."

"Yes," I said with passionate feeling. "The stench is vile, as bad as a monkey house."

We looked at the eagle. The vulture was dozing, its feathers ruffled up.

"The art of controlling the plywitsum," said the stranger, "is both complex and subtle. You must under no circumstances feel distressed or reproach yourself. The course in plywitsum control lasts seven semesters and requires a thorough knowledge of quantum alchemy. As a programmer, you would probably have no difficulty in mastering the electronic-level plywitsum, the so-called PEP-17 . . . but the quantum plywitsum—the hyperfields . . . transgressive materialization . . . the unified Lomonosov-Lavoisier law . . ." He gestured apologetically.

"Why, naturally!" I said hastily. "I would never claim . . . Of course I am entirely unprepared." At this point I suddenly remembered I hadn't offered him a cigarette.

"Thank you," said the stranger. "But I very much regret that I don't."

Then, with a polite shuffling of my fingers, I inquired—I didn't ask, but precisely inquired—"Might I perhaps be permitted to know to what I owe the pleasure of our meeting?"

The stranger lowered his eyes. "I am afraid that I may appear indiscreet," he said, "but I am, alas, obliged to confess that I have been here for quite a long time. I would not wish to name names, but I believe it is clear even to you, Alexander Ivanovich, far removed as you are from this entire business, that a rather unedifying commotion has developed over the sofa: a scandal is in the offing, the atmosphere is growing heated, and the tension is mounting. In such a situation mistakes and highly undesirable accidents are inevitable . . . We need not look too far for examples. A certain person—I repeat, I would not wish to name names, especially as this person is an associate deserving of the highest respect, and in speaking of respect, I have in mind if not perhaps his manners then his great talent and selfless dedication—well then, in his nervous haste, a certain person leaves the plywitsum here by mistake, and the plywitsum becomes the center of a sphere of events, in which there becomes implicated a certain individual having no connection with them whatsoever . . ." He bowed in my direction. "And in such cases it is absolutely essential to take action which will neutralize the harmful effects . . ." He cast a meaningful glance at the prints of my shoes on the ceiling. Then he smiled at me and said, "But I would not wish to appear to be an abstract altruist. Of course, as both a specialist and an administrator I find all these events extremely interesting . . . However, I have no intention of inconveniencing you any further, and since you have given me your assurance that you will not experiment with the plywitsum any further, I shall ask you please to allow me to take my leave." He stood up.

"No, please!" I cried out. "Do not go! It is such a pleasure for me to talk with you, and I have a thousand questions to ask!"

"I am most truly appreciative of your tact, Alexander Ivanovich, but you are exhausted, you are in need of rest . . ."

"Not in the least!" I retorted heatedly. "Quite the contrary!"

"Alexander Ivanovich," said the stranger, smiling kindly and staring hard into my eyes. "You really are feeling tired, and you really do want to take a rest."

And then I realized that I actually was falling asleep. I couldn't keep my eyes open. I didn't want to talk anymore. I didn't want to do anything at all. I just felt terribly sleepy.

"It has been a quite exceptional pleasure to make your acquaintance," the stranger said in a soft voice.

I saw him start to fade, gradually becoming fainter until he dissolved into the air, leaving behind a faint odor of expensive eau de cologne. I spread the bedding out clumsily on the floor, stuck my face into the pillow, and instantly fell asleep.

I was woken by a flapping of wings and an unpleasant screeching. The room was filled with a strange, bluish half-light. The vulture on the brick oven was rustling its feathers, screaming repulsively, and banging its wings against the ceiling. I sat up and looked around. Floating in the air at the center of the room was a big, tough-looking bozo in tracksuit pants and a striped Hawaiian shirt. He was hovering above the cylinder and making passes over it with his massive, bony hands without touching it.

"What's the problem?" I asked.

The bozo glanced briefly at me over his shoulder and then turned away.

"I didn't hear your answer," I said angrily. I was still feeling very sleepy.

"Quiet, mortal," the bozo said in a hoarse voice. He stopped making passes and picked the cylinder up off the floor. I thought his voice sounded familiar.

"Hey, buddy!" I said threateningly. "Put that thing back and clear out."

The bozo looked at me, thrusting out his jaw. I threw the blanket off and stood up.

"All right, put the plywitsum down," I yelled at the top of my voice. The bozo descended to the floor, planted his feet firmly, and assumed a combat stance. The room became a lot lighter, although the lamp was not switched on.

"Sonny boy," said the bozo, "it's nighttime—you ought to be asleep. Why don't you lay yourself down, before I help you do it?"

This guy was obviously no pushover in a fight. But then neither was I. "Shall we go outside, perhaps?" I suggested briskly, pulling up my underpants.

Someone declared with feeling, "With your thoughts directed to the higher Self, free from craving and self-love, cured of spiritual fever, fight, Arjuna!"

I started. So did the young guy.

"Bhagavad Gita!" said the voice. "Chapter 3, verse 30."

"It's the mirror," I said automatically.

"I know that," the bozo growled.

"Put the plywitsum down," I demanded.

"Why are you yelling like an elephant with a sick head?" the guy asked. "As if it was yours!"

"You mean it's yours?"

"Yes, it's mine."

I had a sudden flash of inspiration. "So it was you who took the sofa too!"

"Mind your own business," the young guy advised me.

"Give the sofa back," I said. "I signed a receipt for it."

"Go to hell!" said the bozo, looking around.

At this point another two men appeared in the room, a skinny one and a fat one, both wearing striped pajamas, like inmates of Sing Sing.

"Korneev!" the fat one howled. "So you're the sofa thief! You ought to be ashamed of yourself!"

"You can all go—" said the bozo.

"You lout!" the fat man shouted. "You ought to be thrown out. I'll send in a report on you!"

"Go ahead," Korneev said morosely. "Do what you enjoy doing most."

"How dare you talk to me in that tone of voice! You insolent urchin! You left the plywitsum here! This young man could have suffered as a result!"

"I already have," I interjected. "The sofa's gone, I'm sleeping on the floor like a dog . . . these conversations all night every night . . . That stinking eagle . . ."

The fat man immediately turned toward me. "A quite unprecedented breach of discipline," he declared. "You must complain . . . And you ought to be ashamed of yourself!" he said, turning back to Korneev.

Korneev was gloomily stuffing the plywitsum into his cheek.

The skinny man asked in a low, threatening voice: "Have you extracted the Thesis, Korneev?"

The bozo laughed morosely. "There isn't any Thesis in it," he said. "Why do you keep going on about it? If you don't want us to steal the sofa, then give us another translator."

"Have you read the order about not removing items from the storeroom?" the skinny man asked threateningly.

Korneev stuck his hands in his pockets and gazed up at the ceiling.

"Are you aware of the decision of the Academic Council?" the skinny man asked.

"I am aware, comrade Demin, that Monday starts on Saturday," Korneev said morosely.

"Enough of your demagoguery," said the skinny man. "Return the sofa immediately, and do not dare come back here again."

"I won't return the sofa," said Korneev. "Not until we've finished the experiment."

The fat man made a shocking scene at that. "Unpardonable insubordination," he squealed. "You hooligan!"

The vulture started screeching excitedly again. Without taking his hands out of his pockets, Korneev turned his back and stepped straight through the wall. The fat man dashed after him, yelling, "Oh no, you give back the sofa!"

The skinny man said to me, "It's all a misunderstanding. We'll take measures to prevent it from happening again." He nodded to me and also started moving toward the wall.

"Wait," I exclaimed. "The eagle! Take the eagle! And take the smell with it!"

The skinny man, already halfway into the wall, turned back and beckoned to the bird with his finger. The vulture noisily launched itself off the oven and was sucked in under his fingernail. The skinny man disappeared. The blue light slowly faded and the room went dark. I switched on the light and looked around. Everything in the room was the same as it had been, except for the deep, gaping scratches from the vulture's claws on the oven and the fantastically absurd, dark-ribbed imprints of my shoes on the ceiling.

"The transparent oil found in the cow," the mirror pronounced with idiotic profundity, "does not facilitate the cow's nourishment, but being processed in an appropriate fashion, it provides the finest of nutrition."

I turned the light off and lay down. The floor was hard and there was a cold draft. I'll catch it hot from the old woman tomorrow, I thought.

6

*"No," he said, in answer to the persistent interrogation of my
eye; "I'm not a member—I'm a ghost."*
"Well, that doesn't give you the run of the Mermaid Club."
—H. G. Wells

In the morning the sofa was back where it belonged. I wasn't surprised. I just thought that one way or another the old woman had
gotten what she wanted: the sofa was standing in one corner and
I was lying in another. As I cleared away my bedding and did my
morning exercises, I thought about how there must be some kind of
limit to the capacity for surprise. Clearly I was well past the threshold now. In fact I was feeling pretty close to saturation. I tried to
imagine something that would astonish me at that moment, but
my imagination wasn't up to it. I didn't like that at all, because I
can't stand people who are incapable of being surprised. But my
psychological state was still a long way from *so what's the big deal
anyway*—it was more like Alice in Wonderland, as if I were dreaming
and prepared to accept any miracle as something perfectly natural
that deserved a more adequate response than simply dropping my
jaw and gaping wide-eyed.

I was still doing my exercises when I heard the hallway door
slam. There was a sound of shuffling feet and clattering heels,
someone coughed, something clattered and fell, and an imperious voice called out, "Comrade Gorynych!" The old woman
didn't answer, and the people in the hallway started talking to
each other.

"Which door is this? Ah, I see. And this one?"

"This is the entrance to the museum."

"And this here? What's this? All sealed up, these locks . . ."

"She keeps a very strict house, Janus Polyeuctovich. And here's the phone."

"Then where is the famous sofa? In the museum?"

"No. There should be a storeroom here somewhere."

"That's in here," said a familiar morose voice.

The door of my room swung open to reveal a tall, skinny old man with a magnificent head of snow-white hair, black eyebrows, a black mustache, and intense black eyes. Catching sight of me (I was standing there in my underpants with my arms extended to the sides and my feet planted at shoulder width), he stopped and said in a sonorous voice, "I see."

There were other faces peering into the room on his left and right. I said: "I beg your pardon" and ran to get my jeans. But in fact they took no notice of me. Four people came into the room and arranged themselves around the sofa. I knew two of them: the morose Korneev, unshaven and red-eyed, still wearing that frivolous Hawaiian shirt, and the swarthy, hook-nosed Roman, who winked at me, made a mysterious sign with his hand, and immediately turned away. I didn't know the white-haired man. And I didn't know the tall, stout man with the black suit that was shiny on the back and the sweeping, imperious gestures.

"This sofa here?" the shiny man asked.

"It's not a sofa," Korneev said morosely. "It's a translator."

"To me it's a sofa," said the shiny man, looking in a notebook. "Sofa, soft, small double, inventory number 1123." He leaned down and felt it. "There's a damp spot here, Korneev, you had it out in the rain. You'll see, now the springs will turn rusty and the upholstery will go rotten."

"The value of the item concerned," said Roman in a tone that I thought sounded mocking, "does not depend in any way on its upholstery, or even its springs, because it doesn't have any."

"Now that's enough of that, Roman Petrovich," the shiny man said with dignity. "Don't you go trying to shield your Korneev from me. The sofa's registered to my museum, and that's where it has to stay."

"It's a piece of equipment," Korneev said despairingly. "It's for working with."

"I don't know anything about that," the shiny man declared. "I don't know what you mean by working with a sofa. I've got a sofa at home too, and I know what kind of work gets done on that."

"We know that too," Roman said quietly.

"Now, that's enough of that," said the shiny man, turning to face him. "You're not in the beer hall now—this is an official institution. What exactly are you trying to say?"

"What I'm trying to say is that this is not a sofa," said Roman, "or, to put it in a form that you can grasp, it is not entirely a sofa. It is a piece of equipment with the appearance of a sofa."

"I would ask you please to stop making insinuations," the shiny man said emphatically, "concerning forms that I can grasp and so forth. Let's each of us stick to his own job. My job is to put a stop to maladministration and waste, and that's what I'm doing."

"Right," said the white-haired man in a clear, ringing voice. Suddenly there was silence. "I have had a word with Cristóbal José-evich and Fyodor Simeonovich. They believe that the only value this translator has is as a museum piece. It once belonged to King Rudolf II, which puts its historical value beyond dispute. In addition, if my memory does not deceive me, we have already ordered a serial translator, two years ago . . . Can you remember who put in the order, Modest Matveevich?"

"Just a moment," said the shiny Modest Matveevich, and began leafing rapidly through his notebook. "Just a moment . . . One Kitezhgrad Plant TDK-80E Twin-Cycle Translator . . . At the request of comrade Balsamo."

"Balsamo works on it round the clock," said Roman.

"And that TDK's a load of junk," added Korneev. "Molecular-level discrimination."

"Yes, yes," said the white-haired man. "Now I remember. There was a report on a study of the TDK. The discrimination curve really is rather uneven . . . Yes. What about this . . . er . . . sofa?"

"Handcrafted," Roman put in quickly. "Absolutely reliable. Designed and made by Loew ben Bezalel. It took him three hundred years to assemble it and tune it."

"Now then!" said the shiny Modest Matveevich. "That's the way to do a job! An old man like that and he did everything himself."

The mirror suddenly cleared its throat and said, "All of them became younger after having been in the water for an hour, and

I tiptoed rapidly across into the corner and sat down in front of the mirror. That very moment Modest came bursting excitedly into the room, dragging the youthful Sergeant Kovalyov along by the arm.

"Where?" Modest howled in confusion, gazing around.

"There," said Roman, pointing to the sofa.

"No need to get excited, it's right where it supposed to be," added Korneev.

"I meant, where's that . . . programmer?"

"What programmer?" Roman asked in surprise.

"That's enough of that," said Modest. "There was a programmer here. Wearing trousers with no shoes."

"Oh, that's what you meant," said Roman. "We were just playing a joke, Modest Matveevich. There wasn't any programmer here. It was simply . . ." He made a strange movement with his hands and a man wearing jeans and a T-shirt appeared in the center of the room.

I only saw him from the back, so I can't say what he looked like, but the youthful Kovalyov shook his head and said, "No, that's not him."

Modest walked around the apparition, muttering, "T-shirt . . . trousers . . . no shoes! That's him!" The apparition disappeared.

"No it's not, that's not him," said Sergeant Kovalyov. "He was younger and he didn't have a beard . . ."

"He didn't have a beard?" Modest echoed. He was totally confused now.

"He didn't," Kovalyov confirmed.

"Mmm . . ." said Modest. "I think he did have a beard . . ."

"Here, then, I'll give you the notice," said the youthful Kovalyov, handing Modest an official-looking sheet of paper. "And you can sort this business out with your Privalov and your Gorynych . . ."

"But I tell you, the five-kopeck piece isn't ours!" roared Modest. "I can't say anything about this Privalov. Perhaps there isn't any real Privalov at all . . . But comrade Gorynych is our employee!"

The youthful Kovalyov pressed his hands to his breast as he tried to say something.

"I insist that you get to the bottom of this immediately!" roared Modest. "I won't take any more of this, comrade Sergeant! This notice is a slur on the reputation of the entire collective! I insist that you check for yourself!"

"I have my orders—" Kovalyov began, but Modest threw himself on him with a cry of "That's enough of that! I insist!" and dragged him out of the room.

"He's taken him off to the museum," said Roman. "Sasha, where are you? Take the cap off. Let's go and watch."

"Maybe I ought to keep it on," I said.

"Take it off, take it off," said Roman. "You're a phantom now. Nobody believes in you—not the administration or the militia."

Korneev said, "All right, I'm off to get some sleep. Sasha, come over after lunch. You can have a look at our computers and what have you."

I took the cap off. "Now that's enough of that," I said. "I'm on vacation."

"Come on, let's go," said Roman.

In the hallway Modest was holding on to the sergeant with one hand while he opened a massive padlock with the other. "I'll show you our five-kopeck piece!" he shouted. "Everything's properly registered . . . Everything's in its proper place."

"That's not what I was saying," Kovalyov protested feebly. "All I meant was that there could be more than one five-kopeck piece . . ."

Modest opened the door and we all went into a large hall.

It was a perfectly respectable museum, with stands, diagrams, display cases, models, and plaster casts. The general impression was similar to a museum of crime detection, with lots of photographs and rather off-putting exhibits. Modest immediately dragged the sergeant off somewhere behind the stands, where the two of them started droning away: "There's our five-kopeck piece . . ."

"I'm not saying anything about that . . ."

"Comrade Gorynych . . ."

"But I've got my orders!"

"Now that's enough of that!"

"Take a poke around, Sasha," said Roman with a sweeping gesture, and sat down in an armchair by the door.

I began walking along the wall. I wasn't surprised by anything, I just found it all very interesting. "Living water. Efficiency 52%. Permissible sedimentation 0.3" (an old square bottle containing water, the cork sealed with colored wax). "A diagram of the process of industrial extraction of living water." "A model of a living water still." "Veshkovsky-Traubenbach love potion" (a small chemist's jar containing a poisonous-yellow ointment). "Ordinary bad blood" (a sealed ampoule containing a black liquid) . . . Hanging above this stand was a plaque that read, "Active chemical substances. 12th–17th centuries." There were a lot more bottles, jars, retorts, ampoules, flasks, and working and nonworking models of apparatuses for sublimation, distillation, and condensation, but I moved on.

"Magic Sword" (a very rusty two-handed sword with a wavy blade, attached with a chain to an iron pillar inside a tightly sealed display case). "The right canine (working) tooth of Count Dracula of Transylvania" (I am no Cuvier, but to judge from this tooth, Count Dracula of Transylvania was a very unusual and unpleasant individual). "A mortar on its launching pad. 9th century" (a massive assemblage of gray, porous cast iron) . . . "Gorynych Wyrm, skeleton. 1/25 natural size" (it looked like the skeleton of a diplodocus with three necks) . . . "Diagram of the operation of the fire-breathing gland of the middle head" . . . "Seven-league boots, gravitational, working model" (very large rubber boots) . . . "Flying carpet, antigravitational. Working model" (a carpet about one and a half meters square, showing a Circassian man embracing a young Circassian woman against a background of mountains, also Circassian) . . .

I got as far as the stand "Development of the Idea of the Philosopher's Stone" when Sergeant Kovalyov and Modest Matveevich came back into the hall. As far as I could tell, they hadn't made any progress at all.

"That's enough of that, now," Modest said wearily.

"I've got my orders," Kovalyov responded just as wearily.

"Our five-kopeck piece is in its proper place . . ."

"Then let the old woman come in and make a statement . . ."

"What do you think we are, counterfeiters?"

"I didn't say that . . ."

"A slur on the name of the entire collective . . ."

"We'll get to the bottom of this . . ."

Kovalyov didn't notice me, but Modest stopped, ran his lackluster gaze over me, then raised his eyes and pronounced wearily, "Laboratory ham-munculus, generic view," and went on.

I followed him, with a strange feeling that something bad was about to happen. Roman was waiting for us by the door.

"Well?" he asked.

"Outrageous bureaucracy," Modest said wearily.

"I have my orders," Sergeant Kovalyov repeated stubbornly from the hallway.

"Come on out then, Roman Petrovich, come on," said Modest, jangling the keys.

Roman went out. I was about to dart through after him, but Modest stopped me.

"I beg your pardon," he said. "Where do you think you're going?"

"What do you mean?" I asked, crestfallen.

"You go back to your place."

"What place?"

"Well, where is it you stand? You're one of those . . . hammunculuses, aren't you? Go and stand where you're supposed to."

I thought I was done for. And I probably would have been, because Roman was obviously dismayed as well, but just at that moment Naina Kievna burst into the hall, clattering and stamping and leading a huge black goat on a rope. At the sight of the militia sergeant the goat gave a discordant bleat and made a dash for it. Naina Kievna fell over. Modest dashed out into the hallway and there was an almighty racket as the empty water tub was sent tumbling. Roman grabbed me by the arm, whispered, "Move it! Move it!" and ran for my room. We slammed the door shut behind us and leaned back against it, gasping for breath. We heard voices shouting in the hallway: "Let me see your papers!"

"Good grief, what's going on?"

"Why's that goat here? What's a goat doing on the premises?"

"Me-e-e-eh . . ."

"That's enough of that, you're not in a beer hall now!"

"I don't know anything about any five-kopeck pieces!"

"Me-e-e-eh . . ."

"Citizeness, take the goat outside!"

"That's enough of that, that goat's been properly inventoried!"

"A goat, inventoried?"

"It's not a goat! It's one of our employees!"

"Then let it show me its papers!"

"Out of the window and into the car!" Roman ordered.

I grabbed my jacket and jumped through the window. The cat Vasily darted out from under my feet with a loud *meow*. I crouched over and ran to the car, swung open the door, and jumped into the driver's seat. Roman was already pushing back the massive main gates.

The engine wouldn't start. As I struggled with the ignition I saw the door of the house swing open and the black goat come darting out of the hallway and away around the corner in massive bounds. The engine roared into life. I turned the car around and hurtled out into the street. The oak gates slammed shut with a crash. Roman appeared through the wicket gate and threw himself in beside me.

"Now step on it!" he said cheerfully. "Into the center!"

As we were turning onto Peace Prospect, he asked, "Well, how do you like it round these parts?"

"I like it," I said. "Only it's almost too lively."

"It's always lively at Naina's place," said Roman. "She's a cantankerous old woman. Didn't upset you, did she?"

"No," I said. "We hardly even spoke."

"Hang on," said Roman. "Slow down."

"Why?"

"There's Vladimir. Remember Volodya?"

I stopped the car. The bearded Volodya got into the backseat and shook our hands with a beaming smile. "That's great!" he said. "I was just on my way to see you!"

"That would have just made our day," said Roman.

"So what happened in the end?"

"Nothing," said Roman.

"Then where are you going now?"

"To the Institute," said Roman.

"What for?" I asked.

"To work," said Roman.

"I'm on vacation."

"Makes no difference," said Roman. "Monday starts on Saturday, and this year August starts in July!"

"But the guys are expecting me," I pleaded.

"We can handle that," said Roman. "The guys won't notice a thing."

"I don't believe this," I said.

We drove between shop number 2 and cafeteria number 11. "He already knows the way," remarked Volodya.

"He's a great guy," said Roman, "a colossus!"

"I took a liking to him straightaway," said Volodya.

"You obviously do need a programmer very badly," I said.

"But we don't need just any old programmer," Roman retorted.

I stopped the car in front of the strange building with the sign saying "NITWiT" between the windows. "What does that mean?" I asked. "Am I at least allowed to know where I'm being press-ganged into working?"

"Yes, you are," said Roman. "You're allowed to know everything now. It's the National Institute for the Technology of Witchcraft and Thaumaturgy . . . Well, what are you waiting for? Drive in!"

"In where?" I asked.

"You mean you can't see it?" And then I did see it.

But that's an entirely different story.

Vanity of Vanities

1

*Of all the characters in a story, one or two central heroes stand
out, and all the others are regarded as secondary.*
—The Methodology of Teaching Literature

About two o'clock in the afternoon, when the Aldan's input device
blew its fuse again, the phone started to ring. It was the deputy
director for the administration of buildings and contents, Modest
Matveevich Kamnoedov.

"Privalov," he said sternly, "why aren't you where you're supposed to be again?"

"Why, where am I supposed to be?" I asked petulantly. That
day had been just full of hassle, and I'd forgotten everything.

"Now, that's enough of that," said Modest Matveevich. "You
were supposed to report to me for instructions five minutes ago."

"Holy cow," I said, and put down the phone.

I turned off the computer, took off my lab coat, and told the girls
not to forget to shut off the power. The big corridor was empty,
the windows were half frozen over, and there was a blizzard raging
outside. I put my jacket on as I walked along, then set off at a run
to the Department of Buildings and Contents.

Modest Matveevich, wearing his shiny suit, was waiting imperi-
ously for me in his own waiting room. Behind him a little gnome
with hairy ears was running his fingers over a massive register with
despondent diligence.

"You, Privalov, are like some kind of ham-munculus," said
Modest, "never where you're supposed to be."

Everyone tried to keep on the right side of Modest Matveevich,
because he was a powerful man, absolutely intransigent and quite
incredibly ignorant. So I roared out, "Yes, sir!" and clicked my heels.

"You've always got to be where you're supposed to be," Modest Matveevich continued. "Always. You've got a university education, and glasses, and you've grown that fine beard, but you still can't even grasp a simple theorem like that."

"It won't happen again," I said, opening my eyes wide.

"That's quite enough of that," said Modest Matveevich, softening. He took a sheet of paper out of his pocket and looked at it for a moment. "Right, then, Privalov," he said eventually, "today it's your turn to stand watch. Night watch in an institution over a holiday is a serious responsibility. Not as simple as pressing those buttons of yours.

"First, there's fire safety. That's the first thing, to forestall any occurrences of spontaneous combustion. Ensure that the production facilities entrusted to your care are disconnected from the power supply. And do it in person—none of that doubling-up or tripling-up trickery. None of those doubles of yours. If you discover an incident of combustion, call 01 immediately and start taking measures. For this eventuality you are provided with an alarm whistle to summon the emergency team." He handed me a platinum whistle with an inventory number on it.

"And don't you let anyone in. This is the list of individuals who have permission to use the laboratories at night, but don't you let them in either, because it's a holiday. Not a single living soul in the entire Institute. All those other souls and spirits—that's all right, but not a single living one. Put a spell on the demons at the entrance and the exit. You understand the situation. Not a single living soul must get in, and none of the others must get out. Because we've already had a press-eedent: when a devil got out and stole the moon. A very famous press-eedent it was too—they even made it into a film." He gave me a meaningful look and suddenly asked to see my papers.

I showed them to him. He examined my pass closely, gave it back to me, and said, "All in order. Just for a moment there I suspected you were a double after all. All right, then. At fifteen hundred hours in accordance with the currently applicable labor regulations, the working day will end and everyone will hand in the keys to their production premises. Following which you will personally inspect all the Institute's premises. After that you make your rounds every three hours for purposes of spontaneous combustion. During your period of duty you will visit the vivarium at least twice. If the supervisor is drinking tea, stop him. We've had reports it's not tea he's drinking. That's the way of things. Your post is in the director's waiting room. You can rest on the sofa. Tomorrow at sixteen hundred hours you will be relieved by Vladimir Pochkin from comrade Oira-Oira's laboratory. Is that clear?"

"Absolutely," I said.

"I'll call you during the night and tomorrow afternoon. You may also be checked by comrade head of the Personnel Department."

"I understand," I said, and ran my eye down the list. The first name on the list was the Institute's director, Janus Polyeuctovich Nevstruev, with a penciled note: "Two-off." Second came Modest Matveevich himself, and third was comrade head of the Personnel Department citizen Cerberus Psoevich Demin. They were followed by names I'd never come across anywhere before.

"Is anything unclear?" inquired Modest Matveevich, who had been following my movements suspiciously.

"Just here," I said gravely, jabbing my finger at the list, "I have identified a sequence of . . . twenty-two comrades with whom I am not personally acquainted. I would like to run through these names with you in person." I looked him straight in the eye and said, "As a precautionary measure."

Modest Matveevich took the list and examined it, holding it at arm's length. "All in order," he said condescendingly. "It's just that you, Privalov, are not up to speed. The individuals listed from number 4 to number 25 inclusive have been entered in the list of individuals allowed to work at night posthumously. In acknowledgment of services rendered previously. Is that clear now?"

I felt a little bit freaked. After all, it was pretty hard to get used to all this stuff.

"Take up your post," Modest Matveevich said majestically. "Allow me, comrade Privalov, on behalf of the administration, to wish you every appropriate success in your professional and private life in the New Year."

I wished him appropriate success too and went out into the corridor.

When I had learned the day before that I was going to be on duty, I'd been delighted: I was intending to finish off a calculation for Roman Oira-Oira. But now I realized that things weren't quite that simple. The prospect of spending the night in the Institute suddenly appeared to me in an entirely different light. I'd stayed on to work late before, when the guys on watch had economized by switching off four lamps out of five in every corridor and I had to make my way to the exit past twitching masses of tangled shadows. At first I found this very disturbing, then I got used to it, but then I got unused to it again when one day I was walking down the wide corridor and I heard the regular clicking of claws on parquet flooring and glanced back to see some kind of phosphorescent beast running along behind me, clearly following my tracks. In actual fact, when they brought me down from the cornice, it turned out to have been an ordinary live dog that belonged to one of the staff. The staff member concerned came to apologize and Oira-Oira lectured me on the harmfulness of superstition, but even so it all left a pretty bitter aftertaste. The first thing I'll do, I thought, is put the spell on the demons.

At the entrance to the director's waiting room I ran into the morose Vitka Korneev. He nodded gloomily and was about to walk by, but I caught hold of his sleeve.

"What?" Korneev said rudely, stopping.

"I'm on duty today," I informed him.

"More fool you," said Korneev.

"You're so rude, Vitka," I said. "I don't think I'll bother talking to you any more."

Vitka pulled down the collar of his sweater with one finger and looked at me curiously. "What are you going to do with me, then?"

"I'll think of something," I said, rather uncertainly.

Vitka suddenly livened up. "Hang on," he said. "You mean this is the first time you've done the night watch?"

"Yes."

"Aha," said Vitka. "And just how do you intend to proceed?"

"According to instructions," I replied. "I'll put a spell on the demons and go to sleep. For purposes of spontaneous combustion. Where are you going to be?"

"Oh, there's a few people getting together," Vitka said vaguely. "At Vera's place . . . what's that you've got there?" He took my list. "Ah, the dead souls . . ."

"I won't let anyone in," I said. "Dead or alive."

"A correct decision," said Vitka. "Impeccably correct. Only keep an eye on my lab. There'll be a double working in there."

"Whose double?"

"My double, of course. Who else would give me theirs? I've locked him in there—here, take the key, since you're on duty."

I took the key. "Listen, Vitka, he can work until about ten, but after that I'll disconnect everything. In accordance with regulations."

"OK, we'll sort that out somehow. Have you seen Edik anywhere around?"

"No, I haven't," I said. "And don't you go trying to pull a fast one. I'm disconnecting everything at ten o'clock."

"That's just fine by me. Disconnect away. Disconnect the whole town if you like."

Then the door of the waiting room opened and Janus Polyeuctovich came out into the corridor. "I see," he said when he saw us there.

I bowed respectfully. I could tell from Janus Polyeuctovich's face that he'd forgotten my name.

"Here you are," he said, handing me his keys. "You're on duty, if I'm not mistaken . . . And by the way . . ." He hesitated. "Wasn't I talking to you yesterday?"

"Yes," I said, "you stopped by the computer room."

He nodded. "Yes, yes, that's right . . . we had a talk about train-ees."

"No," I interjected respectfully, "not exactly. It was about our letter to the Central Academic Supplies Committee. Concerning an electronic peripheral device."

"Ah, that's it," he said. "Very well then, I wish you a peaceful night shift . . . Victor Pavlovich, could I see you for a moment?"

He took Vitka by the arm and led him away down the corridor, and I went into the waiting room, where the second Janus Polyeuc-tovich was locking the safes. When he saw me, he said, "I see," and immediately started jangling his keys. It was A-Janus. I'd already learned something about how to tell them apart. A-Janus looked a bit younger; he was unsociable, always formally correct, and not very talkative. He was supposed to be a hard worker, and people who had known him for a long time said that this fair-to-middling administrator was slowly but surely developing into an outstand-ing scientist. S-Janus, on the other hand, was always soft-mannered and very attentive, and he had the strange habit of asking, "Wasn't I talking to you yesterday?" They said he'd been going downhill pretty badly just recently, although he was still a scientist with a serious international reputation. And yet A-Janus and S-Janus were one and the same person. I just couldn't get my head around that. It seemed too artificial somehow. I even suspected it was just a figure of speech.

A-Janus closed the final lock, handed me some of the keys, said good-bye coolly, and went out. I sat at the academic secretary's desk, put my list down in front of me, and dialed my own number in the computer room. There was no answer—the girls must have gone already. It was 1430 hours.

At 1431 hours the great magician and sorcerer the famous Fyodor Simeonovich Kivrin came bursting into the waiting room, panting noisily and setting the parquet floor creaking. As the head of the Department of Linear Happiness, Fyodor Simeonovich was famous for his incorrigible optimism and faith in the bright future. His own past history was extremely turbulent. Under Ivan Vasilyevich—the

czar Ivan the Terrible—the *oprichniki* of the minister of state security, Malyuta Skuratov, had jibed and joked as they burned him in
a wooden bathhouse as a sorceror on the denunciation of his neigh-
bor, a church sexton; under Czar Alexei Mikhailovich the Peaceful
he was beaten mercilessly with rods, and the collected manuscripts
of his works were burned on his bare back; under Czar Peter the
Great he was initially elevated to the role of a specialist in chemistry
and mining but somehow managed to displease Prince Romoda-
novsky and ended up in exile at the Tula Arms Plant, from where he
fled to India, traveled around for a long time, was bitten by poisonous snakes and crocodiles, effortlessly mastered yoga, came back to
Russia at the height of Pugachev's rebellion, was accused of being
the rebels' healer, had his nostrils slit, and was exiled to Solovets
in perpetuity. In Solovets he survived a whole heap of other mis-
fortunes before he eventually became attached to NITWiT, where
he soon became a head of department, and recently he had been
doing a lot of work on the problems of human happiness, waging a
dedicated struggle against those of his colleagues who believed that
the basis of happiness was material abundance.

"Greetings to you!" he boomed, laying the keys to his laboratories in front of me. *"Poor* man, what have you done to *deserve* this? On a night like *this* you ought to be out having fun. I'll call Modest, this is such *nonsense,* I'll take the shift *myself . . ."*

I could see this idea had only just occurred to him and he was really taken by it.

"All right now, where's his *telephone* number? *Curses,* I never remember *telephone* numbers . . . One-one-*five* or *five*-one-one . . ."

"Thank you, Fyodor Simeonovich," I cried. "Please don't bother! I've just settled in to get a bit of work done!"

"Ah, a bit of *work!* That's a *different* matter. 'At's good, 'at's splendid, *well* done! Dammit, I know *nothing* at all about electronics . . . I *must* do some studying, get away from all this *word magic,* this old junk, hocus-pocus with *psychofields,* primitive stuff . . . *Antiquated* methods."

And right there and then he conjured up two big apples, handed one to me, bit off half of the other, and began munching on it with relish.

"Curses, I've made a *worm*-eaten one again. How's yours—is it all right? 'At's good. I'll come *back* and see you later, Sasha. I don't really understand that *system* of computer commands properly . . . I'll just have a glass of *vodka* and then come back . . . The twenty-ninth *command* of that machine of yours . . . Either the machine is lying, or I *don't* understand . . . I'll bring you a *detective* novel: Erle Stanley Gardner. You read English, don't you? He writes well, the rascal, *great* stuff. He's got this real *hard-headed* lawyer, Perry Mason. Do you know him? And then I'll give you something else to read, some *science fiction.* Asimov, maybe, or Ray *Bradbury . . ."*

He went over to the window and exclaimed in delight. "A blizzard, dammit. How I *love* that!"

The slim and elegant Cristóbal Joséevich Junta came in, wrapping himself in a mink coat.

Fyodor Simeonovich turned around. "Ah, Cristó!" he exclaimed. "Just look at this, that *fool* Kamnoedov has locked a young boy in to keep watch on New Year's Eve. Let's let him *off;* the two of us

can stay, we'll remember the *old* times and have a drink, what do you say? Why should *he* have to suffer? He ought to be out *dancing* with the girls . . ."

Junta put his keys on the desk and said casually, "Association with girls affords pleasure only when it is attained through the overcoming of obstacles."

"But of *course!*" boomed Fyodor Simeonovich. "'*Much* blood is spilled and many *songs* are sung for ladies fair' . . . How does that one of yours go? 'Only he shall attain the *goal* who knows not the word *fear* . . .'"

"Precisely," said Junta. "And anyway, I can't stand charity."

"He *can't* stand charity! Who was it who begged Odikhmantiev from me? *Enticed* away a fine laboratory assistant, you did . . . You put up a bottle of *champagne* right now, *nothing* less . . . No, you know *what*, not champagne! Amontillado! Do you have any of the old *Toledo* stock left?"

"They're waiting for us, Teodoro," Junta reminded him.

"Ah yes, *that's* right . . . I've still got to find a *tie* . . . and some felt boots. We'll never get a *taxi* . . . We're off then, Sasha, don't get too *bored* now."

"No one on duty in the Institute on New Year's Eve ever gets bored," Junta said in a low voice. "Especially new boys."

They walked to the door. Junta let Fyodor Simeonovich out first and, before going out himself, he glanced sideways at me and carefully traced out a Star of Solomon on the wall with his finger. The star flared up and then began slowly fading away, like the trace of an electron beam on the screen of an oscilloscope. I spat three times over my left shoulder.

Cristóbal Joséevich Junta, the head of the Department of the Meaning of Life, was a remarkable man, but apparently quite heartless. In his early youth he had spent a long time as a grand inquisitor, but then he'd fallen into heresy, although to the present day he'd retained the habits of those times, and rumor had it that he'd found them very useful during the struggle against the fifth column in Spain. He performed almost all of his abstruse experiments either on himself or on his colleagues, as I had been indignantly informed at the general meeting of the trade union. He was studying the meaning of life, but he hadn't made a great deal of progress so far, although he had produced some interesting results. For instance, he had proved, at least theoretically, that death was by no means a necessary attribute of life. People had expressed their indignation at this discovery, too—at the philosophy seminar.

He allowed almost no one to enter his office, and vague rumors circulated in the Institute about it being full of all sorts of interesting things. They said that standing in one corner was the magnificently stuffed body of an old acquaintance of Cristóbal Joséevich, an SS *Standartenführer* in full dress uniform, with a monocle, dagger, Iron Cross, Oak Leaves, and other paraphernalia. Junta was a magnificent taxidermist and, according to Cristóbal Joséevich himself, so was the *Standartenführer*. But it was Cristóbal Joséevich who had gotten his hand in first. He always liked to get his hand in first, in everything he did. But he was not entirely without skepticism either. A huge poster hanging in one of his laboratories posed the question Do We Really Need Ourselves for Anything? A quite exceptional individual.

At exactly 3:00, in accordance with the labor regulations, doctor of science Ambrosius Ambroisovich Vybegallo brought me his keys. He was wearing felt boots soled with leather and a smelly sheepskin coat like a cab driver's with his gray, dirty beard sticking out through its upturned collar. He wore his hair in a bowl cut, so no one had ever seen his ears.

"It, er . . ." he said as he came up to me. "It could just happen that one of mine will hatch out today. In my laboratory, that is. It, er . . . it would be a good idea to keep an eye out. I've left him plenty of supplies. It's er . . . five loaves of bread, you know, some steamed bran, two buckets of skim milk. But when, er . . . he's eaten all that lot, he'll start kicking up a fuss, you know. So, *mon cher*, if anything happens, you . . . er . . . just give me a jingle, my good man." He set a bunch of barn door keys down in front of me and opened his mouth in some perplexity, with his eyes fixed on me.

His eyes were transparent and he had grains of millet stuck in his beard.

"Where shall I jingle you?" I asked.

Roman Oira-Oira breezed in wearing a green coat with a lamb-skin collar. He twitched his hooked nose and inquired, "Did Vybe-gallo just drop by?"

"He did," I said.

"Yes indeed," he said, "it's the herrings. Take my keys. Do you know where he dumped one truckload? Under Gian Giacomo's windows. Right under his office. A little New Year's present. Might as well have a cigarette now that I'm here."

He slumped into an immense leather armchair, unbuttoned his coat, and lit up.

"All right, try this one," he said. "Given: the smell of salted herring water, intensity sixteen microchokes, cubic volume . . ." He looked around the room. "Well, you can work that out for yourself. The year's on the turn, Saturn's in the constellation of Libra . . . Get rid of that stench!"

I scratched myself behind one ear. "Saturn . . . Why are you telling me about Saturn? What's the magistatum vector?"

"Well, brother," said Oira-Oira, "that's for you . . ."

I scratched behind my other ear, worked out the vector in my head, then stuttered and stammered my way through the acoustic operation (pronounced the incantation). Oira-Oira held his nose. I pulled two hairs out of my eyebrow and polarized the vector. The smell grew stronger again.

"That's bad," Oira-Oira said reproachfully. "What are you doing, sorcerer's apprentice? Can't you see the window's open?"

"Ah," I said, "that's right." I adjusted for the divergence and the curl of the vector, tried to resolve Stokes's equation in my head, got confused, plucked another two hairs out of my eyebrow, breathing through my mouth, sniffed them, mumbled Auer's incantation and was already plucking out another hair when I realized the waiting room had aired itself by natural means and Roman advised me not to waste any more of my eyebrows and close the window.

"Satisfactory," he said. "Let's try some materialization." We worked on materialization for a while. I created some pears, and

Roman insisted that I eat them. I refused, and then he made me create some more. "You'll keep working until you create something edible," he said. "And you can give these to Modest. He can digest stones." Eventually I created a genuine pear—large, yellow, soft as butter, and bitter as quinine. I ate it and Roman allowed me to take a break.

Then fat Magnus Fyodorovich Redkin, bachelor of black magic, brought in his keys, as always preoccupied and greatly affronted. He'd been awarded his bachelor's degree three hundred years earlier for inventing breeches of darkness, and he'd spent all his time since then making improvements to those breeches. The breeches of darkness had first been transformed into pantaloons of darkness, then into trousers of darkness, and just recently they'd become known as pants of darkness. But somehow he just couldn't get them right.

At the most recent session of the black magic seminar, when he gave his regular paper "On Certain New Properties of Redkin's Pants of Darkness," he had suffered yet another fiasco. During the demonstration of the new, improved model something had gotten stuck in the button-and-braces mechanism and instead of making the inventor invisible the trousers had given a resounding click and become invisible themselves. It had been a very awkward moment.

For the most part, however, Magnus Fyodorovich was working on a dissertation under the title "The Materialization and Linear Naturalization of the White Thesis as an Argument for the Adequately Random Sigma Function of Incompletely Representable Human Happiness." In this area he had produced substantial and significant results, from which it followed that humanity would be literally swimming in incompletely representable happiness, if only the White Thesis itself could be located and also—more important—if only we were able to understand what it is and where to look for it.

The only mention of the White Thesis is found in the journals of ben Bezalel, who supposedly isolated the Thesis as a byproduct of some alchemical reaction and, not having any time to waste on such petty matters, incorporated it into one of his devices as an auxiliary element. In one of his later memoirs, written in a dungeon, ben Bezalel noted, "And can you believe it? That White Thesis failed to justify my expectations. It failed. But when I realized the good that it could have done—I am talking about happiness for all people, as many as there are in existence—I had already forgotten where I installed it."

The Institute possessed seven devices that once belonged to ben Bezalel. Redkin had stripped six of them down to the last bolt and not discovered anything special. The seventh device was the sofa-translator. But Vitka Korneev had appropriated the sofa, and Redkin's simple soul had been filled with the very blackest of suspicions. He began following Vitka around. Vitka had immediately flown into a rage. They had argued and become sworn enemies, and still were to that very day. Magnus Fyodorovich was well disposed toward me as a representative of the precise sciences, but he disapproved of my friendship with "that plagiarist."

Redkin was basically not a bad person, very hardworking, very tenacious, entirely devoid of self-interest and avarice. He had done a huge amount of work, assembling a gigantic collection of the most varied definitions of happiness. There were extremely simple negative definitions ("Happiness is not to be found in money"), extremely simple positive definitions ("Supreme satisfaction, total gratification, success, and good luck"), casuistic definitions ("Happiness is the absence of unhappiness"), and paradoxical definitions ("The happiest of all men are jesters, fools, idiots, and the unaware, for they know not the pangs of conscience, have no fear of ghosts and other ghouls and goblins, and are not tormented by fear of future calamities, nor are they deluded by hopes of boons to come").

Magnus Fyodorovich put down his key on the table and, glancing distrustfully at us from under his brows, said, "I've found another definition."

"What is it?" I asked.

"It's like a poem. Only without any rhyme. Would you like to hear it?"

"Of course we would," said Roman.

Magnus Fyodorovich opened his notebook and read it out, stammering and stuttering:

> *You ask me:*
> *What is the greatest happiness on earth?*
> *Two things:*
> *changing my mind*
> *as I'd change a penny for a shilling;*
> *and*
> *listening to the sound*
> *of a young girl*
> *singing down the road*
> *after she has asked me the way.*

"I didn't understand a thing," said Roman. "Let me read it for myself."

Redkin gave him the notebook and explained: "It's Christopher Logue. From the English."

"Great poetry," said Roman.

Magnus Fyodorovich sighed. "Some say one thing, others say something else."

"It's tough," I said sympathetically.

"It really is, isn't it? How can you link it all together? Hear a girl singing . . . And not just any old singing either—the girl has to be young and be off his path, and it must be after someone asks him the way . . . How on Earth can it be done? Is it really possible to reduce things like that to algorithms?"

"Hardly," I said. "I wouldn't like to try."

"You see!" Magnus Fyodorovich exclaimed. "And you're the head of our computer center! So who can do it?"

"Maybe it just doesn't exist at all?" Roman suggested in the voice of a movie villain.

"What?"

"Happiness."

Magnus Fyodorovich immediately took offense at that. "How can it not exist," he said with a dignified air, "when I myself have experienced it on repeated occasions?"

"By changing pennies for a shilling?" asked Roman.

Magnus Fyodorovich took even greater offense at that and grabbed his notebook out of Roman's hands. "You're still too young—" he began.

But at that moment there was a sudden rumbling and crashing, a flash of flame, and a smell of sulfur, and Merlin appeared in the center of the room. Magnus Fyodorovich recoiled all the way to the window in surprise, exclaimed, "Oh, you!" and went running out.

"Good God!" Oira-Oira said in English, wiping the dust out of his eyes. "Canst thou not enter by the usual route as decent people do?" Then he added, "Sir."

"I do beg thy pardon," Merlin said smugly, casting a satisfied glance in my direction. I must have looked pale, because I'd suddenly been terrified by the thought of spontaneous combustion.

Merlin straightened his moth-eaten robe, tossed a bunch of keys onto the desk, and said, "Have you noticed, kind sirs, what the weather is like?"

"As predicted," said Roman.

"Precisely, Sir Oira-Oira! Precisely as predicted!"

"A very handy thing, the radio," said Roman.

"I listen not to the radio," said Merlin. "I have my own methods." He shook the hem of his robe and floated up a meter above
the floor.

"The chandelier!" I said. "Careful!"

Merlin glanced briefly at the chandelier and began speaking,
apropos of nothing at all: "Oh ye imbued with the spirit of Western
materialism, base mercantilism, and utilitarianism, whose spiritual
poverty is incapable of rising above the gloom and chaos of petty,
cheerless cares . . . I cannot help but recall, dear sirs, how last year I
and Sir Chairman of the district soviet, comrade Pereyaslavsky . . ."

Oira-Oira gave a heart-rending yawn, and I suddenly felt
depressed too. Merlin would probably have been even worse than
Vybegallo, if he weren't so archaic and conceited. Through an over-
sight on someone's part he had once managed to rise to be head
of the Department of Predictions and Prophecies, because he had
written in all his questionnaires about his implacable struggle against
Yankee imperialism even back in the Middle Ages, attaching to the
questionnaires notarized typed copies of the relevant pages from
Mark Twain. Later, in connection with the changed internal situation and the improved international climate, he had been moved
back to his position as head of the weather office and now worked,
just as he had a thousand years earlier, at forecasting atmospheric
phenomena, relying on magical means as well as the behavior of
tarantulas, twinges of rheumatism, and the propensity of the pigs
of Solovets to lie down and wallow in the mud or to clamber out
of the aforesaid substance. However, the main source of his fore-
casts was the crude interception of radio signals, performed with the
assistance of a crystal receiver that was widely believed to have been
stolen in the 1920s from a Young Scientist Exhibition in Solovets.
The Institute kept him on out of respect for his age. He was a great
friend of Naina Kievna Gorynych, and the two of them collected
and disseminated rumors about a gigantic woman covered in hair
appearing in the forest and a female student being taken prisoner by
a yeti from Mount Elbrus. It was also said that from time to time he

took part in the nocturnal vigils on Bald Mountain with C. M. Viy, Khoma Brut, and other hooligans.

Roman and I said nothing and waited for him to disappear. But he wrapped his robe around himself, settled in comfortably under the chandelier, and launched into the long, boring story that everyone already knew by heart about how he, Merlin, and the chairman of the Solovets district soviet, Pereyaslavsky, had undertaken a journey of inspection around the local district. The whole story was nothing but a pack of lies, a talentless and opportunistic transposition of Mark Twain. He talked about himself in the third person, sometimes losing the thread and calling the chairman King Arthur.

"Right so the chairman of the district soviet and Merlin departed, and went until a keeper of bees, the Hero of Labor Sir Eremitenko, who was a good knight and a renowned gatherer of honey. So Sir Eremitenko related to them his successes in labor and did cure Sir Arthur of his radiculitis with bee venom. And Sir Chairman was there three days, and his radiculitis was soothed that he might ride and go, and so departed. And as they rode, Ar—Chairman said, I have no sword. No force, said Merlin, hereby is a sword that shall be yours and I may. So they rode till they came to a lake, the which was a fair water and broad, and in the midst of the lake Arthur was ware of a hand hardened by toil, that held a hammer and sickle. Lo, said Merlin, yonder is that sword that I spake of . . ."

Then the phone rang and I grabbed it in delight. "Hello," I said. "Hello, who is it?"

There was a low mumbling in the receiver and Merlin droned on through his nose: ". . . So they rode into Lezhncv, and by the way they met with Sir Pellinor; but Merlin had done such a craft that Pellinore saw not the Chairman . . ."

"Sir citizen Merlin," I said, "could you speak more quietly please? I can't hear."

Merlin stopped speaking, but with the expression of a man ready to continue at any moment.

"Hello," I said into the receiver again. "Who's speaking? Who are you looking for?" I said out of old habit.

"That's enough of that from you. You're not in the circus now, Privalov."

"I'm sorry, Modest Matveevich. Duty staff member Privalov here."

"That's better. Now report."

"Report what?"

"Listen here, Privalov, there you go again behaving like I don't know what. Who's that you're talking with there? Why are there outsiders at your post? Why, in contravention of the labor regulations, are there still people in the Institute after the end of the working day?"

"It's Merlin," I said.

"Throw him out on his ear!"

"Gladly," I said. (Merlin, who had no doubt been listening, broke out in red blotches, exclaimed, "Boorish churl!" and dissolved into thin air.)

"Gladly or otherwise, it makes no difference to me. And I've received a warning here that you're piling up the keys entrusted to you in a heap on the desk, instead of locking them in the box."

Vybegallo ratted on me, I thought.

"Haven't you got anything to say?"

"I'll put that right."

"That's the way of things," said Modest Matveevich. "Unflagging vigilance is absolutely essential. Is that clear?"

"It is."

"That's all from me, then," Modest Matveevich said, and hung up.

"All right, then," said Oira-Oira, "I'll go and start opening cans and uncorking bottles. Cheers for now—I'll drop by again later."

2

I walked on, descending dark passages, in order to ascend again to the floors above. I was alone, I called out, nobody answered, I was alone; there was no one in that house—a house as vast and tortuous as a labyrinth.

—Guy de Maupassant

I dropped the keys into my jacket pocket and set off on my first round. I went down the formal staircase, which I could only ever remember being used on one occasion, when the Institute was visited by a most august personage from Africa, into the vast entrance hall decorated with centuries-old strata of architectural extravagance, and glanced in the window of the doorman's chamber, where I could vaguely make out the two Maxwell's macrodemons through the phosphorescent mist. The demons were playing that most stochastic of games—heads or tails, which was what they did whenever they weren't on duty. Huge, sluggish, and indescribably grotesque, resembling more than anything else colonies of the polio virus under an electron microscope, dressed in worn-out livery, they spent all their lives, as Maxwell's demons are supposed to do, opening and closing doors. These were experienced, well-trained specimens, but one of them—the one in charge of the exits—had already reached retirement age, commensurate with the age of the galaxy, and every now and then he lapsed into senile dementia and started malfunctioning. Then someone from the Technical Service Department had to put on a diving suit, clamber into the chamber, which was filled with compressed argon, and restore the old guy to his senses.

Following instructions, I put a spell on them both—that is, I shut off the information channels and linked the input-output devices to

myself. The demons didn't react; they had other things on their
mind. One was winning and the other, accordingly, was losing, and
that bothered them, because it violated the statistical equilibrium.
I closed the cover over the little window and walked around the
entrance hall. It was damp and gloomy, with a hollow echo. The

Institute building was pretty ancient, but they had obviously started building it from this entrance hall. The bones of chained skeletons gleamed in the mildewed corners, there was a steady *drip-drip* of water from somewhere, in the niches between the columns statues in rusty suits of armor stood in unnatural poses, fragments of ancient idols were heaped up by the wall to the right of the door, and there was a pair of plaster legs in boots jutting out of the top of the heap. Venerable elders gazed down severely from blackened portraits up under the ceiling, with the familiar features of Fyodor Simeonovich, comrade Gian Giacomo, and other grand masters discernible in their faces. They should have thrown out all this archaic garbage ages ago, set windows in the walls and installed daylight fluorescent lighting, but everything was registered and inventoried and Modest Matveevich had personally forbidden its improper exploitation or disposal.

On the capitals of the columns and in the labyrinths of the gigantic chandelier hanging from the blackened ceiling, bats of several varieties, large and small, rustled their wings. Modest Matveevich waged war against them. He doused them with turpentine and creosote, sprinkled them with insecticide, sprayed them with hexachlorophene, and they died in the thousands—but regenerated in the tens of thousands, and mutated. Singing and talking strains appeared, and the descendants of the most ancient species now fed exclusively on a mixture of pyrethrum and chlorophene. The Institute's film technician, Sasha Drozd, swore that one day he'd seen a bat here that was a dead ringer for our comrade head of the Personnel Department.

In a deep niche that gave off an icy stench, someone was moaning and rattling chains. "Now that's enough of that," I said sternly. "None of that mysticism! You ought to be ashamed of yourself!" The niche went quiet. I restored order by adjusting a carpet that was out of position and went back up the stairs.

As you already know, from the outside the Institute looked like a two-story building, but in actual fact it had at least twelve floors. I never went any higher up than the twelfth floor, because they were always repairing the elevator, and I didn't know how to fly yet. Like most facades, the frontage with ten windows was an optical illusion. To the right and left of the entrance hall the Institute extended for at least a kilometer, and yet absolutely all of the windows looked out onto the same crooked street and the same "emporium." I was absolutely astounded by this. At first I used to pester Oira-Oira to explain to me how it could be reconciled with classical or even relativistic concepts of the properties of space. I didn't understand a word of his explanations, but I gradually got used to it and stopped being amazed. I am quite convinced that in ten or fifteen years' time every schoolboy will have a better grasp of the general theory of relativity than our present-day specialists. This by no means requires any understanding of how the deformation of space and time occurs; all that's needed is for the concept to be made familiar in childhood so that it seems normal.

The entire ground floor was occupied by the Department of Linear Happiness. This was Fyodor Simeonovich's kingdom, which smelled of apples and pine forests; this was where the prettiest girls and the grandest boys worked. Here there were no gloomy zealots and adepts of black magic; here no one plucked out his own hair, hissing and grimacing at the pain; no one muttered incantations that sounded like indecent tongue twisters or boiled toads and ravens alive at midnight, for Halloween or on unlucky days of the year. They worked on optimism here. Here they did everything that was possible within the limits of white, submolecular, and infraneuron magic to enhance the spiritual vigor of every individual and entire collectives of individuals. Here they condensed happy, good-natured laughter and disseminated it right around the world; they developed, tested, and applied models of behavior and relationships that reinforced friendship and subverted discord; they sublimated and distilled extracts of sorrow-soothers that didn't contain a single molecule of alcohol or other drugs. At that time they were preparing for the field trials of a portable universal evil-crusher and were developing new grades of the rarest alloys of intellect and kindness.

I unlocked the door of the central hall and stood in the doorway, admiring the operation of the gigantic Children's Laughter Distillation Unit, which looked something like a Van de Graaf generator, except that unlike a generator it worked quite silently and gave off a pleasant smell. According to my instructions, I was supposed to turn two large white switches on the control panel to switch off the golden glow that filled the hall and leave it dark, cold, and still—in other words, my instructions required me to cut off the power to the production premises in question. But without even the slightest hesitation, I backed out into the corridor and locked the door behind me. Shutting down anything at all in Fyodor Simeonovich's laboratories seemed like sacrilege to me.

I set off slowly along the corridor, examining the amusing pictures on the doors of the laboratories, and at the corner I met the brownie Tikhon, who drew the pictures and changed them every night. We shook hands. Tikhon was a lovely little gray brownie from the Ryazan region, whom Viy had exiled to Solovets for some offense or other: he'd either failed to greet someone correctly or refused to eat up his boiled viper . . . Fyodor Simeonovich had taken him in, cleaned him up, and cured him of chronic alcoholism, and he'd settled in here on the ground floor. He drew extremely well, in the manner of Bidstrup, and he was famous among the local brownies for his sensible and sober behavior.

I was about to go up to the second floor when I remembered about the vivarium and set out for the basement instead. The vivarium supervisor, an elderly rehabilitated vampire named Alfred, was drinking tea. When he caught sight of me he tried to hide the teapot under the table and broke his glass. He blushed and lowered his eyes. I felt sorry for him.

"Happy New Year, when it arrives," I said, pretending I hadn't noticed anything.

He cleared his throat, put his hand over his mouth, and replied hoarsely, "Thank you. And the same to you."

"Is everything in order?" I asked, looking around at the rows of cages and stalls.

"Briareos has broken a finger," said Alfred.

"How did he manage that?"

"Some way or other. On his eighteenth right hand. He was picking his nose and he turned awkwardly—they're clumsy, those hecatoncheires—and he broke it."

"Then we need a vet," I said.

"He'll manage without! It's not the first time."

"No, that's not right," I said. "Let's go and take a look."

We walked through into the depths of the vivarium, past the Little Humpbacked Horse, dozing with its nose stuck in a feed bag of oats, past the cage of harpies who watched us go by with eyes dull and heavy from sleep, past the cage of the Hydra of Lerna, morose and incommunicative at that time of year . . . The three hecatoncheir brothers, triplets with a hundred hands and fifty heads each, the firstborn of Heaven and Earth, were housed in a vast concrete cave, closed off by thick iron bars. Gyges and Kottos were asleep, curled up into huge, shapeless bundles from which their blue shaved heads with closed eyes and their relaxed hairy hands protruded. Briareos was suffering. He was squatting on his haunches, huddled up against the bars, sticking the hand with the damaged finger out into the passage and holding it with another seven hands. With his remaining ninety-two hands he was holding on to the bars and propping up his heads. Some of the heads were asleep.

"Well?" I asked. "Does it hurt?"

The heads that were awake started jabbering in ancient Hellenic and woke up a head that knew Russian.

"It hurts really badly," said the head. The other heads fell silent and gaped at me with their mouths open.

I inspected the finger. It was dirty and swollen, but it wasn't broken at all. It was simply dislocated. In our sports hall, injuries like that are cured without any doctor. I grabbed hold of the finger and tugged it toward me as hard as I could. Briareos roared with all of his fifty throats and fell over on his back.

"There, there," I said, wiping my hands on my handkerchief. "It's all over now."

Sniveling with all his noses, Briareos began inspecting the finger. The heads at the back craned their necks avidly and in their impatience bit the ears of the heads in front to make them get out of the way. Alfred chuckled.

"It would do him good to have some blood let," he said with a long-forgotten expression on his face, then he sighed and added, "But what sort of blood has he got in him? It's just pretend. Nonlife, isn't he?"

Briareos stood up. All of his fifty heads were smiling blissfully. I waved to him and began walking back. I paused beside Koschei the Deathless. The great villain lived in his own comfortable cage with carpets, air conditioning, and bookshelves. The walls of the cage were hung with portraits of Genghis Khan, Himmler, Catherine de Médicis, one of the Borgias, and either Goldwater or McCarthy. Koschei himself, wearing a shimmering dressing gown, was standing in front of an immense lectern with one leg crossed over the other, reading an offset-printed copy of the *Malleus Maleficarum*; at the same time he was making unpleasant movements with his fingers—screwing or thrusting something in or ripping something off. He was detained in eternal confinement awaiting trial while a never-ending investigation was conducted into his infinite number of crimes. He was well taken care of in the Institute, since he was used in certain unique experiments and as an interpreter for communicating with Wyrm Gorynych. Gorynych himself was locked away in an old boiler room, where he could be heard snoring metallically and roaring as he dozed.

I stood there, thinking that if at some point in time infinitely removed from us Koschei should ever be convicted, then the judges, whoever they might be, would find themselves in a very strange position: the death penalty can't be applied to an immortal, and if you included detention while awaiting trial, he would already have served an infinite sentence . . .

Then someone grabbed me by the trouser leg and a hoarse drunk's voice asked, "Right, then, guys, who fancies sharing a drink?"

I had to pull myself free. The three vampires in the next cage were staring at me greedily, pressing their grayish-purple faces against the metal mesh that carried two hundred volts of electricity.

"You crushed my hand, you four-eyed beanpole!" said one of them.

"You shouldn't go grabbing hold of people," I said. "Fancy a nice little poplar stake?"

Alfred came running up, cracking a whip, and the vampires withdrew into a dark corner, where they immediately started swearing obscenely and slapping down homemade cards on the floor in a frenzied game.

I said to Alfred, "All right, then. I think everything's in order. I'll get going."

"Safe journey," Alfred replied eagerly.

As I walked upstairs I could hear the rattling and glugging of his teapot.

I glanced into the electrical room to see how the generator was working. The Institute was not dependent on the municipal energy supply. After the principle of determinism had been defined, it had been decided to use the well-known Wheel of Fortune as a source of free mechanical energy. There was only a minute section of the gigantic wheel's gleaming, polished rim rising up above the concrete floor, and since the axis of rotation lay an infinite distance away, the rim looked like a conveyor belt emerging from one wall and disappearing into the other. At one time it was fashionable to present doctoral dissertations on calculating the Wheel of Fortune's radius of curvature, but since all these dissertations produced results with an extremely low degree of accuracy, plus or minus 10 megaparsecs, the Institute's Academic Council had decided not to consider any more dissertations on this topic until such time as intergalactic transportation should make it reasonable to expect a substantial improvement in precision.

Several maintenance imps were playing by the Wheel, leaping onto the rim, riding as far as the wall, leaping off, and running back to the start. I called them to order firmly. "That's enough of that,"

I said. "You're not at the fairground now." They hid behind the housings of the transformers and began pelting me with spitballs. I decided not to get involved with the little babies and set off along the line of control panels. Once I was certain everything was in order, I went up to the second floor.

Here it was quiet, dark, and dusty. A decrepit old soldier wearing the uniform of the Preobrazhensky Regiment and a three-cornered hat was dozing by a low, half-open door, leaning on a long flintlock rifle. This was the Department of Defensive Magic, where for a long time now the staff had not included a single living person. In their day all of our old-timers, with the possible exception of Fyodor Simeonovich, had shown some enthusiasm for this division of magic. Ben Bezalel had made successful use of the Golem in palace coups; the clay monster, indifferent to bribes and impervious to poisons, had guarded the laboratories and with them the imperial treasure house. Giuseppe Balsamo had created the first flying broom squadron, which had given a good account of itself in the battlefields of the Hundred Years' War. But the squadron had fallen apart fairly quickly: some of the witches had married and the others had tagged along with the German cavalry regiments as camp followers. King Solomon had captured and enchanted a dozen times a dozen ifrits and hammered them into a special flame-throwing anti-elephant pursuit battalion. The young Cristóbal Junta had brought the forces of Charlemagne a Chinese dragon trained to fight Moors; on learning, however, that it was not the Moors that the emperor intended to fight but his fellow tribesmen the Basques, he had flown into a fury and deserted.

Throughout many centuries of history various magicians have suggested the use in battle of vampires (for night reconnaissance raids), basilisks (to terrify the enemy into a state of total petrification), flying carpets (for dropping sewage on enemy towns), magic swords of various calibers (to compensate for lack of numbers), and many other things. However, after the First World War, after Big Bertha, tanks, mustard gas, and chlorine gas, defensive magic had gone into decline. Staff began abandoning the department in droves.

The one who stayed longer than all the others was a certain Pitirim Schwarz, a former monk and the inventor of a musket stand, who had labored with selfless devotion on a project for genie bombardments. The essential idea of the project was to bomb the enemy's cities with bottles containing genies who had been held in solitary confinement for at least three thousand years. It is a well-known fact that in a state of freedom, genies are only capable of either destroying cities or building palaces. A fully mature genie, so Pitirim Schwarz reasoned, would not start building palaces when he was freed from his bottle, and the enemy would find himself with a serious problem. A certain obstacle to the realization of this plan was presented by the small number of bottles containing genies, but Schwarz was counting on augmenting the reserves by deep trawling of the Red and Mediterranean Seas. They say that when he learned about the hydrogen bomb and bacteriological warfare, old Pitirim became mentally unbalanced, gave away the genies he had to various departments, and moved over to Cristóbal Junta's team to investigate the meaning of life. No one had ever seen him again.

When I stopped in the doorway, the soldier looked up at me with one eye and croaked, "Not allowed, on your way . . ." and dozed off again. I glanced around the unoccupied room, cluttered with fragments of bizarre models and scraps of botched drawings, nudged a file lying by the entrance with the toe of my shoe, reading the blurred inscription TOP SECRET. BURN BEFORE READING, and went on. There was nothing here to switch off, and as for spontaneous combustion, everything that could combust spontaneously had done so many years ago.

The book depository was on the same floor. It was a rather gloomy, dusty space a bit like a lobby, but with substantially larger dimensions. They said that well inside, half a kilometer from the entrance, there was a fairly decent highway running along the shelves, complete with posts showing distances in versts. Oira-Oira had gone as far as post number 19, and the persistent Vitka Korneev, in search of technical documentation on the sofa-translator, had gotten hold of some seven-league boots and run as far as post number 124. He would have gone even farther, but his way was blocked by a brigade of Danaids in padded work jackets with jackhammers. Under the supervision of the fat-faced Cain, they were breaking up the asphalt and laying some kind of pipes. The Academic Council had several times raised the question of building a high-voltage power line along the highway to transmit clients of the depository through the wires, but every positive proposal had foundered on a lack of funding.

The depository was crammed full of extremely interesting books in all languages of the history of the world, from the tongue of the ancient Atlanteans to pidgin English inclusive. But what interested me most of all was a multivolume edition of the *Book of Fates*.

The *Book of Fates* was printed in brevier type on super-thin rice paper and contained in chronological order more or less complete data on the 73,619,024,511 members of the genus *Homo*. The first volume began with the pithecanthropus Aiuikh. ("Born 2 Aug. 965543 BC, died 13 Jan. 965522 BC. Parents ramapithecines. Wife a ramapithecus. Children: male Ad-Amm, female E-Ua. Lived nomadically with a tribe of ramapithecines in the valley of Mount Ararat. Ate, drank, and slept to his heart's content. Drilled the first hole in stone. Eaten by a cave bear during a hunt.") The last name in this publication's latest volume, published the year before, was Francisco Caetano Agostinho Lucia e Manuel e Josefa e Miguel Luca Carlos Pedro Trinidad ("Born 16 Jul. 1491 AD, died 17 July 1491 AD. Parents: Pedro Carlos Luca Miguel e Josefa e Manuel e Lucia Agostinho Caetano Francisco Trinidad and Maria Trinidad. Portuguese. Acephaloid. Cavalier of the Order of the Holy Spirit, Colonel of the Guards").

The publishing data informed me that the *Book of Fates* was published in an edition of 1 (one) copy and this latest volume had been sent to press at the time of the Montgolfier brothers' flights. Evidently in order to satisfy the demand of their own contemporaries, the publishers had begun issuing the occasional special edition, which listed only the years of birth and death. In one of these volumes I found my own name. However, hasty work has led to many errors finding their way into these volumes, and I was amazed to learn that I would die in 1611. Eight volumes of misprints have been identified to date, but they still haven't gotten as far as my name yet.

The *Book of Fates* used to be consulted by a special group in the Department of Predictions and Prophecies, but now the department was impoverished and deserted. It had never really recovered following the brief reign of sir citizen Merlin. The Institute had repeatedly advertised to fill the vacant position of head of department, and every time the only person to apply had been Merlin. The Academic Council always conscientiously reviewed the application and safely rejected it—43 votes "against" and 1 "for." (By tradition Merlin was also a member of the Academic Council.)

The Department of Predictions and Prophecies occupied the entire third floor. I walked past the doors with the plaques that read COFFEE GROUNDS GROUP, AUGURS' GROUP, PYTHIAS' GROUP, METEOROLOGICAL GROUP, SOLITAIRE GROUP, SOLOVETS ORACLE. I didn't have to disconnect anything here, since the department worked by candlelight. On the doors of the weather forecasting group a fresh inscription in chalk had already appeared: "Dark waters in the clouds." Every morning Merlin, cursing the intrigues of the envious, wiped this inscription away with a damp rag, and every night it was renewed.

I simply couldn't understand what the authority of this department rested on. From time to time its members gave papers on strange subjects such as "Concerning the Expression of the Augur's Eye" or "The Predictive Qualities of Mocha Coffee from the Harvest of 1926." Sometimes the group of Pythias managed to predict something correctly, but every time it happened the Pythias themselves seemed so astonished and frightened by their success that the whole effect was totally ruined. S-Janus, an individual of supreme tact, was remarked on numerous occasions to be unable to restrain an ambiguous smile whenever he attended the augurs' and Pythias' seminars.

On the fourth floor I eventually found something to do: I switched off the light in the cells of the Department of Eternal Youth. There were no young people in this department, and these old men suffering from a thousand years of arteriosclerotic dementia were always forgetting to turn the lights off after themselves. I suspected that in fact it wasn't just a matter of forgetfulness. Many was a smell of sulfur, scorched wool, and streptocide ointment in the air. I lingered for a while, examining them, because in our latitudes ifrits are rare beings. But the one standing on the right, with unshaven cheeks and a black eye patch, began glaring at me with his one eye. There were bad rumors about him—supposedly he used to eat people—so I hurried on my way. I could hear him snuffling and smacking his lips behind my back.

In the premises of the Department of Absolute Knowledge all the small upper windows were open, because the smell of Professor Vybegallo's herring heads was seeping in. There was snow heaped up on the windowsills and there were dark puddles under the radiators of the central steam heating system. I closed the windows and walked between the virginally clean desks of the department's staff members. Standing on the desks were brand-new ink sets that had never seen ink, but there were cigarette butts spilling out of the inkwells. This was a strange department. Its motto was "The cognition of infinity requires an infinite amount of time." I could hardly dispute that assertion, but the staff drew an unexpected conclusion from it: "And therefore it makes no difference whether you work or not." So in the interest of not adding to the amount of entropy in the universe, they didn't work. At least, most of them didn't. Not *en masse*, as Vybegallo would have said. Reduced to essentials, their task consisted of analyzing the curve of relative cognition in the region of its asymptotic approximation of absolute truth. Therefore some members of the department were always occupied with dividing zero by zero on their desktop calculators, and others kept requesting study assignments to eternity. They returned from their trips cheerful and overfed and immediately took time off on health grounds. In the gaps between assignments they wandered around from department to department, sat on other people's desks smoking cigarettes, and told jokes about evaluating indeterminate forms with L'Hopital's rule. They were easy to recognize from the empty look in their eyes and the cuts on their ears from constant shaving. In the six months I'd been at the Institute they'd only come up with a single job for the Aldan, and that boiled down to the same old division of zero by zero and involved absolutely no truth quotient at all. Perhaps some of them also did some real work, but I didn't know anything about it.

At half past ten I stepped onto Ambrosius Ambroisovich Vybegallo's floor. Covering my face with my handkerchief and trying to

Every old magazine and book,
We want everything you've got.

I blushed and went on. As I set foot on the sixth floor, I immediately saw that the door of Vitka's laboratory was slightly ajar and I heard hoarse singing. I crept stealthily toward it.

3

THEE *for my recitative,*
Thee in the driving storm even as now, the snow,
the winterday declining,
Thee in thy panoply, thy measur'd dual throbbing
and thy beat convulsive . . .
                                    —Walt Whitman

Vitka had told me he was going to join a group of friends and he was leaving a double working in the lab. A double is a very interesting kind of thing. As a rule it is a rather specific copy of its creator. Let's say someone has too much to handle—he creates himself a double, mindless and submissive, who only knows how to solder contacts or carry heavy weights, or write to dictation, but who does it well. Or say someone requires a model anthropoid for some kind of experiment—he creates himself a double, mindless and submissive, who only knows how to walk on the ceiling or receive telepathemes, but who does it well. Or take the simplest case. Let's say someone wants to collect his pay, but he doesn't want to waste any time, and he sends a double in his place, one who knows nothing except how to make sure no one jumps the line, sign the register, and count the money without leaving the cash desk. Of course, not everyone can create doubles. I still couldn't, for instance. What I'd managed to produce so far didn't know how to do anything, not even walk. And I'd be standing there in the line, and Vitka and Roman and Volodya Pochkin would all apparently be there, but there was no one to talk to. They just stood there like stones, not blinking or breathing, not shifting their feet, and there wasn't even anyone to ask for a cigarette.

The genuine masters can create highly complex, multipro-grammed, self-teaching doubles. Roman sent one of those super

127

models off in the car instead of me in the summer. And not one of the guys even guessed it wasn't me. The double drove my Moskvich magnificently, swore when the mosquitoes bit him, and really enjoyed a good sing-along. When he got back to Leningrad he dropped everyone off at their homes, returned the rented car, paid the bill, and immediately disappeared in front of the very eyes of the astounded director of the car rental office.

At one time I used to think that A-Janus and S-Janus were a double and an original. But that wasn't it at all. First, both directors had passports, diplomas, passes, and other essential documents. Not even the most complex doubles could possess any identity documents. At the sight of an official stamp on their photographs they flew into a rage and immediately tore the documents to shreds. Magnus Redkin had spent a lot of time studying this mysterious property of doubles, but the task was clearly beyond him.

In addition, the Januses were protein-based entities. To this day the philosophers and cyberneticists haven't managed to agree whether doubles should be regarded as alive or not. Most of the doubles were organo-silicon structures; there were also germanium-based doubles, and just recently aluminium polymer doubles have become fashionable.

Finally, and most important, neither A-Janus nor S-Janus was ever artificially created by anyone. They weren't a copy and an original; they weren't twin brothers. They were one man—Janus Polyeuctovich Nevstruev. Nobody in the Institute understood this, but they all knew it so well that they didn't even try to understand.

Vitka's double was standing leaning with his open palms on the lab table and staring fixedly at a small Ashby homeostat. At the same time he was purring a song set to a tune that was once popular:

> For us Descartes or Newton would be gross misnomers,
> Science for us is such a tight-closed book,
> We daren't even look.
> We're just plain ordinary astronomers
> It's only stars down from the sky we pluck

I'd never heard any doubles sing before, but you could expect anything at all from Vitka's doubles. I remember one of them who even dared to wrangle with Modest Matveevich himself over the excessive consumption of psychic energy—and even the pitiful specimens I created, without any arms or legs, were pathologically afraid of Modest Matveevich. It was clearly instinctive.

Standing under a canvas cover in the corner to the right of the double was the TDK-80E translator, the useless product of the Kitezhgrad Magotechnical Plant. Beside the laboratory table was my old friend the sofa, its patched leather gleaming in the light of three spotlights. Perched on top of the sofa was a child's bathtub full of water, and floating belly up in the water was a dead perch. The laboratory also contained shelves crammed with instruments and, right beside the door, a large green-glass carboy covered in dust. There was a genie sealed inside the carboy; you could see him swirling around inside with his eyes glittering.

Vitka's double stopped watching the homeostat, sat down on the sofa beside the bath, and, fixing the same stony stare on the dead fish, sang the following verse:

> *In order to achieve nature's pacification,*
> *The absolute and total dissipation*
> *Of dark mystification*
> *You need an accurate, precise representation*
> *Of the whole world's complex concatenation . . .*

The perch remained as it was. Then the double thrust his hand deep into the sofa and began breathing hard and straining as it twisted something inside there.

The sofa was a translator. It created around itself an M-field that, putting it simply, translated genuine reality into fairy tale reality. I had experienced the result that memorable night when I lodged with Naina Kievna, and the only thing that had saved me then was that the sofa was operating at a quarter power, on dark current, otherwise I would have woken up as some little Tom Thumb in thigh boots. For Magnus Redkin the sofa was the possible receptacle of the long-sought White Thesis. For Modest Matveevich, it was a museum exhibit, inventory number 1123, the improper appropriation and exploitation of which was prohibited. For Vitka it was instrument number 1. That was why Vitka stole the sofa every night, Magnus Fyodorovich jealously reported this to comrade

Demin, the head of personnel, and Modest Matveevich directed his energies to putting an end to all of the foregoing. Vitka had carried on stealing the sofa until Janus Polyeuctovich intervened. Acting in close cooperation with Fyodor Simeonovich, with the support of Gian Giacomo, on the authority of an official letter from the Presidium of the Academy of Sciences signed in person by four academicians, the director had eventually managed to neutralize Redkin completely and shift Modest Matveevich slightly from his entrenched position.

Modest Matveevich declared that he, as the individual bearing material responsibility, wouldn't hear of anything else but the sofa, inventory number 1123, being located in the premises specifically designated for it. And if that was not done, Modest Matveevich threatened, then be it on the heads of all of them, up to and including the academicians. Janus Polyeuctovich agreed to take it on his own head, and so did Fyodor Simeonovich, and Vitka quickly moved the sofa into his own laboratory. Vitka was a serious scientist, not like those idle loafers from the Department of Absolute Knowledge, and his intention was to transform all the water in the seas and oceans of our planet into living water. As yet, however, he was still at the experimental stage.

The perch in the bathtub began to stir and turned belly down. The double removed his hand from the sofa. The perch fluttered its fins apathetically, yawned, slumped over onto its side, and turned belly up again.

"*Bastard!*" the double said emphatically.

That immediately put me on my guard. It had been said with feeling. No lab double could have said it like that. The double stuck its hands in its pockets, slowly stood up, and saw me. We looked at each other for a few seconds. Then I inquired acidly, "Working, are we?"

The double stared at me stupidly.

"OK, drop it, drop it," I said. "Your cover's blown."

The double said nothing. He stood there like stone, not even blinking.

"I'll tell you what," I said. "It's well after ten already. I'll give you ten more minutes. Tidy everything up, dump that carrion, and go off dancing. I'll disconnect everything myself."

The double thrust out its lips as if it were playing the flute and began backing away. It stepped back very carefully, rounded the sofa, and stood so that the lab table was between us. I glanced pointedly at my watch. The double muttered an incantation and a calculator, a fountain pen, and a pile of clean paper appeared on the desk. Bending his knees and floating into the air, the double began writing something, glancing warily at me from time to time. It was all very convincing, and it almost had me fooled for a moment. But in any case, I had a sure way of finding out the truth. As a rule, doubles are entirely insensitive to pain. I fumbled in my pocket, pulled out a small pair of sharp pincers, and advanced on the double, clicking them suggestively. The double stopped writing. Looking him hard in the eyes, I snipped off the head of a nail that was protruding from the tabletop and said: "*Weeell?*"

"Why couldn't you just leave me alone?" Vitka asked. "Can't you see when someone's working?"

"You're a double," I said. "Don't you dare make conversation with me."

"Put away the pincers," he said.

"You shouldn't go playing the fool," I said. "Some double you are."

Vitka sat on the edge of the table and rubbed his ears wearily. "Nothing's going right for me today," he declared. "Today I'm an idiot. I created a double and it turned out absolutely brainless. Dropped everything, sat on the plywitsum, a real brute. I smashed it over the head, broke its arm off . . . And the perch just keeps on dying all the time."

I went across to the sofa and glanced into the bathtub. "What's wrong with it?"

"How should I know?"

"Where did you get it?"

"At the market."

I picked the perch up by the tail. "What did you expect? It's just an ordinary dead fish."

"Blockhead," said Vitka. "That's living water."

"Aha," I said, and started wondering what advice to give him. I have only the vaguest idea about the effects of living water. Mostly from the fairy tale about Tsarevich Ivan and the Gray Wolf.

Every now and then the genie in the carboy would start trying to wipe away the dust on the outside of the glass with his hand. "You could at least wipe the bottle," I said when I failed to come up with anything.

"What?"

"Wipe the dust off the bottle. He's bored in there."

"To hell with him, let him be bored," Vitka said absentmindedly. He thrust his hand back into the sofa and twisted something in there again. The perch came to life.

"See that?" said Vitka. "When I give it maximum intensity, there's no problem."

"It's a bad specimen," I said, guessing in the dark.

Vitka pulled his hand out of the sofa and fixed his gaze on me.

"The specimen . . ." he said. "Is a bad one . . ." His eyes glazed over like a double's. "*Specimen specimini lupus est.*"

"And then it was probably frozen," I said, growing bolder. Vitka wasn't listening to me.

"Where can I get a fish?" he said, gazing around and slapping his pockets. "I need a little fishie . . ."

"What for?" I asked.

"That's right," said Vitka. "What for? Since there isn't any other fish," he reasoned, "then why not change the water? That makes sense, doesn't it?"

"Er, no," I objected. "That won't do it."

"What will then?" Vitka asked eagerly.

"Clear out of here," I said. "Get off the premises."

"Where to?"

"Wherever you like."

He clambered over the sofa and grabbed me by the lapels. "You listen to me, all right?" he said threateningly. "Nothing in the world is identical to anything else. Everything's distributed according to the Gaussian curve. Water's not like other water . . . This old fool forgot all about the dispersion of qualities . . ."

"Come on, old man," I appealed to him. "It's almost New Year's! Don't get so carried away."

He let go of me and started fumbling about. "Where did I put it? What a dumb hick! Where did I stick it? Ah, there it is . . ."

He dashed across to the table, where the plywitsum was standing upright. The same one. I jumped back to the door and said imploringly, "Come to your senses! It's after eleven already! They're waiting for you! Vera's waiting!"

"*Naah*," he answered. "I sent them a double. A fine double, a good talker . . . The life and soul . . . tells jokes, stands on his hands, dances like a lunatic . . ." He twisted the plywitsum in his hands, figuring something out, weighing something up, screwing up one eye.

"Clear out of here, I told you," I roared in desperation.

Vitka shot me a rapid glance and I bit my tongue. The joking was over. Vitka was in that state of mind in which magicians obsessed with their work turn the people around them into spiders, wood lice, lizards, and other quiet animals. I squatted down beside the genie and watched.

Vitka froze in the classical pose for a material incantation. A pink vapor rose up from the table, shadows that looked like bats began flitting up and down, the calculator disappeared, the paper disappeared, and suddenly the entire surface of the table was covered with vessels full of transparent liquids. Vitka dumped the plywitsum on a chair without looking, grabbed one of the vessels, and started examining it closely. He was obviously never going to leave the place now. He grabbed the bathtub off the sofa, then leaped across to the shelves in a single bound and lugged a cumbersome copper aquavitometer back to the table. I was about to make myself more comfortable and clean off a little observation window for the genie when I suddenly heard voices, the clattering of feet, and doors slamming in the corridor. I leaped up and dashed out of the lab.

The huge building's aura of nocturnal emptiness and tranquil darkness had disappeared without a trace. There were lamps blazing brightly in the corridor. Someone was dashing crazily up the stairs; someone else was shouting, "Valka! The voltage has dropped! Run to the electrical room!"; someone was shaking off a fur coat on the landing, sending wet snow flying in all directions. Walking toward me with a thoughtful expression on his face was Gian Giacomo, and trotting along behind him with his huge portfolio under its arm and his cane in its mouth was a gnome. We exchanged bows. The great prestidigitator smelled of good wine and French fragrances. I didn't dare try to stop him, and he walked straight through the locked door into his office. The gnome stuck his briefcase and cane through the closed door and then dived into the radiator.

"What the hell?" I shouted, and ran toward the stairs.

The Institute was overflowing with members of staff. There seemed to be even more of them than on an ordinary working day. In the offices and laboratories lights were blazing; doors were standing wide open. The usual buzz of work filled the air: crackling electrical discharges, monotonous voices dictating figures and intoning spells, the sharp chatter of typewriters. And above it all Fyodor Simeonovich's booming, triumphant growl: "'At's good, 'at's just grand! Well done there, good boy! But what *fool* turned off the *generator?*"

Somebody poked me in the back with the hard corner of something and I grabbed hold of the banister, feeling really furious now. It was Volodya Pochkin and Edik Amperian, carrying a coordinate-measuring machine that weighed half a ton.

"Ah, Sasha," Edik said pleasantly. "Hi there, Sasha."

"Sashka, get out of the way!" yelled Volodya Pochkin, edging along backward. "Higher, higher!"

I grabbed him by the collar. "Why are you in the Institute? How did you get in?"

"Through the door, through the door, let go . . ." said Volodya. "Edka, more to the right! Can't you see it's not fitting through?"

I let go of him and dashed down to the entrance hall, seething with administrative indignation. "I'll teach you," I muttered, jumping four steps at a time. "I'll teach you, you idle loafers, I'll teach you to go just letting in all and sundry!"

Instead of doing their job, the macrodemons Entrance and Exit were playing roulette, trembling with excitement and phosphorescing feverishly. In front of my very eyes Entrance, totally oblivious to his duties, broke the bank to win about seventy billion molecules from the equally oblivious Exit. I recognized the roulette wheel immediately. It was mine; I had made it myself for a party and kept it behind a cupboard in the computer room, and the only person who knew about it was Vitka Korneev. A conspiracy, I thought. I'll sling the whole lot of you out now. But the red-cheeked, jolly, snow-covered members of staff just kept on pouring in through the vestibule.

"It's really blowing out there! My ears are all clogged up . . ."

"So you left too, then?"

"Well, it's so boring . . . Everyone got drunk. So I thought, why don't I go in and do a bit of work instead. I left them a double and took off . . ."

"You know, there I am dancing with her and I can just feel myself turning hairy all over. I took a shot of vodka, but it didn't do any good . . ."

"What about an electron beam? A large mass? Try photons, then . . ."

"Alexei, have you got a laser you're not using? Even a gas one would do . . ."

"Galka, how come you left your husband?"

"I left an hour ago, if you must know. I fell into a snowdrift, you know, almost got buried in it . . ."

I realized I'd failed in my duty. There was no point now in taking the roulette wheel away from the demons. The only thing I could do was go and have a blazing fight with that agent provocateur Vitka; the rest was out of my hands. I waved my fist at the demons and set off back upstairs, trying to imagine what would happen if Modest Matveevich happened to drop into the Institute just then.

On my way to the director's waiting room I stopped in the test lab, where they were pacifying a genie released from a bottle. The huge genie, blue with rage, was dashing around inside a cage walled off with shields of Jan ben Jan and closed off above by a powerful magnetic field. They were zapping the genie with high-voltage shocks. He howled, cursed in several dead languages, bounded about, and belched tongues of flame. In his vehement fury he began building palaces and then immediately destroying them, until finally he gave up, sat down on the floor, shuddering from the electrical discharges, and howled plaintively. "That's enough, no more, I'll behave myself . . . Hey, hey, hey . . . Look, see how calm I am . . ."

The imperturbable, unblinking young men standing at the control panel of the discharge generator were all doubles. The originals were crowded around the vibration table, glancing at their watches and opening bottles.

I went over to them. "Ah, Sashka!" "Sashentsiya, they tell me you're on watch today . . . I'll drop by your room a bit later." "Hey, someone create him a glass, my hands are full here . . ."

I was so dumbfounded I didn't even notice the glass appear in my hand. The corks clattered against the shields of Jan ben Jan; the ice cold champagne hissed as it flowed. The discharges stopped crackling, the genie stopped wailing and began sniffing, and at that very second the Kremlin clock started chiming twelve.

"Right, guys! Long live Monday!"

Glasses clinked together. Then someone cast an eye over the bottles and said, "Who created the wine?"

"I did."

"Don't forget to pay tomorrow."

"Well, how about another bottle?"

"No, that's enough, we'll catch a chill."

"Some genie we've got here . . . Seems a bit high strung."

"Never look a gift horse . . ."

"Never mind, he'll fly like a good'un. Forty turns and his nerves will soon be in order."

"Guys," I said timidly, "it's night outside, and a holiday. Why don't you all just go home?"

They looked at me, slapped me on the shoulder, and told me, "Don't worry about it, it'll pass"—and the whole gang moved across to the cage. The doubles rolled aside one of the shields and the originals surrounded the genie, took a firm grasp of his arms and legs, and carried him across to the vibration table. The genie muttered timidly and uncertainly, promising everyone the treasures of the kings of the Earth.

I stood alone at one side and watched as they strapped him down and attached microsensors to various parts of his body. Then I touched the shield. It was immense and heavy, pitted with dents from the impact of ball lightning, and some spots were carbonized. The shields of Jan ben Jan were made of seven dragon skins, glued together with the bile of a patricide, and were designed to resist a direct lightning strike. All the shields in the Institute had originally been taken from the treasure house of the Queen of Sheba by either Cristóbal Junta or Merlin. Junta never spoke about it, but Merlin boasted about it at every opportunity, always citing the dubious authority of King Arthur. There were tin-plate inventory-number tags attached to each shield with upholstery nails. In theory there ought to have been images of all the famous battles of the past on the fronts of the shields and images of all the great battles of the future on the reverse. In practice, what I could see on the front side of the shield I was looking at was something like a jet plane strafing a refueling station, and its inside was covered with strange swirls and streaks reminiscent of an abstract painting. They started shaking up the genie on the vibration table. He giggled and squealed: "Hey, that tickles! Hey, stop it!"

I went back into the corridor. It smelled of fireworks. There were firecrackers zooming around in circles under the ceiling, and rockets darting about, banging against the walls and leaving trails of colored smoke behind them. I ran into a double of Volodya Pochkin lugging along a gigantic incunabulum with brass clasps, two doubles of Roman Oira-Oira struggling under the weight of a massively heavy metal C beam, then Roman himself with a heap of bright blue files from the archives of the Department of Unsolvable Problems, and then a fierce-looking lab assistant from the Department of the Meaning of Life, herding a flock of cursing ghosts in crusaders' cloaks to an interrogation with Junta . . . Everybody was working hard.

The labor regulations were being deliberately and ubiquitously flouted, but I no longer felt the slightest desire to combat these infringements, since these people had fought their way here through a blizzard at midnight on New Year's Eve because they were more interested in finishing up some useful job of work or starting up a completely new one than in dissolving their wits in vodka, jerking their legs about moronically, playing forfeits, and flirting with varying degrees of frivolity.

These people had come here because they preferred being together to being apart and because they couldn't stand Sundays of any kind, because on Sunday they felt bored. These were Magicians, People with a capital *P*, and their motto was "Monday starts on Saturday." Yes, they knew a few spells, they could turn water into wine, and it would have been no problem for any one of them to feed a thousand people with five loaves. But that wasn't why they were magicians. That was just the shell, the exterior. They were magicians because they knew a great deal, so much indeed that this huge quantity of theirs had made the leap of conversion into quality, and their relationship with the world had become different from that of ordinary people. They worked in an institute that was concerned first and foremost with the problems of human happiness and the meaning of human life, but even in their ranks there was no one who knew for certain what happiness is and what exactly is the meaning of life. And they had accepted as a working hypothesis that happiness lies in the constant cognition of the unknown, which is also the meaning of life. Every man is a magician in his heart, but he only becomes a magician when he starts thinking less about himself and more about others, when his work becomes more interesting to him than simply amusing himself according to the old meaning of that word. And their working hypothesis must have been close to the truth, because just as labor transformed ape into man, so the absence of labor transforms man into ape or something even worse, only far more rapidly.

We don't always notice this in life. The idler and sponger, the debauchee and careerist, continue to walk on their hind extremities and articulate speech quite clearly (although their range of subjects becomes extremely narrow), and as for the drainpipe trousers and passion for jazz that used to be cited as a measure of the extent of an individual's anthropoidicity, it became clear fairly quickly that these are to be found even among the very finest magicians. But in the Institute it was impossible to disguise retrogression.

The Institute offered unlimited opportunities for the transformation of man into magician. However, it was ruthless with apostates and marked them out unfailingly. A member of staff only had to indulge for an hour in egotistical and instinct-driven activity (or sometimes merely thoughts) and he would be horrified to notice that the fluff in his ears was growing thicker. It was a warning. Just as the militiaman's whistle warns of a possible fine and pain warns of a possible injury. It was all left up to you.

A man is frequently incapable of resisting his embittered thoughts, for as a man he embodies the transitional stage between Neanderthal and Magician. But he can act despite these thoughts, and then he still has a chance. Or he can give way, give up on everything ("You only live once," "You have to take what life has to offer," "*Nihil humanum mihi alienum est*") and then there's only one thing left for him to do: leave the Institute as soon as possible. Outside it, he can at least still be a respectable philistine, earning his wages honestly, if somewhat listlessly. But it's hard to bring yourself to leave. The Institute's a warm, cozy place, the work's clean and it's respectable, the pay's not bad, and the people are wonderful, so you can put up with the shame—after all, it won't kill you. They slouch along the corridors and through the laboratories, followed by sympathetic or disapproving glances, their ears covered with coarse gray fur, confused and incoherent, gradually losing the power of articulate speech, growing stupider. And these are the ones you can still pity and still try to help; you can still hope to restore their humanity . . .

There are others. With empty eyes. Who know for certain which side their bread is buttered on. In their own way very far from stupid. In their own way accomplished connoisseurs of human nature. Calculating and unprincipled, acquainted with the full power of human weaknesses, able to turn any evil to their own advantage and indefatigable in so doing. They shave their ears thoroughly and frequently invent wonderful potions for eliminating body hair. They wear corsets made of dragons' whiskers to disguise the curvature of their spines; they envelop themselves in immense medieval robes and boyars' fur coats, proclaiming their devotion to national tradition. They complain loudly in public of chronic rheumatic pains and wear tall felt boots soled with leather in both winter and summer. They are undiscriminating as to their means and as patient as spiders in achieving their ends. And very often they achieve truly significant results and major successes in their basic goal—the construction of a bright future in a single apartment and on a single village plot, fenced off from the rest of humanity by electrified barbed wire . . .

I went back to my post in the director's waiting room, dumped the useless keys in the box, and read a few pages of J. P. Nevstruev's classic work *Equations of Mathematical Magic*. This book read like an adventure novel, because it was absolutely chock-full of unsolved problems. I felt a burning desire to do some work, and I had just decided to say nuts to the management and go back to my Aldan when Modest Matveevich phoned.

Munching and crunching down the line, he inquired angrily, "Where have you been wandering about, Privalov? This is the third time I've called. It's outrageous!"

"Happy New Year, Modest Matveevich," I said.

He chewed without saying anything for a while, then answered in a voice one tone lower: "Likewise. How's the shift going?"

"I've just completed a round of the premises," I said. "Everything's fine."

"There weren't any cases of spontaneous combustion?"

"None at all."

"Is the power off everywhere?"

"Briareos has broken a finger," I said.

He was alarmed. "Briareos? Hold on just a moment . . . Aha, inventory number 1489 . . . Why?"

I explained.

"What measures did you take?"

I told him.

"A correct decision," said Modest Matveevich. "Continue with your watch. That's all."

Immediately after Modest Matveevich, Edik Amperian called from the Department of Linear Happiness and politely asked me to calculate the optimal coefficient of frivolity for managerial staff. I agreed, and we arranged to meet in the computer room in two hours' time. Then a double of Oira-Oira came in and asked in a colorless voice for the keys to Janus Polyeuctovich's safe. I refused. It tried to insist. I refused and threw it out.

A minute later Roman himself came dashing in. "Give me the keys."

I shook my head. "I won't."

"Give me the keys!"

"You can go soak your head. I'm the individual with material responsibility."

"Sashka, I'll take the safe away!"

I chuckled and said, "Be my guest."

Roman glared at the safe and strained hard, but the safe was either under a spell or bolted to the floor.

"What is it you want in there?" I asked.

"The documentation on the RU-16," said Roman. "Come on, give me the key!"

I laughed and reached out a hand toward the box of keys. But at that very instant there was a blood-curdling howl from somewhere upstairs. I leaped to my feet.

Ц

Woe is me, I am not a strong fellow
And the upyr will gobble me right up . . .

—A. S. Pushkin

"He's hatched," Roman said calmly, looking up at the ceiling.

"Who?" I was really on edge: it was a woman who had screamed.

"Vybegallo's upyr," said Roman. "Or rather, cadaver."

"But why did that woman scream?"

"You'll see soon enough," said Roman.

He took hold of my arm and jumped into the air, and we went soaring up through the stories of the Institute building, piercing the ceilings and slicing through the floors like a hot knife through frozen butter, bursting out into the air with a plopping sound and tearing into the next ceiling. In the darkness between the floors little gnomes and mice shied away from us with startled squeaks, and as we flew through laboratories and offices Institute staff looked up with puzzled faces.

In the "Nursery" we elbowed our way through a crowd of curious onlookers and saw Professor Vybegallo sitting at the laboratory table, absolutely naked. His bluish-white skin glistened damply, his wet wedge-shaped beard drooped limply, and his wet hair was glued to his low forehead, on which an actively volcanic pustule blazed bright red. His empty, transparent eyes blinked occasionally as they roamed senselessly around the room.

Professor Vybegallo was eating. On the table in front of him steam was rising from a large photographic developing tray, filled up to the top with steamed bran. Without paying any particular attention to anyone else, he scooped the bran up with his broad palm, kneaded it in his fingers like pilaf, and dispatched

143

the resulting lump into the cavity of his mouth, sprinkling his beard liberally with crumbs in the process. At the same time he crunched, squelched, grunted, and snorted, inclining his head to one side and grimacing as though in immense delight. From time to time, without stopping his swallowing and choking, he would get excited and grab hold of the edges of the tub of bran and one of the buckets of skim milk that were standing on the floor beside him, every time pulling them closer and closer to himself. Standing at the other end of the table, pale and tearful, her lips trembling, was the pretty young trainee witch Stella, with her pristine pink ears. She was slicing loaves of bread in immense slabs and presenting them to Vybegallo, turning her face away from him. The central autoclave was open and there was a wide green puddle surrounding it.

Vybegallo   suddenly   muttered   indistinctly,   "Hey, girl . . . er . . . give me some milk! Pour it . . . you know . . . right in here, in the bran . . . *S'il vous plaît* . . ."

Stella hastily snatched up the bucket and splashed skim milk into the tray.

"Eh!" exclaimed Professor Vybegallo. "The crock's too small, you know. You, girl, whatever your name is . . . er . . . pour it straight in the tub. We'll eat, you know, straight from the tub."

Stella began emptying the bucket into the tub of bran, and the professor grabbed the tray like a spoon and began scooping up bran and dispatching it into his jaws, which had suddenly opened incredibly wide.

"Phone him, will you!" Stella shouted plaintively. "He'll finish everything in a minute!"

"We have phoned him already," said someone in the crowd. "But you'd better move away from him. Come over here."

"Well, is he coming? Is he coming?"

"He said he was just leaving. Putting on his galoshes . . . you know . . . and leaving. Come away from him, I told you."

I finally realized what was going on. It wasn't Professor Vybegallo, it was a newborn cadaver, a model of Gastrically Unsatisfied Man. Thank God for that—there I was thinking the professor had developed palsy as a result of his intensive labors. Stella cautiously moved away. People grabbed her by the shoulders and pulled her into the crowd. She hid behind my back, clutching my elbow tight, and I immediately straightened up my shoulders, although I still didn't understand what the problem was and what she was afraid

of. The cadaver guzzled. The lab was full of people, but an astonished silence reigned and the only sound that could be heard was
the cadaver snorting and munching like a horse and the scraping
of the tray on the walls of the tub. We watched. He got down off
his chair and stuck his head into the tub. The women turned away.
Lilechka Novosmekhova began to feel unwell, and they took her
out into the corridor. Then Edik Amperian's clear voice spoke up:
"All right. Let's be logical. First he'll finish the bran, then he'll eat
the bread. And then?"

There was a movement in the front rows. The crowd pressed
toward the doors. I began to understand. Stella said in a thin little
voice, "There are the herring heads as well . . ."

"Are there a lot of them?"

"Two tons."

"*Riiight*," said Edik, "And where are they?"

"They're supposed to be delivered by the conveyor," said Stella.
"But I tried and the conveyor's broken."

"By the way," Roman said loudly, "I've been trying to pacificate
him for two minutes now, with absolutely no result."

"Me too," Edik.

"Therefore," said Roman, "it would be a very good idea if one
of the more squeamish among us were to try to repair the conveyor
belt. To give us a bit of time. Are there any of the masters here? I
can see Edik. Is there anybody else? Korneev! Victor Pavlovich, are
you here?"

"He's not here. Maybe someone ought to go for Fyodor Simeonovich?"

"I don't think there's any need to bother him yet. We'll manage
somehow. Edik, let's try focusing on it together."

"What mode?"

"Physiological inhibition mode. All the way down to tetanic contraction. All of you guys who can, give us a hand."

"Just a moment," said Edik. "What happens if we damage him?"

"Oh yes, yes," I said. "You'd better not do that. Better just let
him eat me instead."

"Don't worry, don't worry. We'll be careful. Edik, let's do it with rapid strokes. In a single flurry."

"OK, let's go," said Edik.

It went even quieter. The cadaver was scrabbling in the tub, and on the other side of the wall the volunteers were talking as they fiddled with the conveyor. A minute went by. The cadaver pulled his head out of the tub, wiped his beard, looked at us sleepily, and suddenly, stretching out his arm an unbelievable distance, grabbed up the last loaf of bread. Then he belched thunderously and leaned back against his chair, folding his arms across his massive, swollen belly. Bliss flooded across his features. He snuffled and smiled inanely. He was undoubtedly happy, in the way an extremely tired man is happy when he finally reaches his longed-for bed.

"Looks like it worked," someone in the crowd said with a sigh of relief.

Roman pressed his lips together doubtfully.

"That's not quite the impression I get," Edik said politely.

"Perhaps his spring's run down?" I said hopefully.

Stella announced plaintively, "It's just temporary relaxation . . . an acute fit of satisfaction. He'll wake up again soon."

"You masters are a useless waste of time," said a manly voice. "Let me through there, I'll go and call Fyodor Simeonovich."

Everyone looked around, smiling uncertainly. Roman was toying pensively with the plywitsum, rolling it around on his palm. Stella shuddered and whispered, "What's going to happen? Sasha, I'm afraid!" As for me, I thrust out my chest, knitted my brows, and struggled with a compulsive urge to phone Modest Matveevich. I desperately wanted to shift the responsibility on to somebody else. It was a weakness, and I was powerless against it. Modest Matveevich appeared to me now in a very special light, and I recalled with a feeling of hope the master's degree thesis someone had recently defended on the subject of "The Correlation Between the Laws of Nature and the Laws of Administration," which attempted to demonstrate that by virtue of their specific inflexibility, administrative laws are frequently more efficacious than the laws of nature and magic. I was convinced that Modest Matveevich only had to turn up and yell at the upyr, "Now that's enough of that, comrade Vybegallo!" for the upyr to decide it really was enough.

"Roman," I said casually, "I suppose that in an emergency you can dematerialize it?"

Roman laughed and slapped me on the shoulder. "Don't be such a coward," he said. "This is just a bit of fun and games. Only I don't much fancy getting involved with Vybegallo . . . It's not this guy you ought to be afraid of, but that one!" He pointed to the second autoclave crackling peacefully in the corner.

Meanwhile the cadaver suddenly began stirring uneasily. Stella squealed quietly and pressed herself against me. The cadaver's eyes opened. First he leaned over and glanced into the tub. Then he rattled the empty buckets. Then he froze and sat there for a while without moving. The expression of satisfaction on his face was replaced by an expression of bitter resentment. He half-raised himself out of his chair and sniffed the table rapidly, flaring his nostrils, then stretched out his long red tongue and licked up the crumbs.

"Watch out now, guys," someone whispered in the crowd.

The cadaver stuck his hand into the tub, pulled out the tray, examined it from every angle, and cautiously bit off the edge. His eyebrows shot up in a martyred expression. He bit off another piece and began crunching it. His face turned blue as though from extreme exasperation and his eyes became moist, but he bit again and again until he had chewed up the entire tray. He sat there thoughtfully for about a minute, running his fingers over his teeth, then slowly ran his gaze over the motionless crowd. It was not a nice gaze; it seemed too appraising and selective. Responding automatically, Volodya Pochkin said, "Now then, calm down . . ." And then the empty transparent eyes locked on to Stella, and she let out a howl, that same blood-curdling howl bordering on ultrasonic frequencies that Roman and I had already heard in the director's waiting room three stories below. I shuddered. It embarrassed the cadaver too: he lowered his eyes and began drumming nervously on the table with his fingers.

There was a noise in the doorway, everybody squeezed together, and Ambrosius Ambroisovich Vybegallo, the real one, came walking through the crowd, pushing aside the dawdlers and pulling the icicles out of his beard. He smelled of vodka, a coarse cloth overcoat, and frost.

"My dear fellow!" he yelled. "What is all this? *Quelle situation?* Stella, what are you . . . er . . . thinking of! Where are the herrings? He has needs! And they're expanding! You should read my works!"

He approached the cadaver and the cadaver immediately started sniffing him. Vybegallo gave him his coat.

"Needs have to be satisfied!" he said, hastily clicking the switches on the conveyor's control board. "Why didn't you give him them straightaway? Oh, always *les femmes, les femmes!* Who said it was broken? It's not broken at all, it's bewitched. So, you know, not just anybody can use it, because . . . er . . . everybody has needs, but the herrings are for the model."

A little window opened in the wall, the conveyor started muttering, and a stream of fragrant herring heads poured straight out onto the floor. The cadaver's eyes glittered. He went down on all fours, trotted smartly over to the little window, and got to work. Vybegallo stood beside him, clapping his hands, crying out in delight, and just occasionally, overcome by his feelings, scratching the cadaver behind the ear.

The crowd sighed in relief and began shuffling about. It turned out that Vybegallo had brought with him two correspondents from the regional newspaper, our old acquaintances G. Pronitsatelny and B. Pitomnik. They also smelled of vodka. They blitzed away with their flashguns, taking photographs and making notes in their little books. G. Pronitsatelny and B. Pitomnik specialized in science. G. Pronitsatelny was renowned for the phrase "Oort was the first to glance up at the starry sky and notice that the galaxy rotates." He was also the author of a literary account of Merlin's journey with the chairman of the district soviet and an interview (conducted out of ignorance) with one of Oira-Oira's doubles. The interview was called "'Man' with a Capital Letter" and began, "Like any genuine scientist he was sparing with words . . ." B. Pitomnik was parasitical on Vybegallo. His militant essays on self-donning footwear, carrots that were self-pulling and self-loading-into-trucks, and other projects undertaken by Vybegallo were well known throughout the district, and his article "The Wizard from Solovets" had even appeared in one of the major national magazines.

When the cadaver's next acute fit of satisfaction set in and he dozed off, Vybegallo's lab assistants, who had turned up after being dragged away from their festive New Year's tables and were not in a very friendly mood, hastily dressed him in a black suit and shoved a chair underneath him. The journalists stood Vybegallo beside him, put his hands on the cadaver's shoulders, pointed their lenses at him, and asked him to continue.

"What is the most important thing of all?" said Vybegallo, readily complying. "The most important thing is for man to be happy. Let me observe in parenthesis: happiness is a human concept. And what is man, philosophically speaking? Man, comrades, is *Homo sapiens*, the creature who can achieve and who desires. He can achieve everything that he desires, and he desires everything that he can achieve. *N'est-ce pas*, comrades? If he—that is, man—can achieve everything that he desires and desires everything that he can achieve, then he is happy. This is how we shall define him. What is this that we have here before us, comrades? We have here a model. But this model, comrades, desires, and that is already good. *Exquis, excellent, charmant*, so to speak. And again, comrades, you can see for yourselves that it can achieve. And that is even better, because . . . because in that case it—he, that is—is happy. There is a metaphysical transition from unhappiness to happiness and this comes as no surprise to us, because people are not born happy, they . . . er . . . become happy. Thanks to proper care and attention being paid. Look, now it's waking up . . . it desires. And therefore for the moment it is unhappy. But it can achieve, and this ability can produce a sudden dialectical leap. There, there! Look! See how it can achieve! Oh, you little darling, my happy little one! Look! Look! See how well it can achieve. It can achieve for a whole ten or fifteen minutes . . . You

there, comrade Pitomnik, put down your little camera and pick up
the movie camera, because here we have a process . . . everything
we have here is in motion! For us the state of rest is relative, as
it ought to be, and movement is absolute. Indeed so. Now it has
achieved and it is making the dialectical transition to happiness. To
satisfaction, that is. Look, it has closed its eyes. It is delighted. It feels
good. I can tell you quite scientifically that I would gladly change
places with it. At the present moment, of course . . . You, comrade
Pronitsatelny, write down everything I say, and then give it to me.
I'll straighten it out and put in the references . . . There, it's dozing
now, but that's not all there is to this process. Our needs must grow
and expand in depth as well as in breadth. Otherwise, you know,
the process will not be correct. *On dit que* Vybegallo is supposedly
against the world of the mind. That, comrades, is a crude label. It is
high time for us, comrades, to forget such manners in scientific discussion. We all know that the material comes first and the spiritual
comes afterward. *Satur venter*, as we all know, *non studet libenter.**
Which, with regard to the present case, we can translate thus: a
hungry fox is always thinking of bread."

"The opposite way round," said Oira-Oira.

Vybegallo stared vacantly at him for a short while, then said,
"Comrades, we shall dismiss that undisciplined remark from the
audience with the contempt it deserves. Let us not be distracted
from the main thing—from practice. Let us leave the theory to those
who have not yet mastered it sufficiently. To continue, I now move
on to the next stage of the experiment. Let me elucidate for the
press. Proceeding from the materialist idea that the temporary satisfaction of material needs has taken place, we may proceed to the
satisfaction of spiritual needs. That is, watching films and television, listening to folk music or singing it yourself, and even reading
some kind of book or, let's say, the magazine *Crocodile* or a newspaper . . . Comrades, we do not forget that you have to possess the
abilities for all of this, whereas the satisfaction of material needs does

---

* AUTHORS' NOTE: "A full belly is deaf to learning."

not require any special abilities—they are always present, for nature follows materialism. As yet we can say nothing about the spiritual abilities of this particular model, insofar as the rational core of its being is gastric dissatisfaction. But we will now identify its spiritual abilities."

The morose laboratory assistants laid out a tape recorder, a radio, a film projector, and a small portable library on the tables. The cadaver cast an indifferent eye over these instruments of culture and tried the magnetic tape to see how it tasted. It became clear that the model's spiritual abilities would not manifest themselves spontaneously. Then Vybegallo gave the order to commence what he called the forcible inculcation of cultural skills. The tape recorder began crooning sweetly, "My darling and I parted, swearing eternal love . . ." The radio began whistling and hooting. The film projector began showing the cartoon *The Wolf and the Seven Little Goats* on the wall. Two laboratory assistants holding magazines stood on each side of the cadaver and began reading out loud across each other . . .

As was only to be expected, the gastric model remained absolutely indifferent to all this racket. Just as long as it wanted to gobble it couldn't give a damn for its spiritual world, because its desire was to gobble and it could achieve that desire. But when it was sated, it totally ignored its spiritual world, because it was feeling drowsy and for the time being it didn't want anything else. Even so, the sharp-eyed Vybegallo managed to spot an undeniable connection between the beating of a drum (on the radio) and a reflex twitching of the model's lower extremities. This twitching threw him into raptures of delight.

"The leg!" he shouted, grabbing hold of B. Pitomnik's sleeve. "Film the leg! In close-up! *La vibration de son mollet gauche est un grand signe.* That leg will sweep aside all their machinations and tear away all the labels that they hang on me! *Oui, sans doute,* a man who is not a specialist might perhaps be surprised by my reaction to that leg. But after all, comrades, all the great things are manifested in small things, and I must remind you that the model in question is a model with limited needs—to be specific, only one need, and to put it simply, our way, calling things by their own names, without any of these veiled hints: it is a model of gastric need. That is why it is so limited in its spiritual needs. Let me elucidate for the press, using a clear example. If, let us say, it were to have a strongly pronounced need for the given 'Astra-7' tape recorder for 140 rubles—which need must be understood by us as material—and if it were to acquire that tape recorder, then it would play the tape recorder in question, because, as you know yourselves, there is nothing else you can do with a tape recorder. And if it were to play it, then it would be with music, and if there is music, then you have to listen to it and perhaps dance . . . and what, comrades, is listening to music, either dancing or not dancing? It is the satisfaction of spiritual needs. *Comprenez-vous?"*

I had noticed quite a while before this that the cadaver's behavior had changed significantly. Perhaps something inside it had stopped functioning properly, or perhaps it was the way things were supposed to happen, but its relaxation times were getting shorter and shorter, so that by the end of Vybegallo's speech it was no longer leaving the conveyor even for a moment. Or perhaps it had simply begun to find it difficult to move.

"May I ask a question?" Edik said politely. "How do you account for the cessation of the acute fits of satisfaction?"

Vybegallo stopped speaking and looked at the cadaver. The cadaver was guzzling. Vybegallo looked at Edik.

"I'll tell you how," he said smugly. "That is a correct question, comrades. Yes, I would even call it an intelligent question, comrades. We have before us a concrete model of constantly expanding material needs. And only the superficial observer can believe that the acute fits of satisfaction have supposedly ceased. In actual fact they have made the dialectical transition from quantity to a new quality. They have extended, comrade, to the very process of the satisfaction of needs. Now it is not enough for it to be satisfied. Its needs have grown, so that now it has to eat all the time—now it has self-educated itself and it knows that chewing is also good. Is that clear, comrade Amperian?"

I looked at Edik. Edik was smiling politely. Standing beside him, hand in hand, were doubles of Fyodor Simeonovich and Cristóbal Joséevich. Their heads had wide-set ears and they were turning on their axes, like the radar antennae at airports.

"May I ask another question?" said Roman.

"By all means," said Vybegallo with an expression of weary condescension.

"Ambrosius Ambroisovich," said Roman, "what will happen when it has consumed everything?"

Vybegallo's gaze became wrathful. "I ask everyone present to take note of this provocative question, which reeks a mile away of Malthusianism, neo-Malthusianism, pragmatism, existentio- . . . -oa- . . . -nalism, and disbelief, comrades, in the inexhaustible powers of humanity. What is it you are suggesting by asking this question, comrade Oira-Oira? That a moment can come in the activity of our scientific institution, a crisis, a retrogressive development, when there will not be enough consumer products for our consumers? Wrong, comrade Oira-Oira! You haven't thought it through properly! We cannot permit labels to be hung on our work and aspersions cast upon it. And we shall not permit it, comrades."

He took out a handkerchief and wiped his beard. G. Pronitsatelny asked the next question, screwing up his face with the intellectual effort: "Of course, I'm not a specialist. But what future has the model in question? I understand that the experiment is proceeding successfully. But it is consuming very energetically."

Vybegallo laughed bitterly. "There, you see, comrade Oira-Oira, that's the way unsavory sensations are started. You asked a question without thinking. And our rank-and-file comrade here is already disoriented. Facing toward the wrong ideal . . . You are facing toward the wrong ideal, comrade Pronitsatelny!" he said, addressing the journalist directly. "The model in question represents a stage that is already past! Here is the ideal toward which we must turn our faces!" He went across to the second autoclave and set his ginger-haired hand against its polished side. His beard jutted out. "This is our ideal!" he declared. "Or, to be more precise, this is the model of our ideal, yours and mine. Here we have the universal consumer who desires everything and can, accordingly, achieve everything he desires. All the needs that exist in the world are embodied in him. And he can satisfy all those needs. With the help of our science, naturally. Let me elucidate for the press. The model of the universal consumer contained in this autoclave—or, to use our term, self-sealing vessel—desires without any limitation. We are all of us, comrades, with all due respect to ourselves, simply nothing in comparison with it. Because it desires things that we have absolutely no concept of. And it will not wait for favors from nature. It will take from nature everything that it needs for its complete happiness—that is, for satisfaction. Material-magic forces will simply extract from surrounding nature everything that it needs. The happiness of this model will be indescribable. It will know neither hunger nor thirst, nor toothache, nor other unpleasantnesses. All of its needs will be instantly satisfied as they arise."

"Excuse me," Edik said politely, "but will all of its needs be material?"

"Well, of course," Vybegallo yelled, "its intellectual needs will develop accordingly! As I have already remarked, the more material needs there are, the more varied the intellectual needs will be. It will be a mental giant and an intellectual luminary!"

I looked around at the people there. Many of them looked absolutely dumbfounded. The correspondents were scribbling away desperately. I noticed that some people were glancing from the autoclave to the incessantly guzzling cadaver and back again, with a strange expression on their faces. Stella was pressing her forehead against my shoulder, sobbing and whispering, "I've got to get out of here, I can't take any more . . ." I think I was also beginning to understand just what Oira-Oira was afraid of. I pictured an immense maw gaping wide to receive a magically generated stream of animals, people, cities, continents, planets, the sun . . .

"Ambrosius Ambroisovich," said Oira-Oira. "Could the universal consumer create a stone so heavy that even he would be unable to lift it, no matter how strong his desire?"

Vybegallo pondered that, but only for a second. "That isn't material need," he replied. "That's caprice. That's not the reason I created my doubles, for them to go getting, you know, capricious."

"Caprice can be a need too," Oira-Oira objected.

"Let's not get involved in scholastics and casuistry," Vybegallo proposed. "And let's not start drawing analogies with religious mysticism."

"No, let's not," said Oira-Oira.

B. Pitomnik glanced around and addressed Vybegallo again: "When and where will the demonstration of the universal model take place, Ambrosius Ambroisovich?"

"The answer," said Vybegallo, "is that the demonstration will take place right here in my laboratory. The press will be informed of the time later."

"But will it be just a matter of a few days?"

"It could well be a matter of a few hours. So it would be best for the comrades of the press to stay and wait."

At this point, as though on command, the doubles of Fyodor Simeonovich and Cristóbal Joséevich turned and walked out of the room. Oira-Oira said, "Does it not seem to you, Ambrosius Ambroisovich, that holding such a demonstration in the Institute, here in the center of town, is dangerous?"

"We have nothing to be concerned about," said Vybegallo. "It's our enemies who should be feeling concerned."

"Do you remember I told you there might possibly—"

"You, comrade Oira-Oira, possess an inadequate, you know, grasp of the matter. It is essential, comrade Oira-Oira, to distinguish possibility from reality, theory from practice, and so forth . . ."

"Nonetheless, perhaps the firing range—"

"I am not testing a bomb," Vybegallo said haughtily. "I am testing a model of the ideal man. Are there any other questions?"

Some bright spark from the Department of Absolute Knowledge began asking about the operating mode of the autoclave, and Vybegallo happily launched into explanations. The morose lab assistants were gathering up their spiritual needs satisfaction technology. The cadaver was guzzling. The black suit he was wearing was splitting and coming apart at the seams. Oira-Oira watched him closely. Suddenly he said in a loud voice, "I have a suggestion. Everyone who is not directly involved should leave the premises immediately."

Everyone turned to look at him.

"It's going to get very messy," he explained. "Quite incredibly messy."

"That is provocation," Vybegallo responded pompously.

Roman grabbed me by the hand and dragged me to the door. I dragged Stella after me. The other onlookers hurried after us. People in the Institute trusted Roman. They didn't trust Vybegallo. The only outsiders left in the laboratory were the journalists; the rest of us crowded together in the corridor.

"What's happening?" we asked Roman. "What's going to happen? Why is it going to get messy?"

"He's about to blow," Roman answered, keeping his eyes fixed on the door.

"Who is? Vybegallo?"

"I feel sorry for the journalists," said Edik. "Listen, Sasha, is our shower working today?"

The door of the lab opened and two lab assistants came out, carrying the tub and the empty buckets. A third lab assistant was fussing around them, glancing behind him apprehensively and muttering, "Let me help, guys, let me help, it's heavy . . ."

"Better close the doors," Roman advised.

The nervous lab assistant hastily slammed the door shut and came over to us, pulling out his cigarettes. His eyes were rolling and staring wildly. "Any moment now . . ." he said. "The smart-ass, I tried to tip him off . . . The way it guzzles! It's insane, the way it guzzles."

"It's twenty-five past two—" Roman began.

Suddenly there was a loud *boom* and a jangling of broken glass. One of the lab doors gave a sharp crack and flew off its hinges. A camera and someone's tie were blown out through the gap. We jumped back. Stella squealed again.

"Keep calm," said Roman. "It's all over now. There's one less consumer in the world."

The lab assistant, his face as white as his coat, dragged incessantly on his cigarette. From inside the lab we heard sniveling, coughing, and muttered curses. There was a bad smell. I murmured uncertainly, "Perhaps we ought to take a look."

No one replied. Everyone just looked at me pityingly. Stella was crying quietly, holding on to my jacket. Someone explained to someone else, "He's on watch today, get it? Someone has to go and clear it all up."

I took a few hesitant steps in the direction of the doorway, but just then the journalists and Vybegallo came stumbling out of the lab, clutching onto each other.

My God, the state they were in!

Recovering my wits, I pulled the platinum whistle out of my pocket and blew it. The brownie emergency sanitation team came dashing to my side on the double, pushing their way through the crowd of staff.

5

Believe, that it was the most horrible spectacle that ever one saw.

—François Rabelais

What astounded me most of all was that Vybegallo was not discouraged in the least by what had happened. While the brownies worked on him, spraying him with absorbing agents and plastering him with fragrances, he piped in a falsetto voice, "You, comrades Oira-Oira and Amperian, you were apprehensive as well. Wondering what would happen, and how he could be stopped . . . You suffer, comrades, from a certain unhealthy, you know, skepticism. I'd call it a certain distrust of the forces of nature and human potential. And where is it now, this distrust of yours? It has burst! It has burst, comrades, in full view of the wider public, and splattered me and these comrades of the press."

The press maintained a dismayed silence as it obediently presented its sides to the hissing jets of absorbents. G. Pronitsatelny was shuddering violently. B. Pitomnik was shaking his head and involuntarily licking his lips.

When the brownies had restored a first approximation of order in the lab, I glanced inside. The emergency team was briskly replacing windows and burning what was left of the gastric model in a muffle furnace. There wasn't much left: a little heap of buttons with the English inscription For Gentlemen, the sleeve of a jacket, a pair of incredibly stretched suspenders, and a set of false teeth resembling the fossilized jaws of *Gigantopithecus*. Everything else had apparently been reduced to dust in the blast. Vybegallo inspected the second autoclave, the so-called self-sealing vessel, and declared that everything was in order. "Would the press please join me?" he said. "And I suggest that everyone else should return to their own duties."

The press pulled out its notebooks; the three men sat down at a table and set about defining the details of an essay titled "The Birth of a Discovery" and an article titled "Professor Vybegallo's Story." The audience dispersed. Oira-Oira left after taking the keys to Janus Polyeuctovich's safe from me. Stella left in despair because Vybegallo had refused to let her transfer to a different department. The lab assistants left, noticeably more cheerful now. Edik left, surrounded by a crowd of theoreticians, figuring out in their heads as they walked along what was the minimum stomach pressure at which the cadaver could have exploded. I left too, and went back to my post, having first made sure that the testing of the second cadaver would not take place before eight o'clock in the morning.

The experiment had left me feeling very unsettled. I lowered myself into an immense armchair in the director's waiting room and tried for a while to understand whether Vybegallo was a fool or a cunning demagogue and hack. The total scientific value of all his cadavers was quite clearly zero. Any member of the Institute who had successfully defended his master's thesis and taken the two-year special course in nonlinear transgression was capable of creating models based on his own doubles. And it was no problem either to endow these models with magical properties, because there were handbooks, tables, and textbooks for use by postgraduate magicians. In themselves these models had never proved anything, and from a scientific point of view they were of no more interest than card tricks or sword swallowing.

Of course, I could understand all these pitiful journalists who stuck to Vybegallo like flies on a dung heap. Because from the viewpoint of the nonspecialist it all looked very impressive; it inspired a frisson of admiration and vague presentiments of immense possibilities. It was harder to understand Vybegallo, and his morbid obsession with organizing circus performances and public explosions to satisfy people who could not possibly understand (and had no desire to understand) the essence of what was happening. Apart from two or three Absolutists who were exhausted by their research trips and loved to give interviews on the state of affairs in infinity, no one else in the Institute abused their contacts with the press. It was considered bad form—and that disapproval derived from a profound internal logic.

The problem is that the most interesting and elegant scientific results frequently possess the property of appearing abstruse and drearily incomprehensible to the uninitiated. In our time people who have no connection with science expect it to produce miracles and nothing but miracles, but they're practically incapable of distinguishing a genuine scientific miracle from a conjuring trick or intellectual acrobatics. The science of sorcery and wizardry is no exception. There are plenty of people who can organize a conference of famous ghosts in a television studio or drill a hole in a fifty-centimeter wall just by looking at it, which is no good at all to anyone, but it produces an ecstatic response from our highly esteemed public, which has no real idea of the extent to which science has interwoven and blended together the concepts of fairy tale and reality. But just you try to define the profound internal connection between the drilling capacity of the human glance and the philological characteristics of the word *concrete*—just try to answer this one discrete little question, which is known as Auer's Great Problem! Oira-Oira solved it by creating the theory of fantastical totality and founding an entirely new branch of mathematical magic. But almost no one has ever heard of Oira-Oira, and everyone knows all about Professor Vybegallo. ("Ah, so you work at NITWiT? How's Vybegallo doing? What else has he discovered now?") This happens because there are only two or three hundred people in the entire world capable of grasping Oira-Oira's ideas, and while these two or three hundred include many corresponding members of the Academy of Sciences, they do not, alas, include a single journalist. But in its time Vybegallo's classic work "Fundamentals of Technology for the Production of Self-Donning Footwear," which is crammed full of demagogic nonsense, was a great sensation, thanks to the efforts of B. Pitomnik. (It later emerged that self-donning shoes cost more than a motorcycle and are easily damaged by dust and moisture.)

It was getting late. I was seriously tired and I dozed off without realizing it. I dreamed about some kind of fantastic vermin—gigantic multilegged mosquitoes with beards like Vybegallo's—talking buckets of skim milk, a tub with short little legs running down the stairs. Occasionally some indiscreet brownie glanced into my dream, but when he saw these horrors, he bolted in fright. I was woken by a pain and opened my eyes to see beside me a macabre bearded mosquito trying to sink its proboscis, as thick as a ballpoint pen, into my calf.

"Shoo!" I roared, and punched it in its bulging eye.

The mosquito gurgled resentfully and ran away a few steps. It was as big as a dog, ginger with white spots. I must have pronounced the materialization formula without realizing it while I was asleep and unwittingly summoned this macabre beast out of nonexistence. I tried to drive it back into nonexistence but failed. Then I armed myself with the heavy volume *Equations of Mathematical Magic*, opened the small window, and drove the mosquito out into the frost. The blizzard immediately whirled it away, and it disappeared into the darkness. That's the way unsavory sensations are started, I thought.

It was six in the morning and the Institute was absolutely quiet. Either everyone was working hard or they'd all gone home. I was supposed to make one more round, but I didn't want to go anywhere and I wanted something to eat, because the last time I'd eaten was eighteen hours earlier. So I decided to send a double instead.

I'm really still a very weak magician. Inexperienced. If there'd been anybody else there with me, I'd never have taken the chance of exposing my ignorance. But I was alone, and I decided to risk it and get in a bit of practice at the same time. I found the general formula in *Equations of Mathematical Magic*, entered my own parameters into it, performed all the required manipulations, and pronounced all the required expressions in ancient Chaldean. Hard study really does pay dividends. For the first time in my life I managed to make a decent double. He had everything in the right place and he even looked a little bit like me, except that for some reason his left eye didn't open and he had six fingers on his hands. I explained his task to him and he nodded, shuffled one foot across the floor, and set off, staggering as he walked. We never met again. Perhaps he somehow ended up in the Gorynych Wyrm's bunker, or perhaps he embarked on an infinite journey on the rim of the Wheel of Fortune—I don't know, I just don't know. But as a matter of fact, I very quickly forgot all about him, because I decided to make myself breakfast.

I'm not a very fussy person. All I wanted was a piece of bread with a slice of "doctor's" sausage and a cup of black coffee. I don't understand how it happened, but what first appeared on the table was a doctor's white coat thickly spread with butter. When the first shock of natural amazement had passed, I took a close look at the white coat. The greasy substance wasn't actually butter and it wasn't vegetable oil either. At this point I ought to have destroyed the white coat and started all over again. But in my heinous conceit I imagined I was God the Creator and chose the route of sequential transformations. A bottle of black liquid appeared beside the white coat, and after a brief pause the coat itself began charring at the edges. I hastily refined my conceptual formulations, laying special emphasis on the images of the mug and the meat. The bottle changed into a mug but the liquid remained unchanged; one of the coat's sleeves bent up, extended, turned reddish, and began twitching. I broke into a sweat when I saw it was a cow's tail. I got up out of the armchair and moved away into the corner. The change didn't go any further than the tail, but even so it was a pretty horrendous sight. I tried again, and the tail sprouted ears of grain. I got a grip on myself, squeezed my eyes shut, and tried to picture as clearly as possible a slice of ordinary rye bread being sliced off the loaf and spread with butter from a crystal butter dish, and a round slice of sausage being set on it.

Never mind the "doctor's" sausage, it could be ordinary Poltava sausage, semismoked. I decided to wait for a while with the coffee. When I cautiously half-opened my eyes, there was large piece of rock crystal lying on the white coat, with something dark inside it. I picked up the crystal and the coat came with it, having become attached to it in some mysterious way, and inside the crystal I could make out my much-coveted sandwich, looking very much like the real thing. I groaned and mentally attempted to shatter the crystal. It became covered with a dense network of cracks, so that the sandwich was almost hidden from view. "You dunce," I said to myself, "you've eaten thousands of sandwiches and you can't even manage a half-decent visualization of one. Don't worry, there's no one here—no one can see you. It's not a test or a piece of course work or an exam. Try it again." So I did.

It would have been better if I hadn't. My imagination somehow began running riot, and the most unexpected associations flared up and faded away in my brain. As I continued my efforts, the reception room filled up with the most peculiar objects. Many of them had clearly emerged from my subconscious, out of the teeming jungles of hereditary memory, from behind the primordial terrors long ago suppressed by higher education. They had limbs on which they moved about restlessly; they made repulsive sounds; they were obscene; they were aggressive and kept fighting all the time. I gazed around me, worn out. The scene reminded me very vividly of old engravings showing the temptations of Saint Anthony. One especially unpleasant item was an oval plate on spider's legs with thin, coarse fur around its edge. I don't know what it wanted from me, but it kept retreating into the far corner of the room, taking a run at me, and smashing into me full steam below the knees, until I finally trapped it against the wall with my armchair. Eventually I managed to eliminate some of the items and the rest wandered off into the corners and hid. I was left with the plate, the white coat with the crystal, and the mug with the black liquid, which had expanded to the size of a jug. I picked it up with both hands and took a sniff. I believe it was black ink for fountain pens.

The dish wriggled behind my armchair, scratching at the patterned
linoleum with its feet and hissing loathsomely. Things were looking very bleak.

I heard footsteps and voices in the corridor, and the door
opened. Janus Polyeuctovich appeared in the doorway and, as
always, said, "I see." I was thrown into confusion. Janus Polyeuctovich walked through into his office, having liquidated my
entire cabinet of curiosities on the way with a single multifunction
movement of one eyebrow. He was followed by Fyodor Simeonovich, Cristóbal Junta with a thick black cigar in the corner
of his mouth, a sullen, scowling Vybegallo, and a determined-
looking Roman Oira-Oira. They were all greatly preoccupied and
in a great hurry, so they paid no attention at all to me. The office
door was left open. With a sigh of relief, I settled back into my
former position, only to discover a large porcelain mug of steaming hot coffee and a plate of sandwiches waiting for me. One of
the titans at least must have felt some concern for me, but I don't
know which. I tucked into my breakfast, listening to the voices
coming out of the office.

"Let us begin," said Cristóbal Junta, speaking with icy disdain,
"with the fact that your 'Nursery'—begging your pardon—is located
directly below my laboratory. You have already succeeded in pro-
ducing one explosion, with the result that I was obliged to wait for
ten minutes while the shattered windows in my office were replaced.
I strongly suspect that you will not pay any attention to arguments
of a more general nature, and I am therefore basing my comments
on purely egotistical considerations—"

"My dear fellow, what I do in my own lab is my own business,"
Vybegallo replied in a thin falsetto. "I don't interfere with your
floor, although just recently living water's been leaking through
continuously. It's soaked my entire ceiling, and it encourages bed-
bugs. But I don't interfere with your floor, so don't you interfere
with mine."

"Dear *fellow*," rumbled Fyodor Simeonovich, "Ambrosius Ambroisovich! You must take into account the *possible*

complications . . . After all, no one works with the *dragon*, for instance, in the building, even though we have *heatproof* materials, and—"

"I don't have a dragon, I have a happy human being! A giant of the mental life! Your reasoning is rather strange, comrade Kivrin: you draw rather strange comparisons, not our kind at all! A model of an ideal man—and some déclassé fire-breathing dragon!"

"Dear *fellow*, the point is not that he *has* no social class, it's that he could cause a *fire*—"

"There you go again! An ideal man could cause a fire! You haven't bothered to think it through, Fyodor Simeonovich!"

"I was *talking* about the *dragon*."

"And I'm talking about your incorrect orientation! You're blurring boundaries, Fyodor Simeonovich! Doing everything possible to plaster over differences! Of course, we do eliminate contradictions between . . . the mental and the physical . . . between town and country . . . between man and woman, even . . . But we won't allow you to plaster over an abyss, Fyodor Simeonovich!"

"*What* abyss? What sort of idiocy is this, *Roman*, tell me? I was there when you *explained* it to him! I am *saying*, Ambrosius Ambroisovich, that your experiment is *dangerous*, do you understand? It could do damage to the town, do you *understand?*"

"I understand everything, all right. And I won't allow the ideal man to hatch out in a bare, windswept field!"

"Ambrosius Ambroisovich," said Roman, "I can run through my arguments again. The experiment is dangerous because—"

"There you are, Roman Petrovich. I've been watching you for a long time and I just can't understand how you can use expressions like that about the ideal man. Hah, he thinks the ideal man is dangerous!"

At this point Roman ran out of patience, no doubt due to his youth. "It's not the ideal man!" he yelled. "It's just your ultimate consumer genius!"

There was an ominous silence.

"What did you say?" Vybegallo inquired in a terrible voice. "Repeat that. What did you call my ideal man?"

"Janus Polyeuctovich," said Fyodor Simeonovich, "this really won't *do*, my friend—"

"It certainly won't!" exclaimed Vybegallo. "Quite right, comrade Kivrin, it won't do! We have an experiment of global scientific significance! This titan of the mental world must make his appearance here, within the walls of our Institute! It is symbolic! Comrade Oira-Oira with his pragmatic deviation from the party line is taking a narrow, utilitarian view, comrades! And comrade Junta is also adopting a lowbrow approach! Don't you look at me like that, comrade Junta, the czar's gendarmes didn't frighten me, and you won't frighten me either! Is it really in the spirit of our work, comrades, to be afraid of an experiment? Of course it is excusable for comrade Junta, as a former foreigner and employee of the Church, to go astray at times, but you, comrade Oira-Oira, and you, Fyodor Simeonovich, you are simple Russian folk!"

"Enough of your *demagogy*!" Fyodor Simeonovich finally exploded. "Aren't you *ashamed* to spout such gibberish? *What* kind of simple man of the people am I? And what kind of word is that— *simple*? It's your doubles that are simple!"

"I have just one thing to say," Cristóbal Joséevich stated indifferently. "I am a simple former grand inquisitor, and I shall block all access to your autoclave until such time as I receive a guarantee that the experiment will take place on the firing range."

"And at *least* five kilometers away from the *town*," added Fyodor Simeonovich. "Or even *ten*."

Evidently the last thing Vybegallo wanted to do was to drag all his equipment and himself all the way out to the firing range, while there was a blizzard raging and the light was too poor to film the event. "I see," he said. "I understand. You're fencing our science off from the people. In that case, why ten kilometers, why not ten thousand kilometers, Fyodor Simeonovich? Somewhere on the other side? Somewhere in Alaska, Cristóbal Joséevich, or wherever it is you're from? Just tell us straight out. And we'll note it down!" Silence fell again, and I could hear Fyodor Simeonovich, deprived of the gift of speech, breathing loudly and menacingly through his nose.

"Three hundred years ago," Junta said in a chill voice, "for those words I would have invited you to take a walk in the country, where I would have shaken the dust off your ears and run you through."

"Oh no, oh no," said Vybegallo. "You're not in Portugual now. You don't like criticism. Three hundred years ago I wouldn't have wasted any more time on you than all the rest of the Catholics." The feeling of hate was choking me. Why didn't Janus say anything? How long could this go on?

I heard footsteps in the silence, then Roman came out into the reception room, pale and scowling. With a click of his fingers, he created a double of Vybegallo. Then with obvious pleasure he grabbed the double by the chest, shook it rapidly, then grabbed its beard and yanked it passionately several times before annihilating the double and going back into the office.

"You should be thrown out, *Vybegallo*," said Fyodor Simeonovich in an unexpectedly calm voice. "It turns out you are a *most* unpleasant character."

"Criticism—you can't stand criticism," answered Vybegallo, puffing himself up.

And then at last Janus Polyeuctovich spoke. His voice was as powerful and steady as the voices of Jack London's sea captains. "As Ambrosius has requested, the experiment will be held today at ten hundred hours. In view of the fact that the experiment will be accompanied by extensive destruction, which will come close to causing human casualties, I set the site of the experiment as a point fifteen kilometers from the town boundary, in the farthest sector of the firing range. I wish to take this opportunity to thank Roman Petrovich in advance for his resourcefulness and courage."

For some time they were evidently all digesting this decision. There was certainly no doubt that Janus Polyeuctovich expressed his thoughts in a strange manner. But everyone willingly accepted that he knew best. There had been precedents.

"I'll go and call for a truck," Roman said suddenly, and he must have gone out through the wall, because he didn't appear in the reception room again.

Fyodor Simeonovich and Junta no doubt nodded in agreement, and Vybegallo recovered his wits and cried, "A correct decision, Janus Polyeuctovich! You have given us a very timely reminder of the need to restore vigilance. As far away as possible from prying eyes. Only I shall need porters. My autoclave is heavy, you know— five tons, after all . . ."

"Of course," said Janus. "Issue instructions."

The armchairs in the office began moving, and I hurriedly finished off my coffee.

For the next hour I hung around the entrance with the other people still left in the Institute and watched the autoclave and the stereoscopic telescopes being loaded up, with the armored shields and some warm old coats just in case. The blizzard had died down and it was a clear, frosty morning.

Roman drove up a truck on caterpillar treads. The vampire Alfred brought the loaders, who were the hekatonheirs. Kottos and Gyges came willingly, chattering excitedly with all their hundred throats and rolling up their numerous sleeves on the way, but Briareos lagged behind, thrusting out his gnarled finger ahead of him and whining that it hurt, that several of his heads were feeling dizzy and he hadn't gotten any sleep last night. Kottos took the autoclave and Gyges took all the rest. When Briareos saw that there was nothing left for him, he started giving instructions and helpful advice. He ran ahead and opened doors, now and then squatting on his haunches and glancing underneath, shouting, "That's got it! That's got it!" or "Farther to the right! You're getting snagged!" Eventually his hand got trodden on and he himself got jammed between the autoclave and the wall. He burst into sobs, and Alfred led him back down to the vivarium.

There were quite a number of people squeezed into the truck. Vybegallo climbed into the driver's seat. He was feeling very dissatisfied and kept asking everyone what time it was. The truck set off, only to return five minutes later because they realized they'd forgotten the journalists. While they were looking for them, Kottos and Gyges started a snowball fight to keep warm and broke

two windows. Then Gyges got into a tussle with an early drunk, who shouted, "All of you against just one of me, eh?" They pulled Gyges off and shoved him back into the truck. He rolled his eyes and swore menacingly in ancient Hellenic. G. Pronitsatelny and B. Pitomnik appeared, still yawning and shivering with sleep, and the truck finally left.

The Institute was left empty. It was half past nine. The entire town was asleep. I'd really wanted to go off to the firing range with everyone else, but there was nothing to be done about it. I sighed and set off on my second round.

I walked along the corridors, yawning and turning lights off everywhere until I reached Vitka Korneev's lab. Vitka took no interest in Vybegallo's experiments. He said that people like Vybegallo ought to be summarily handed over to Junta for experimental investigation to determine whether they were lethal mutants. So Vitka hadn't gone anywhere; he was sitting on the sofa-translator, smoking a cigarette and chatting idly with Edik Amperian. Edik was lying beside him, staring pensively at the ceiling and sucking on a fruit drop. On the table the perch was swimming around cheerfully in its bathtub.

"Happy New Year," I said.

"Happy New Year," Edik replied affably.

"Let's ask Sashka, then," Korneev suggested. "Sasha, is there such a thing as nonprotein life?"

"I don't know," I said. "I haven't seen it. Why?"

"What does that mean, you haven't seen it? You've never seen an M-field either, but you calculate its intensity."

"So what?" I said. I looked at the perch in the bathtub. The perch was swimming round and round, banking steeply on the tight corners, and then you could see it had been gutted. "Vitka," I said, "so it worked after all?"

"Sasha doesn't want to talk about nonprotein life," said Edik. "And he's right."

"You can live without protein," I said, "but how come he's alive without any insides?"

"Well, comrade Amperian here says that life isn't possible without protein," said Vitka, making a jet of tobacco smoke curl into a tornado and wander around the room, avoiding objects.

"I say that life is protein," protested Edik.

"I don't see what the difference is," said Vitka. "You say that if there's no protein, there's no life."

"Yes."

"Right, then what's this?" asked Vitka. He gestured vaguely with his hand.

A repulsive creature appeared on the table beside the bathtub. It looked like a hedgehog and a spider at the same time.

Edik lifted himself up and glanced toward the table. "Ah," he said, and lay back down again. "That's not life. That's nonlife. Koschei the Deathless isn't a nonprotein being, surely?"

"Just what do you want?" asked Korneev. "Can it move? It can. Can it eat? It can. And it can reproduce too. Would you like it to reproduce now?"

Edik raised himself up again and glanced toward the table. The hedgehog-spider was marking time on the spot. It looked as though it wanted to run off in all four directions at once. "Nonlife is not life," said Edik. "Nonlife only exists insofar as rational life exists. I can put it even more precisely: insofar as magicians exist. Nonlife is a product of the activity of magicians."

"All right," said Vitka. The hedgehog-spider disappeared. In its place a little Vitka Korneev appeared on the table, a precise copy of the real one, but only the size of his hand. He snapped his little fingers and created a microdouble that was even smaller. The microdouble snapped his fingers and a double the size of a fountain pen appeared, then one the size of a matchbox. Then one the size of a thimble.

"Is that enough?" asked Vitka. "Each one of them is a magician. But not one contains a molecule of protein."

"A poor example," Edik said regretfully. "First, in principle they are in no way different from a programmable lathe. Second, they are not products of development but of your protein-based skills.

It's hardly worth arguing about whether self-reproducing lathes with programmable controls are capable of generating evolution."

"You don't have a clue about evolution," said the loutish Korneev. "Some Darwin you are! What difference does it make whether it's a chemical process or conscious activity? Not all of your ancient ancestors are protein-based either. I'm prepared to admit that your great-great-great-great-foremother was pretty complex, but she wasn't a protein molecule. And maybe our so-called conscious activity is just another variety of evolution. How do we know that the goal of nature is to create comrade Amperian? Maybe the goal of nature is to create nonlife with the hands of comrade Amperian? Maybe—"

"I get it, I get it. First a protovirus, then a protein, then comrade Amperian, and then the entire planet is populated with nonlife."

"Precisely," said Vitka.

"And then we're all extinct because we've outlived our usefulness."

"And why not?" said Vitka.

"There's a friend of mine," said Edik, "who claims that man is only an intermediate link required by nature to create the crown of creation: a glass of cognac with a slice of lemon."

"Well, after all, why not?"

"Because I don't want it," said Edik. "Nature has its goals, and I have mine."

"Anthropocentrist!" Vitka said in disgust.

"Yes," Edik said proudly.

"I don't wish to engage in discussion with anthropocentrists," said the coarse Korneev.

"Then let's tell jokes instead," Edik suggested calmly, and stuck another fruit drop in his mouth.

On the table Vitka's doubles carried on working. The smallest was already only the size of an ant. While I was listening to the dispute between the anthropocentrist and the cosmocentrist, a thought occurred to me.

"Guys," I said with bogus vivacity, "why didn't you go to the firing range?"

"What for?" asked Edik.

"Well, surely it's interesting."

"I never go to the circus," said Edik. *"Ubi nihil vales, ibi nihil velis."**

---

* AUTHORS' NOTE: "Where you can do nothing, you should want nothing."

"Do you mean yourself?" asked Vitka.

"No. I meant Vybegallo."

"Guys," I said, "I'm just crazy about the circus. And what difference does it make to you where you tell your jokes?"

"Meaning?" said Vitka.

"You cover my shift, and I'll dash over to the firing range."

"What do we have to do?"

"Cut the power off, put out any fires, and remind everyone about the labor regulations."

"It's cold," Vitka reminded me. "It's frosty. It's Vybegallo."

"I really want to go," I said. "It's all very mysterious."

"Shall we let the child go out to play?" Vitka asked Edik.

Edik nodded.

"Off you go then, Privalov," said Vitka. "It'll cost you four hours of machine time."

"Two," I said quickly. I'd been expecting something of the kind.

"Five," Vitka said cheekily.

"OK, three," I said. "I spend all my time working for you anyway."

"Six," Vitka said coolly.

"Vitka," said Edik, "you'll grow fur in your ears."

"Ginger," I said gloatingly. "With a greenish tinge, maybe."

"OK," said Vitka, "go on the cheap, then. Two hours will do for me."

We walked down to the director's waiting room together. On the way the two masters struck up an incomprehensible argument about "cyclotation" or some such thing, and I had to interrupt to get them to transgress me to the firing range. They were fed up with me by then and in their haste to get rid of me they performed the transgression with such high energy that before I even had time to put on my coat I found myself flying backward into the crowd of onlookers.

At the firing range everything was ready. The audience was sheltering behind the armored shields. Vybegallo's head protruded from a freshly dug trench, peering rakishly into a large stereoscopic telescope. Fyodor Simeonovich and Cristóbal Junta were conversing quietly in Latin, holding 40x magnification binoculars. Janus Polyeuctovich was standing indifferently at one side in his large fur coat and prodding at the snow with his cane. B. Pitomnik was squatting on his haunches beside the trench with an open notebook and fountain pen at the ready. And G. Pronitsatelny was standing behind him, hung all over with still cameras and movie cameras, rubbing his frozen cheeks, grunting, and knocking his feet together.

A full moon was sinking toward the west in a clear sky. The nebulous streaks of the northern lights appeared, glimmering between the stars, and then disappeared again. The snow gleamed white on the level land, and the large, rounded cylinder of the autoclave was clearly visible a hundred meters away from us.

Vybegallo tore himself away from the stereoscopic telescope, cleared his throat, and said, "Comrades! Comrades! What do we observe in this stereoscopic telescope? In this stereoscopic telescope, comrades, we, overwhelmed by an entire complex of feelings, rooted to the spot in anticipation, observe the protective hood beginning automatically to unscrew itself . . . Write, write," he said to B. Pitomnik. "And get it right . . . Automatically, you know, unscrew itself. In a few minutes the ideal man will make his appearance among us—a *chevalier*, you know, *sans peur et sans reproche*. We shall have here with us our model, our symbol, our most exalted dream! And we, comrades, must greet this giant of needs and capacities in an appropriate manner, with no polemics, petty wrangling, or other outbursts. Let our dear giant see us as we really are, drawn up in closed ranks in tight formation. Let us conceal our capitalist birthmarks, comrades, those of us who still have them, and reach out our arms to our dream!"

Even with my unaided eye I saw the hood of the autoclave unscrew itself and fall soundlessly into the snow. A long jet of steam shot up out of the autoclave, all the way to the stars.

"Allow me to elucidate for the press—" Vybegallo began, when suddenly there was a hideous bellow.

The ground shifted and began to tremble. An immense cloud of snow flew up into the air. Everyone fell on top of everyone else and I was thrown over and sent rolling. The bellowing kept growing louder, and when I managed to clamber to my feet by clutching at the caterpillar tracks of the truck, I saw the edge of the horizon creeping toward me horrifyingly, like the rim of a gigantic chalice in the dead light of the moon, folding over and in on itself, the armored shields swaying menacingly, onlookers scattering and running, falling and jumping up again, covered in snow. I saw Fyodor Simeonovich and Cristóbal Junta, standing under the rainbow hoods of a defensive field, stagger back under the impact of the hurricane as they raised their hands, struggling to extend the protection over all the others, but the whirlwind ripped their defenses to shreds, and the shreds went hurtling off across the plain, like huge soap bubbles, and then burst in the starry sky. I saw the raised collar of Janus Polyeuctovich, who was standing with his back to the wind and his cane firmly braced against the denuded earth, looking at his watch. And now where the autoclave had been there was a dense, swirling cloud of steam lit with a red light from within, and the horizon was curling back in on itself tighter and tighter, and we all seemed to be on the bottom of a colossal jug.

And then suddenly, right beside the epicenter of this cosmic outrage, there was Roman with his green coat almost torn off his shoulders by the wind. He swung his arm out wide and tossed something large that glinted like a bottle into the steam, then immediately fell flat on his face, covering his head with his hands. The ugly features of a genie, contorted in frenzied rage, appeared out of the cloud, his eyes rolling in silent fury. Opening his jaws in soundless laughter, he flapped his massive, hairy ears, there was a smell of burning, the transparent walls of a magnificent palace flashed above the blizzard, quivered, and collapsed, and the genie, transformed into a long tongue of orange flame, disappeared into the sky. For a few seconds it was quiet, and then the horizon settled back down with a heavy rumbling. I was thrown high into the air, and when I came to I found I was sitting not far from the truck with my hands braced against the ground.

The snow had disappeared. All around us the ground was black. Where the autoclave had stood only a minute ago there was a large gaping crater with white smoke rising out of it. The air was filled with the smell of burning.

The onlookers began getting to their feet, everyone with grimy and contorted faces. Many had lost their voices. They were coughing, spitting, and groaning quietly. They began cleaning themselves off and discovered that some had been left in nothing but their underwear. First there was murmuring, and then shouts: "Where are my pants? Why don't I have any pants? I was wearing pants!"; "Comrades, has anyone seen my watch?"; "And mine?"; "And mine's missing too!"; "My platinum tooth's gone, I only had it put in last summer . . ."; "Hey, and my ring's disappeared . . . And my bracelet!"; "Where's Vybegallo? This is an outrage! What does it all mean?"; "To hell with the watches and the teeth! Is everybody all right? How many of us were there?"; "But what was it that happened? Some kind of explosion . . . A genie . . . And where's the titan of the mental world?"; "Where's the consumer?"; "Where's Vybegallo, come to think of it?"; "Did you see the horizon? Do you know what it was like?"; "A folding of the spatial continuum, I know about these things . . ."; "I'm cold in this vest, give me something . . ."; "*Where's* that *Vybegallo*? Where has that *fool* gone to?"

The earth stirred and Vybegallo climbed out of his trench. His felt boots were gone.

"Allow me to elucidate for the press," he said hoarsely.

But he wasn't allowed to elucidate. Magnus Fyodorovich Redkin, who had come especially to find out at last what genuine happiness was, bounded up to him, waving his clenched fists, and howled, "You charlatan! You'll answer for this! This circus! Where's my cap? Where's my fur coat? I'm going to make an official complaint about you! Where's my cap, I said!"

"In complete conformity with the program of the project," Vybegallo muttered, gazing around, "our dear titan—"

Fyodor Simeonovich advanced on him: "You, my *dear* chap, have been hiding your *talent* in the ground. You ought to reinforce the ranks of the Department of Defensive Magic. Your ideal *people* should be dropped on enemy *bases*. To strike *terror* into the aggressor."

Vybegallo staggered back, shielding himself with the sleeve of his rough coat. Cristóbal Joséevich approached him, looked him over from head to toe, tossed a pair of soiled gloves at his feet, and walked away. Gian Giacomo, who was hastily creating the appearance of an elegant suit for himself, shouted from a distance, "This is absolutely phenomenal, *signore*! I have always felt a certain antipathy toward him, but I could never even imagine anything like this . . ."

At this point G. Pronitsatelny and B. Pitomnik finally grasped the situation. So far they had been smiling uncertainly and gaping at everyone in the hope of understanding something. But now they realized that things were not proceeding "in complete conformity" after all. G. Pronitsatelny walked up to Vybegallo with a firm stride, tapped him on the shoulder, and said in a voice of iron, "Comrade Professor, where can I get my cameras back? Three still cameras and one movie camera."

"And my wedding ring," added B. Pitomnik.

"Pardon," said Vybegallo pompously. "*On vous demandera quand on aura besoin de vous.** Wait for the explanations."

The journalists' courage failed them. Vybegallo turned and walked toward the crater. Roman was already standing at the top of it. "There's everything you could possibly imagine in here," he said from afar.

The titanic consumer was not in the crater. But everything else was, and a great deal more besides. There were cameras and movie cameras, wallets, fur coats, rings, necklaces, trousers, and a platinum tooth. Vybegallo's felt boots were there, and so was Magnus Fyodorovich's cap. My platinum whistle for summoning the

---

* AUTHORS' NOTE: "You will be called upon when you are needed."

emergency brigade was in there too. And in addition we found two Moskvich automobiles, three Volga automobiles, an iron safe with seals from the local savings bank, a large piece of roasted meat, two crates of vodka, a crate of Zhigulevskoye beer, and an iron bed frame with nickel-plated knobs.

Vybegallo pulled on his felt boots and declared with a condescending smile that now they could proceed with the discussion. "I'll take questions," he said. But the discussion never got going. The infuriated Magnus Fyodorovich had called the militia, and young Sergeant Kovalyov came racing up in a little jeep. We all had to give our names as witnesses. Sergeant Kovalyov walked around the crater, trying to discover any traces of the criminal. He found an immense set of false teeth that set him pondering deeply.

Their equipment having been restored to them, the journalists had suddenly begun to see things in a different light and were listening attentively to Vybegallo, who was once again spouting his demagogic trash about unlimited and diversified needs. Things were getting boring and I was freezing.

"Let's go home," said Roman.

"Yes, let's," I said. "Where did you get the genie from?"

"I signed him out of the store yesterday. For entirely different purposes."

"But what actually happened? Did this one overeat as well?"

"No, Vybegallo's just an idiot," said Roman.

"Well that's obvious," I said. "But what caused the cataclysm?"

"The same reason," said Roman. "I told him a thousand times: 'You're programming a standard super egocentric. He'll just grab all the material valuables he can lay his hands on, then he'll roll up space, wrap himself up like a pupa, and halt time.' But Vybegallo just can't grasp that a genuine mental giant is less interested in consuming than in thinking and feeling."

"That's all simple stuff," he continued after we'd flown to the Institute. "It's quite clear enough to everyone. But can you tell me how S-Janus knew that everything would turn out exactly that way, and not any other? He foresaw it all. The massive destruction, and me suddenly realizing how to put an end to the giant in the cradle."

"That's right," I said. "He even expressed his gratitude to you. In advance."

"That is strange, isn't it?" said Roman. "It all needs thinking through very carefully."

So we started thinking it through very carefully. It took us a long time. In fact it wasn't until spring—and then only by chance—that we managed to figure everything out.

But that's an entirely different story.

All Kinds of Commotion

1

"When God made time," the Irish say, *"He made plenty of it."*
—Heinrich Böll

Eighty-three percent of all the days in the year start the same way: the alarm clock rings. The ringing insinuates itself into my final dreams as the frenetic clattering of an automatic card punch or Fyodor Simeonovich's booming, thunderous bass, or the rasping of a basilisk playing in the constant temperature cabinet.

That morning I was dreaming about Modest Matveevich Kamnoedov. He'd been made head of the computer center and was training me to work on the Aldan. "Modest Matveevich," I was telling him, "all this advice you're trying to give me is nothing but crazy gibberish."

And he kept yelling, *"Thaaat's* quite *eeenough* of that *frrrom* you! Everything you've got here *iiis* absolute nonsense, *toootal* rubbish!"

Then I realized it wasn't Modest Matveevich but my "Friendship" alarm clock with its eleven stones and picture of a little elephant with its trunk raised. "I hear you, I hear you," I muttered, and started slapping away at the tabletop, trying to hit the clock.

The window was wide open: I caught a glimpse of clear blue spring sky and felt the sharp breath of a cool spring breeze. There were pigeons clattering along the sheet metal of the cornice. Three flies were fluttering exhaustedly around the glass dome of the ceiling light—they must have been the first flies of the year. Every now and then they suddenly began dashing frenziedly from side to side, and in my half-awake state the brilliant idea occurred to me that the flies were probably trying to break free of a plane that transected them. I sympathized with their hopeless struggle. Two flies settled on the light cover and the third disappeared, and then I finally woke up completely.

First of all I threw off the blanket and attempted to rise into the air above the bed. As always, without my morning exercises, shower, and breakfast, the only result I achieved was that the moment of reaction drove me back down hard into the sofa bed, unhooking the springs and setting them jangling plaintively somewhere beneath me. Then I remembered the previous evening and felt really upset, because I knew I'd be left without any work to do all day long. Yesterday at eleven o'clock in the evening Cristóbal Junta had come into the computer room and, as always, connected himself to the Aldan so that the two of them together could tackle the latest problem of the meaning of life. Five minutes later the Aldan had burst into flames. I don't know what there was inside it that could have burned, but the Aldan was going to be out of action for a long time, which meant that instead of working I would be doing the same thing that all the hairy-eared parasites did: wandering aimlessly from one department to another, complaining about life and telling jokes.

I frowned, sat on the edge of the bed, and began by filling my lungs up to the top with *prāṇa* mingled with the cold spring air. I waited a while for the *prāṇa* to be absorbed and followed the standard recommendations by thinking bright and happy thoughts. Then I breathed out the cold spring air and began performing a sequence of morning exercises. I'd been told that the old school used to prescribe yoga exercises, but the yoga sequence, like the now almost forgotten maya sequence, used to take from fifteen to twenty hours a day, and when a new president of the USSR Academy of Sciences was appointed, the old school had been forced to give way. NITWiT's young generation had been only too glad to break with the old traditions.

At the 115th leap my roommate Vitka Korneev came floating into the room. As always in the morning, he was cheerful and full of energy, even good humored. He lashed me across my bare back with a wet towel and began flying around the room, making movements with his arms and legs as if he were swimming the breaststroke, telling me as he did so about his dreams and interpreting them as he went along according to Freud, Merlin, and

Mademoiselle Lenormand. I went and got washed, then we both got ready and set out for the cafeteria.

In the cafeteria we took our favorite table under a large, faded poster ("Be bold, comrades, and snap your jaws! —Gustave Flaubert"), opened our bottles of kefir, and started eating while we listened to the local news and gossip:

The traditional spring rally had taken place the night before on Bald Mountain, and the participants had behaved quite deplorably. Viy and Khoma Brut had gotten drunk and gone wandering through the dark streets of the town, pestering passersby and using foul language, then Viy had stepped on his own left eyelid and flown into a furious rage. He and Khoma had gotten into a fight, knocked over a newspaper kiosk, and ended up in the militia station, where they were both given fifteen days for being drunk and disorderly. It had taken six men to hold Khoma Brut so that his head could be shaved, and meanwhile the bald-headed Viy had sat in the corner giggling offensively. The case was being passed on to the people's court because of what Khoma Brut had said while his hair was being cut.

Vasily the cat had taken a spring vacation—to get married. Soon Solovets would be blessed once again with talking kittens suffering from hereditary amnesia.

Louis Sedlovoi from the Department of Absolute Knowledge had invented some kind of time machine, and he was going to give a paper about it at a seminar today.

Vybegallo had reappeared in the Institute. He was going around boasting that he'd been inspired by an absolutely titanic idea. It seemed that the speech of many monkeys resembled human speech recorded on tape and played backward at high speed. So he'd, you know, recorded the conversations of the baboons in the Sukhumi nature reserve and listened to them back to front at low speed. The result, he claimed, was something absolutely phenomenal, but exactly what he wasn't saying.

The computing center's Aldan had burned out again, but it wasn't Sashka Privalov's fault, it was Junta's: just recently he'd made it a matter of principle to take an interest only in problems that had already been proved not to have any solution.

The decrepit old sorcerer Perun Markovich Neunyvai-Dubino from the Department of Militant Atheism had taken leave for his next reincarnation.

In the Department of Eternal Youth the model of immortal man had died following a protracted illness.

The Academy of Sciences had allocated the Institute a massive amount of money to improve the facilities on its site. Modest Matveevich intended to use this sum to surround the Institute with fancy cast-iron railings supported by columns with allegorical images and pots of flowers, and in the backyard, between the transformer shed and the fuel store, he was going to install a fountain with a jet nine meters high. The sports committee had requested money for a tennis court, but he had refused, declaring that a fountain was required for scholarly cogitation, and tennis was nothing but a pointless jiggling of arms and joggling of legs.

After breakfast everyone went off to their labs. I stopped by the computer room and shuffled miserably around the Aldan while the sullen, unfriendly technicians from the Technical Service Department fiddled around inside its gaping entrails. They didn't want to talk to me and suggested morosely that I should go somewhere else and mind my own business. I wandered off to visit friends.

Vitka Korneev threw me out because he couldn't concentrate with me around. Roman was giving a lecture to some trainees. Volodya Pochkin was chatting with some journalists. When he caught sight of me he looked delighted and shouted, "Aha, there he is! Let me introduce the head of our computer center, he'll tell you all about how . . ." I gave a very cunning imitation of my own double, which gave the journalists a real fright, and managed to escape. At Edik Amperian's place they treated me to fresh cucumbers and we'd just struck up a lively conversation about the advantages of the gastronomical view of life when their distillation apparatus exploded and they forgot all about me.

I went out into the corridor in absolute despair and ran into S-Janus, who said, "I see," and then after a pause inquired whether we'd spoken yesterday. "No," I said, "unfortunately we didn't." He carried on, and I heard him ask Gian Giacomo the same standard question at the end of the corridor.

Eventually I wound up with the Absolutists, arriving there just before the beginning of the seminar. The members of the department were taking their seats in the small conference hall, yawning and gently stroking their ears. Sitting in the chairman's seat with his fingers calmly clasped together was the head of department, master academician of all white, black, and gray magic, the all-knowing Maurice Johann Laurentius Pupkov-Zadny. He was gazing benignly at the fidgety efforts of the speaker, assisted by two clumsily made doubles with hairy ears, to set up a machine with a saddle and pedals on the display stand. It looked like an exercise machine for the overweight. I took a seat in the corner as far away as possible from everyone else, pulled out a notebook and a pen, and assumed an interested expression.

"Very well, then," said the master academician, "do you have everything ready?"

"Yes, Maurice Johannovich," Louis Sedlovoi replied. "It's all ready, Maurice Johannovich."

"Then perhaps we should begin? I don't see Smoguly anywhere . . ."

"He's away on a research trip, Johann Laurentievich," said a voice from the hall.

"Ah yes, now I remember. Exponential investigations? Right, right . . . Well, then. Today Louis Ivanovich will present a brief report concerning certain possible types of time machines . . . Am I right, Louis Ivanovich?"

"Er . . . actually . . . actually, the title I would have given to my talk is—"

"Very well then. Call it that."

"Thank you. Er . . . I would call it 'The Feasibility of a Time Machine for Traveling in Artificially Structured Temporal Dimensions.'"

"Very interesting," put in the master academician. "However, I seem to recall there was a case when one of our colleagues—"

"Excuse me, that is the very point I'd like to start with."

"Oh, I see . . . Then please carry on."

I listened attentively at first. I even got quite engrossed. It seemed that some of these guys were working on very peculiar things. It turned out that some of them were still wrestling with the problem of movement in physical time, but without actually getting anywhere. But someone—I didn't catch the name, someone old and famous—had proved it was possible to displace material bodies into ideal worlds, that is, into worlds created by the human imagination. It seemed that apart from our usual world with its Riemannian metrics, uncertainty principle, physical vacuum, and boozy Khoma Brut, there were other worlds that possessed a very distinctly defined reality. These were the worlds that had been produced by the creative imagination throughout the course of human history. For instance, there was the world of mankind's cosmological ideas; the world created by painters; even a semiabstract, subtly structured world created by generations of composers.

Some years ago, it seemed, a pupil of that someone old and famous had put together a machine on which he had set off on a journey to the world of cosmological ideas. Unidirectional telepathic contact had been maintained for a while, and he had managed to report that he was on the edge of a flat Earth and below him he could see the coiling trunk of one of the three great elephants, and he was about to make the descent to the great tortoise. No further communications had been received from him.

The speaker, Louis Ivanovich Sedlovoi, was clearly not a bad scientist (he had a master's degree) but he suffered from vestigial elements of Paleolithic consciousness, so that he was obliged to shave his ears regularly. He had constructed a machine for traveling in described time. According to him, a world actually existed that was populated by Anna Karenina, Don Quixote, Sherlock Holmes, Grigory Melekhov, and even Captain Nemo. This world possessed its own extremely curious properties and laws, and the degree of vividness, reality, and individuality of the people who inhabited it depended on the talent, passion, and veracity with which they had been depicted by the authors of the relevant works. I found all this very interesting, because Sedlovoi got quite carried away and spoke in a lively and engaging manner. But then he suddenly got the idea that all this didn't sound very scientific, so he hung up a load of diagrams and charts on the stage and launched into a tedious exposition in highly specialized language about decremental bevel gears, multiple temporal transmissions, and some kind of permeative steering device.

I soon lost track of the thread of his reasoning and started gazing around at the other people there. The master academician was sleeping majestically, occasionally raising his right eyebrow in a pure reflex reaction, as if he were expressing some doubt concerning what the speaker was saying. The people in the back rows were engrossed in a furious game of battleships in Banach space. Two extramural students working as lab assistants were studiously noting down every word, their faces frozen in hopeless despair and abject submission to their fate. Someone furtively lit up a cigarette, blowing the smoke down between his knees under the desk. In the front row the masters and bachelors listened with their customary close attention, preparing their questions and comments. Some were smiling sarcastically; others looked perplexed. Sedlovoi's research supervisor nodded approvingly after each phrase. I began looking out the window, but there was nothing to see but the same boring old emporium and occasional boys running by with fishing rods.

I livened up a bit when the speaker declared that he had finished his introduction and now he would like to demonstrate his machine in action.

"Interesting, interesting," said the master academician, who had woken up. "Righty-ho . . . Will you go yourself?"

"Well, you see," said Sedlovoi, "I'd prefer to stay here to provide clarification in the course of the journey. Perhaps someone here would . . . ?"

Everyone there shrank back, obviously remembering the mysterious fate of the traveler who had journeyed to the edge of the flat Earth. One of the masters offered to send his double. Sedlovoi said that wouldn't be interesting, because doubles were rather insensitive to external stimuli and would be poor transmitters of information. Someone in the back rows asked what kinds of external stimuli there might be. Sedlovoi said the usual ones: visual, olfactory, tactile, acoustic. Then someone else in the back rows asked what kind of *tactile* stimuli would predominate. Sedlovoi shrugged and said that depended on how the traveler behaved in the places he reached.

Someone in the back rows said, "Ah . . ." and no more questions were asked. The speaker gazed around helplessly. Everyone in the audience was looking somewhere else, anywhere but at him. The master academician kept repeating good-naturedly, "Well? Well then? You young people! Well? Who will it be?"

I got to my feet and walked up to the machine without speaking. I simply can't bear the sight of a speaker dying the death; it's just too shameful, too pitiful and painful.

Someone in the back rows called out, "Sashka, what are you doing? Get a grip!" Sedlovoi's eyes glittered.

"May I?" I asked.

"By all means, most certainly!" Sedlovoi muttered, grabbing hold of my finger and dragging me toward the machine.

"Just a moment," I said, freeing myself gently. "Will it take long?"

"Just as long as you want!" exclaimed Sedlovoi. "You just tell me what you want, and that's what I'll do . . . And anyway, you'll be driving yourself! It's all very simple." He grabbed hold of me and dragged me toward the machine again. "You steer with these handlebars. Here's the reality-clutch pedal. This is the brake. And this is the accelerator. Do you drive a car? That's fine then! This control key . . . Which way do you want to go—into the future or the past?"

"The future," I said.

"Ah," he said, and I thought he sounded a little disappointed. "Into the described future . . . All those science fiction novels and utopias. Well of course, that's interesting too. Only don't forget that the future is bound to consist of discrete elements; there must be huge gaps of time that haven't been filled in by any authors. But then, that doesn't matter . . . All right then, you press this key twice. Once now, to start, and the second time when you want to come back. Do you understand?"

"Yes," I said. "But what if something goes wrong with it?"

"It's absolutely safe!" he said with a flutter of his hands. "The very instant anything goes wrong with it, if so much as a single speck of dust gets in between the contacts, you'll come straight back here."

"Be bold, young man," said the master academician, "and you'll be able to tell us what lies out there in the future, *ha-ha-ha . . .*"

I clambered into the saddle, feeling very stupid and trying not to catch anyone's eye.

"Press it, press it," the speaker whispered urgently.

I pressed the key. It was obviously some kind of starter. The machine jerked, snorted, and began trembling gently.

"The shaft's bent," Sedlovoi whispered in annoyance. "Never mind, never mind . . . Engage the gear. That's it. And now the accelerator, step on it."

I pressed on the accelerator, at the same time smoothly releasing the clutch. The world started to fade away. The last thing I heard in the hall was the master academician's voice asking, "And how exactly are we going to observe his progress?" And then the hall disappeared.

2

There is no difference between Time and any of the three dimensions of Space except that our consciousness moves along it.

—H. G. Wells

At first the machine progressed in short leaps and bounds, and it was all I could do to stay in the saddle by wrapping my legs around the frame and clinging to the arched steering bar as tightly as possible. Out of the corner of my eye I glimpsed magnificent spectral buildings, dull yellow plains, and a cold, cheerless sun shining through gray mist from close to its zenith. Then I realized that all the juddering and shuddering was because I'd taken my foot off the accelerator and the engine wasn't providing enough power (exactly the same as with a car), so the machine was moving along in jerks, and in addition every now and then it kept running into the ruins of ancient and medieval utopias. I pushed the accelerator down a bit, the machine immediately started moving smoothly, and at last I was able to make myself more comfortable and take a look around.

I was surrounded by a spectral world. Immense buildings of multicolored marble with decorative colonnades towered up among little village-type houses. All around me fields of grain swayed to and fro although there was not a breath of wind. Plump herds of transparent beasts grazed on grass, and handsome gray-haired shepherds sat on little hillocks. They were all, every single one, reading books and ancient manuscripts. Then two transparent men appeared beside me, struck poses, and began talking. They were both barefoot and wrapped in pleated tunics, with wreaths on their heads. One had a spade in his right hand and a scroll of parchment in his left. The other was leaning on a mattock and toying absentmindedly with a huge copper inkwell dangling from his belt. They spoke strictly in turn and at first I thought they were talking to each other. But very soon I realized they were talking to me, although neither of them had even glanced in my direction. I started listening.

The one with the spade was expounding at monotonous length the fundamental political principles of the wonderful country of which he was a citizen. This system was exceptionally democratic, and any coercion of citizens was quite out of the question (he repeated this several times with special emphasis); everyone was rich and free of care, and even the lowliest of plowmen had at least three slaves to his name. When he halted to catch his breath and lick his lips, the other one, with the inkwell, started speaking. He boasted that he had just worked his three hours as a ferryman on the river, hadn't taken a penny from anyone because he didn't even know what money was, and now was on his way to devote himself to composing poetry in a shady nook by a babbling brook.

They spoke for a long time—judging by the speedometer, it must have been several years—and then they disappeared and there was no one. The motionless sun shone through the spectral forms of the buildings. Suddenly, flying machines with webbed wings like pterodactyls began drifting slowly across the sky high above the earth. For a moment I thought they were all on fire, then I noticed that the smoke was coming out of large conical funnels. They flew over me, flapping their wings ponderously, ashes came showering down, and someone up there dropped a knobbly log of wood on me.

Changes began taking place in the magnificent buildings around me. There were just as many columns, and the architecture remained as sumptuously absurd as ever, but new patterns of color appeared. I think the marble was replaced by some more modern material, and the blind-eyed statues and busts on the roofs were replaced by gleaming devices that looked like the dish antennae of radio telescopes. There were more people on the streets, and a huge number of cars appeared. The herds of beasts and the reading shepherds had disappeared, but the fields of grain carried on swaying, even though there was still no wind. I pressed on the brake and came to a halt.

Looking around, I realized that the machine and I were standing on the belt of a moving sidewalk. Swarming all around me were people of the most varied possible kinds. For the most part, though, these people were somehow unreal—far less real than the powerful, complex, almost soundless machines. So when one of the machines accidentally ran into a person, there wasn't any actual collision. The machines didn't interest me much, no doubt because each of them had an inventor inspired to a state of semitransparency sitting on its frontal casing and expounding the structure and function of his creation at great length. Nobody was listening to the inventors, and they themselves didn't seem to be addressing anyone in particular.

It was more interesting to watch the people. I saw great hulking fellows in overalls walking along arm in arm, swearing and roaring out tuneless songs with badly written verse for words. Now and then I saw people only partially dressed, perhaps with nothing but a green hat and a red jacket on their naked bodies, or with elegant shoes but bare legs and ankles. The other people there didn't seem concerned, and I stopped feeling embarrassed when I recalled that some authors are in the habit of writing things like "The door opened and on the threshold appeared a slim, sinewy man in a shaggy cap and dark glasses." There were also some people dressed normally, although their clothes were cut in an odd fashion, and here and there, elbowing their way through the crowd, there were suntanned men with beards in long, spotless white robes with a rough hoe or some kind of yoke in one hand and an easel or pencil case in the other. The robe-wearers looked bewildered, and they shied away from the multilegged machines and gazed around them with a hunted expression.

Apart from the muttering of the inventors, it was fairly quiet. Most of the people weren't saying anything, but on the corner two youths were fiddling with some mechanical device. One was saying firmly, "Design concepts can't just stand still. That is a law of social development. We shall invent it. We shall definitely invent it. Despite the bureaucrats like Chinushin and the reactionaries like Tverdolobov." The other youth was saying, "I've figured out how to make use of the wear-resistant tires of polystructural fiber with

degenerate amine bonds and incomplete oxygen groups. But I still
don't know how to use the subthermal neutron regeneration reactor. Misha! Misha! What are we going to do about the reactor?"
Glancing at their device, I had no difficulty in recognizing it as a
bicycle.

The sidewalk brought me out into an immense square crammed
with spaceships of the most varied designs with people packed
tightly around them. I got off the moving sidewalk and lifted the
machine off after me. At first I couldn't understand what was going
on. Music was playing, speeches were being made, and here and
there, towering up above the crowd, curly-haired, rosy-cheeked
youths struggled to restrain the long locks of hair that kept falling
across their foreheads as they declaimed poetry with deep feeling.
The poetry was either familiar or quite awful, but as they listened
the eyes of the multitude overflowed with the grudging tears of
men, the bitter tears of women, and the lucid tears of children.
Rugged men embraced each other tightly, twitching the taut mus-
cles on their temples and slapping each other on the back. Since
many of them were not dressed, the slapping sounded like clapping. Two smart-looking lieutenants with tired, kind-looking eyes
dragged a nattily dressed man past me with his arms twisted
behind his back. The man was squirming and shouting something
in broken English. He seemed to be betraying everybody he could
think of and explaining who had paid them to plant a bomb in the
engine of a starship and how they did it. A few boys clutching
little volumes of Shakespeare glanced around stealthily as they
stole across to the thruster nozzles of the nearest astroplane. The
crowd didn't notice them.

I soon realized that one half of the crowd was saying good-bye
to the other half. It was a bit like a general mobilization. From the
speeches and conversations I gathered that the men were setting
out into space, some for Venus, some for Mars—and some, with
expressions of detached resignation on their faces, were even going
to other stars or as far as the center of the galaxy. The women were
staying behind to wait for them. Many of them were standing in a

line to a massive, ugly building that some called the Pantheon and others called the Refrigerator. I realized I had arrived just in time. If I had been just an hour late, there would have been no one left in the city but women frozen for a thousand years. Then my attention was caught by a tall, gray wall bounding the square on its western side. There were swirling clouds of black smoke rising up from behind it.

"What's that over there?" I asked a beautiful woman in a head scarf who was wandering dejectedly toward the Pantheon-Refrigerator.

"The Iron Wall," she answered without stopping.

I grew more and more bored with every minute that passed. Everyone was crying and the orators had all gone hoarse. Beside me a youth in sky-blue overalls was saying good-bye to a girl in a rose-pink dress. The girl said in a monotonous voice, "I wish I were stardust; I'd form a cosmic cloud and envelop your ship . . ." The youth listened to her words. When the sound of the combined orchestras thundered out above the roar of the crowd, my nerves couldn't take any more and I jumped into the saddle and stepped on the accelerator. I just had time to see the starships, planet cruisers, astroplanes, ion ships, photon ships, and star gliders go roaring up into the sky above the city before everything except the gray wall was enveloped in phosphorescent mist.

After the year 2000 the gaps in time began, and I flew through time without any matter. It was cold in those places, with only the occasional eruption of an explosion and a bright glow flaring up behind the gray wall. Now and then the city surrounded me again, and every time its buildings became taller, the spherical domes became more transparent, and there were fewer starships on the square. Smoke rose uninterruptedly from behind the wall. I stopped for a second time when the final star glider had disappeared from the square. The sidewalks were moving, but there were no noisy young fellows in overalls. No one was swearing. A few colorless individuals strolled along the streets in twos or threes, dressed either strangely or meagerly.

As far as I could tell, they were all talking about science. They intended to bring someone back to life, and a professor of medicine, an intellectual with the build of an athlete who looked very unusual dressed in nothing but a waistcoat, was expounding the reanimation procedure to a lanky biophysicist, whom he introduced to everyone they met as the initiator and main executor of this scheme. They were preparing to drill a hole through the Earth somewhere. The project was being discussed right there in the street by a large knot of people, and schemata were sketched out in chalk on walls and on the sidewalk. I tried listening, but it turned out to be so incredibly boring, as well as being interspersed with attacks on some reactionary I'd never heard of, that I hoisted the machine onto my shoulders and left. I wasn't surprised in the least that discussion of the project immediately halted and everybody started doing something useful. But the moment I stopped, a citizen of indeterminate professional status began spouting verbiage, launching out of the blue into a discourse on music. Listeners came running up immediately, gawping at him and asking questions that revealed their profound ignorance.

Suddenly a man came running down the street, shouting. Chasing after him was a spiderlike machine. According to the shouts of its quarry, it was "a self-programming cybernetic robot with trigenic quator feedback that has slipped out of sync . . . Oh no, it's going to tear me limb from limb!" But curiously enough, no one even turned a hair. Apparently no one really believed in the revolt of the machines.

Two other spiderlike machines, not as big and not as ferocious looking, leaped out of a side street. Before I even had time to gasp, one of them had polished my shoes and the other had washed and ironed my handkerchief. A big white tank with winking lights on caterpillar tracks trundled up to me and sprayed me with perfume. I was just about to get out of there when there was a thunderous roar and a huge rusty rocket tumbled down out of the sky into the square. People in the crowd started talking:

"It's *Dream Star!*"

"Yes, so it is!"

"But of course it is! It set out 218 years ago and everyone's forgotten about it, but thanks to the Einsteinian contraction of time that results from movement at near-light speeds, the crew has only aged two years!"

"Thanks to what? Ah, Einstein . . . Yes, yes, I remember. We did that in our second year at school."

A one-eyed man with his left arm and right leg missing clambered out of the rocket with some difficulty.

"Is this Earth?" he asked irritably.

"It is! It is!" the people in the crowd replied, with smiles beginning to blossom on their faces.

"Thank God for that," said the man, and everyone glanced at each other. Either they didn't understand what he meant or they were pretending they didn't.

The maimed astropilot struck a pose and launched into a speech in which he appealed to every last member of the human race to fly to the planet of Willee-Nillee in the Eoella star system of the Small Magellanic Cloud to liberate their brothers in reason, who were groaning under the tyrannical yoke of a bloodthirsty cybernetic dictator. The roar of thruster nozzles drowned out his words as two more rockets, also rusty, landed in the square. Women covered in hoarfrost came running out of the Pantheon-Refrigerator. The crowd began pressing together. I realized I'd arrived in the age of returns, and hastily stepped on the accelerator.

The city disappeared and didn't reappear for a long time. The wall was still there, with fires blazing and lightning flashing behind it with depressing monotony. It was a strange sight: absolute emptiness with just a wall in the west. But at long last a bright light dawned again and I immediately halted.

On every side the land stretched out, deserted but flourishing. Fields of grain swayed and plump herds roamed, but there was no sign of any educated shepherds. I could see the familiar transparent-silver domes on the horizon, the viaducts and spiral slipways. To the west the wall towered up as before.

Someone touched my knee and I started. Standing beside me was a small boy with deep-set, blazing eyes. "What do you want, kid?" I asked.

"Is your device defective?" he inquired in a melodic voice.

"You should speak more politely to grown-ups," I replied in a didactic tone.

He looked very surprised, then his face lit up. "Ah yes, now I remember. If my memory does not deceive me, that was the way things used to be in the Era of Compulsory Courtesy. Insofar as direct forms of address disharmonize with your emotional rhythms, I am willing to adopt any rhythmic formulae to address you."

I couldn't think of anything to say to that. He squatted down in front of the machine, touched it in various places, and spoke several words that I didn't understand at all. He was a really great kid, very clean and healthy and well groomed, but he seemed far too serious for his age to me.

There was a deafening explosion behind the wall and we both turned toward it. I saw a terrible scaly hand with eight fingers clutch at the crest of the wall, strain, release its grip, and disappear.

"Tell me, kid," I said, "what's that wall for?"

He gave me a serious, bashful look. "It's called the Iron Wall," he said. "Unfortunately, I am not familiar with the etymology of those two words, but I know that it separates two worlds—the World of the Humane Imagination and the World of Fear of the Future." He paused and then added, "I am not familiar with the etymology of the word *fear* either."

"Interesting," I said. "Can't we take a look? What's the World of Fear like?"

"Of course you can. There's the communications port. Satisfy your curiosity."

The communications port looked like a low archway closed off by an armor-plated door. I walked up to it and laid a hesitant hand on the bolt.

The boy called after me: "I am obliged to warn you that if anything happens to you in there, you will have to appear before the United Council of the Hundred and Forty Worlds."

I opened the door a little way. *Zap! Boom! Ke-rang! Wheeeee! Da-da-da-da-da-da-da-da!* All five of my senses were traumatized simultaneously. I saw a beautiful, long-legged, naked blonde with an obscene tattoo between her shoulder blades, blasting away with two automatic pistols at an ugly man with dark hair.

Splashes of red spurted out of him every time he was hit. I heard the thunder of explosions and the bloodcurdling roar of monsters. I smelled the indescribable stench of rotten, burning nonprotein-aceous flesh. The incandescent blast of a nearby nuclear explosion scorched my face, and my tongue caught the repulsive taste of protoplasm dispersed through the air. I staggered back and franti-cally slammed the door shut, almost trapping my head in it. The air here tasted sweet and the world looked beautiful. The boy had disappeared. I took a little while to recover my wits, then suddenly felt frightened in case that lousy little sneak might have gone running to complain to his United Council. I made a dash for the machine.

Again the twilight of time without space closed in around me, but I kept my eyes fixed on the Iron Wall. I was burning up with curiosity. In order not to waste any time, I jumped forward a mil-lion years. Thickets of atomic mushrooms sprouted up behind the wall, and I was glad when the light dawned once again on my side of it. I braked and then groaned in disappointment. The massive Pantheon-Refrigerator still towered up close by. A rusty spherical starship was descending from the sky. There was no one to be seen. The fields of grain were swaying to and fro. The sphere landed, the pilot in sky blue I'd seen only recently got out of it, and the girl in rose pink appeared on the threshold of the Pantheon, covered in red bedsores. They dashed toward each other and clasped hands. I looked away—I was beginning to feel rather awkward. Standing close by was a slightly embarrassed-looking old man, indifferently fishing goldfish out of an aquarium. The sky-blue pilot and the rose-pink girl launched into a long joint disquisition.

I got off the machine to stretch my legs and only then noticed that the sky above the wall was unusually clear. I couldn't hear any rumble of explosions or crackle of shots. I took heart and set off toward the communications port.

On the other side of the wall the land stretched out in an abso-lutely level plain, divided all the way to the horizon by the deep gash of a trench. On the left of the trench I couldn't see a single living soul, and the surface was covered with low metal domes that looked like the manhole covers of sewers. On the right of the trench were several horsemen prancing along the line of the horizon. Then I noticed a stocky, dark-faced man in metal armor sitting on the edge of the trench with his legs dangling into it. He had something that looked like a submachine gun with a very thick barrel hanging on a long strap around his neck. The man was chewing slowly and spitting constantly. He looked at me without any particular interest. I looked at him too, holding the door open, unable to bring myself to speak. His appearance was simply too strange. Abnormal, somehow. Wild. Who could tell what sort of man he was?

After he'd taken a good look at me, he drew a flat bottle out from under his armor, tugged the cork out with his teeth, took a swig, spat into the trench again, and spoke in a hoarse voice, in English: "Hello! You from the other side?"

"Yes," I replied, also in English.

"And how's it going out there?"

"So-so," I said, closing the door just a little. "And how's it going out here?"

"It's OK," he said phlegmatically, and fell silent.

I waited for a while and then asked what he was doing there. He answered me reluctantly at first, but then he warmed to his subject. Apparently on the left side of the trench humanity was living out its final days under the oppressive yoke of relentlessly ferocious robots. The robots there had become cleverer than humans and seized power. They enjoyed all the good things of life and had driven people underground and set them to work on assembly lines. On the right of the trench, on the land that he was guarding, people had been subjugated by aliens from a neighboring universe. They had also seized power, then established a feudal society and made unrestricted use of the right of the first night. The aliens lived it up, but a few crumbs also came the way of those who were in their good graces. Twenty miles farther along the trench there was a region where people had been enslaved by aliens from Altaic, intelligent viruses who infected a person's body and then made him or her do whatever they wanted. Even farther to the west there was a large Galactic Federation colony. The people there were enslaved too, but their life wasn't all that bad, because His Excellency the vice regent kept them fed so that he could recruit the personal bodyguards of His Majesty the Galactic Emperor A-u the 3,562nd from among them. There were also areas that had been subjugated by intelligent parasites, intelligent plants, and intelligent minerals, and even Communists. And finally, somewhere far away in the distance, there were regions enslaved by someone else, but no serious person would ever believe the tales that were told about them.

Our conversation was interrupted at this point by several saucer-shaped devices flying low across the flat plain, raining down bombs that swirled and tumbled through the air. "Here we go again," the man growled, then he lay back with his legs pointing toward the detonations, raised his gun, and opened fire on the horsemen prancing along the horizon.

I got out of there fast, slamming the door shut and slumping back against it, then listening for a while to the bombs screeching, roaring, and rumbling. The pilot in sky blue and the girl in rose pink still hadn't managed to bring their dialogue to a conclusion, and the indifferent old man, having caught all the goldfish, was looking at them and wiping his eyes with a handkerchief. I took another cautious peep through the door. The huge fireballs of explosions were slowly expanding above the plain. The metal covers were being thrown open one by one and pale, ragged people with savage, bearded faces were climbing out of them, holding iron bars at the ready. The horsemen in armor had galloped up and were cutting my recent conversation partner to pieces with their long swords. He was screaming and fending them off with his submachine gun. A gigantic tank was crawling along the trench toward me with its cannon and machine guns firing. The saucer-shaped flying devices came diving back out of the radioactive clouds.

I closed the door and carefully pulled the bolt shut.

Then I went back to my machine and got into the saddle. I wanted to fly on another million years and take a look at the Earth as it was dying, the way Wells had described it. But just then for the first time something in the machine jammed: I couldn't get the clutch to separate. I pressed it once, twice, then kicked the pedal with all my might. Something snapped and jangled, the swaying fields of grain stood erect, and I seemed to wake up. I was sitting on a demonstration stand in a small lecture hall in our Institute, and everyone was looking at me in awe.

"What's wrong with the clutch?" I asked, gazing around to find the machine. The machine wasn't there. I'd come back alone.

"Never mind that!" cried Louis Sedlovoi. "Thank you very, very much! You really bailed me out there . . . And it was very interesting, wasn't it, comrades?"

The audience buzzed its agreement that yes, it was interesting.

"But I've read all of it somewhere," one of the masters sitting in the front row said doubtfully.

"But of course you have! Of course!" exclaimed Sedlovoi. "After all, he was in the *described* future!"

"There weren't very many adventures," said the battleships players in the back rows. "Nothing but talk and more talk."

"Well, I'm not to blame for that," Sedlovoi said firmly.

"Pretty serious talk, though," I said, climbing down off the stand. I remembered my swarthy conversation partner getting hacked to pieces and suddenly felt unwell.

"But I suppose there are a few interesting bits," said one of the bachelors. "That machine . . . Remember it? With the trigenic quator feedback . . . You know, I like that."

"Well, gentlemen," said Pupkov-Zadny, "we seem to have already commenced our discussion. But does anyone have a question for the speaker?"

The fastidious bachelor immediately asked a question about the multiple temporal transmission (he was interested in the coefficient of volumetric expansion) and I slipped out of the room.

I felt very strange. Everything seemed so material, so solid and substantial. When people walked by I could hear their shoes squeaking and feel the draft from their movements. Everyone was very taciturn, everyone was working, everyone was thinking—no one was chatting or reading poetry or declaiming passionate speeches. Everyone knew that a lab is one thing and a trade union meeting is another thing altogether, and a public rally is something else again. And when I saw Vybegallo coming toward me, shuffling his leather-soled felt boots along the floor, I even felt a surge of something like sympathy for him, because he had the usual grains of boiled millet stuck in his beard, because he was picking his teeth with a long, thin nail, and he walked past without saying hello. He was a living, material, visible boor; he didn't brandish his hands in the air or strike academic poses.

I dropped in on Roman, because I was dying to tell someone about my adventure. He was standing over his lab table clutching his beard in his hand and looking at a small green parrot lying in a petri dish. The parrot was dead, its eyes glazed over with a dull, lifeless white film.

"What happened to it?" I asked.

"I don't know," said Roman. "It's expired, as you can see."

"How did a parrot end up in here?"

"I find that rather remarkable myself," said Roman.

"Maybe it's artificial?" I suggested.

"No, it's a genuine, honest-to-goodness parrot."

"Vitka must have sat on the plywitsum again."

We leaned down over the parrot and began inspecting it carefully. There was a ring on one of the black legs tucked in close to its body.

"'Photon,'" Roman read. "And then some figures . . . One nine zero five seven three."

"I see," said a familiar voice behind us.

We turned around and drew ourselves erect.

"Hello," said S-Janus, coming across to the table. As he emerged from the door of his lab at the back of the room he looked somehow tired and very sad.

"Hello, Janus Polyeuctovich," we chorused with all the deference we could muster.

Janus caught sight of the parrot and said "I see" again. He picked the small bird up very carefully and gently, stroked its bright red crest, and said quietly: "What happened then, my little Photon?"

He was about to say something else, but he glanced at us and stopped. We stood there watching as he walked slowly across to the far corner of the lab like an old man, opened the door of the electric furnace, and lowered the little green corpse into it.

"Roman Petrovich," he said. "Would you please be so kind as to throw the switch?"

Roman did as he was asked. He looked as though he had been struck by an unusual idea.

S-Janus stood over the furnace for a moment, hanging his head, then he carefully scraped out the hot ashes, opened the window, and scattered them to the wind. He looked at the window for a while, then told Roman he would be expecting him in his office in half an hour and went out.

"Strange," said Roman, staring at the door.

"What's strange?"

"Everything's strange," said Roman.

The appearance of this dead green parrot that Janus Polyeuctovich clearly knew very well seemed strange to me too, and so did the rather too unusual ceremony of cremation and scattering the ashes to the wind, but I was impatient to tell Roman about my journey into the described future, so I started. Roman listened very absentmindedly, gazing at me with a blank expression and nodding in all the wrong places, then suddenly he said, "Carry on, carry on, I'm listening," and dived under the table. He dragged out the wastepaper basket and started rummaging through the crumpled sheets of paper and scraps of recording tape.

When I finished telling my story, he asked, "Hasn't this Sedlovoi ever tried traveling into the described present? I think that would be much more amusing."

While I was pondering this suggestion and admiring Roman's quick wit, he turned the basket over and tipped its contents out onto the floor.

"What's wrong?" I asked. "Lost a dissertation?"

"You know, Sashka," he said, gazing at me with unseeing eyes, "this is a remarkable business. Yesterday I was cleaning the furnace and I found a singed green feather. I threw it in the wastepaper basket, but today it's not there."

"Whose feather?" I asked.

"You know, green birds' feathers are extremely rare items in this part of the world. But the parrot that was just cremated was green."

"That's nonsense," I said. "You found the feather yesterday."

"That's just the point," said Roman, putting the rubbish back in the basket.

3

Poetry's unnat'ral; no man ever talked poetry 'cept a beadle on boxin'-day, or Warren's blackin', or Rowland's oil, or some of them low fellows; never you let yourself down to talk poetry, my boy.

—Charles Dickens

They worked on the Aldan all night. When I turned up in the computer room the next morning the engineers were sitting around on the floor in a sleepy fury, monotonously reviling Cristóbal Joséevich. They called him a Scythian, a barbarian, and a Hun who had invaded the field of cybernetics. They were so desperate that for a while they even listened to my advice and tried to follow it. But then their boss, Sabaoth Baalovich Odin, turned up and they immediately dragged me away from the machine. I walked over to my desk, sat down, and began observing Sabaoth Baalovich's efforts to assess the nature of the damage.

He was very old but sturdy and sinewy, with a suntan, a shiny bald patch, and smoothly shaved cheeks, dressed in a blindingly white suit of raw silk. He was a man everyone regarded with profound respect. I myself had once seen him reprimand Modest Matveevich for something or other in a low voice, and the fearsome Modest had stood there in front of him, leaning forward ingratiatingly and intoning, "Very well . . . I'm sorry. It won't happen again . . ."

Sabaoth Baalovich radiated a monstrously powerful energy. It had been observed that in his presence clocks began running fast and the tracks of elementary particles curved by a magnetic field straightened out again. And yet he wasn't a magician. Or at least not a practicing magician. He didn't walk through walls, he never transgressed anyone, and he never created doubles of himself, although he did a quite exceptional amount of work. He was the head of the Technical Service Department, he knew all of the Institute's equipment inside and out, and he was one of the consultants at the Kitezhgrad Magotechnical Plant. He was also involved with the most unexpected matters of all kinds that were far removed from his immediate professional area.

I had learned Sabaoth Baalovich's story only recently. In ancient times S. B. Odin had been the foremost magician in the entire world. Cristóbal Junta and Gian Giacomo were pupils of his pupils. His name was used for exorcising evil spirits and sealing genies into bottles. King Solomon wrote him rapturously enthusiastic letters and built shrines in his honor. He seemed omnipotent. And then somewhere in the middle of the sixteenth century he really did become omnipotent. By implementing a numerical solution to an integral-differential equation of supreme perfection that had been derived by some Titan before the Ice Age began, he acquired the ability to perform any miracle. Every magician has his limitations. Some are incapable of ridding themselves of the growth in their ears. Others have completely mastered the unified Lomonosov-Lavoisier law but are powerless in the face of the second law of thermodynamics. Still others—there are not very many of these—can, for instance, stop time, but only in Riemannian space and not for long. Sabaoth Baalovich was all powerful. He could do anything at all. And yet he was unable to do anything at all. Because the limiting condition of the equation of perfection was that no miracle may cause any harm to anyone. To any rational being. Not here on Earth nor in any other part of the universe. And no one, not even Sabaoth Baalovich, could even imagine a miracle like that. So S. B. Odin abandoned magic forever and became the head of the Technical Service Department at NITWiT.

Once he arrived in the room the engineers soon got their act together. They started moving with greater purpose and cut out the malicious witticisms. I took out my current business file and was just getting down to work when Stella, the pretty young witch with the snub nose and gray eyes who was Vybegallo's trainee, turned up to collect me to work on the Institute's wall newspaper. Stella and I were on the editorial board and wrote the satirical poems, the moral fables, and the captions for the drawings. And in addition to that, I did the clever drawing of a mailbox requesting comments, with winged letters flying toward it from every direction.

The actual artistic designer of the wall newspaper was my name-sake, another Alexander Ivanovich, with the surname of Drozd, a film technician who had somehow ended up at the Institute. He was a specialist in headlines. The newspaper's senior editor was Roman Oira-Oira, and his deputy was Volodya Pochkin.

"Sasha," said Stella, gazing at me with her honest gray eyes. "Let's go."

"Where?" I asked, although I already knew where.

"To do the newspaper."

"What for?"

"Roman asked us specially, because Cerberus is getting nasty about it. He says there's only two days left and nothing's ready yet." Cerberus Psoevich Demin, comrade head of the Personnel Department, was the managerial supervisor of our newspaper, our head slave driver and censor.

"Listen," I said, "why don't we do it tomorrow?"

"I can't tomorrow," said Stella. "I'll be on a plane to Sukhumi. To record baboons. Vybegallo says I have to record the group leader, because he's the most important . . . He's afraid to go near him himself, because the leader's very jealous. Come on, Sasha, let's go."

I sighed, put away my work, and followed Stella, because I can't write poems on my own; she always provides the first line and the basic idea, and I think that's the most important thing in poetry. "Where shall we do it?" I asked as we walked along. "In the trade union committee room?"

"The committee room's occupied—they're busy reprimanding Alfred. For his tea. But Roman said we could use his place."

"What do we have to write about? Is it the bathhouse again?"

"Yes, and a few other things. The bathhouse, Bald Mountain. We have to hold Khoma Brut up to public shame."

"Our Khoma Brut is not too cute," I said.

"*Et tu, Brute,*" said Stella.

"That's an idea," I said. "We should develop that."

The newspaper was laid out on the table in Roman's lab—an immense sheet of virginally white Whatman paper. Lying beside it, surrounded by jars of gouache, airbrushes, and copy for the newspaper, was our artist and film technician Alexander Drozd, with a cigarette glued to his lower lip. His shirt, as always, was unbuttoned, and we could see the little bulge of his hairy belly.

"Hey," I said.

"Hi," said Sasha. There was a burst of music. He was fiddling with a portable radio.

"All right, what have we got here?" I asked, raking up the copy.

There wasn't very much of it. There was a lead article, "The Forthcoming Holiday." There was a brief piece from Cerberus Psoevich, "The Results of an Investigation into the Implementation of the Directors' Instructions Concerning Labor Discipline During the Second Half of the First Quarter and the First Half of the Second Quarter." There was an article by Professor Vybegallo, "Our Duty Is a Duty to Our Sponsored Enterprises and Farms in the Town and the District." There was one by Volodya Pochkin, "On the All-Union Electronic Magic Conference." There was a contribution from some brownie, "When Will They Scavenge the Steam Heating on the Fourth Floor?" There was an article from the chairman of the cafeteria committee, "Neither Flesh nor Fowl"—six single-spaced typed pages. It began with the words "Man needs phosphorous like the air he breathes." There was a piece by Roman about the work of the Department of Unsolvable Problems. There was an article from Cristóbal Junta for the section Our Veterans. It was called "From Seville to Granada, 1547." There were a few more short texts criticizing the following: the lack of proper order in the mutual-help fund; ineptitude in the work of the volunteer fire brigade; the toleration of gambling in the vivarium (written by the Little Humpbacked Horse, who'd lost a week's ration of oats playing chemin de fer with Koschei the Deathless). There were a few caricatures. One of them showed Khoma Brut in a state of sartorial disarray with a bright purple nose. Another took a dig at the bathhouse—a blue naked man freezing solid under an icy shower.

"This is all dead boring," I said. "Maybe we don't need any poems?"

"Yes we do." Stella said with a sigh. "I've already tried laying out the copy this way and that way, but there's always some empty space left."

"Sasha here can draw something. A few ears of wheat, or some pansies . . . How about it, Sasha?"

"You do some work," said Drozd. "I've got the masthead to do."

"Big deal," I said. "Three words to write."

"Against the background of a starry sky," said Drozd impressively. "And a rocket. And all the headlines for the articles. And I haven't had any lunch yet. Or breakfast."

"Then go and get something to eat," I said.

"I can't afford to," he said irritably. "I bought a tape recorder. Secondhand. Instead of wasting time on this nonsense, why don't you conjure me up a couple of sandwiches? With butter and jam. Better still, create me a ten-spot."

I pulled out a ruble and showed it to him from a distance. "When you've done the masthead, you can have it."

"For keeps?" Drozd asked keenly.

"No. As a loan."

"Makes no difference anyway," he said. "Just bear in mind that I'm at death's door. I've started getting spasms. My hands and feet are turning cold."

"He's lying," said Stella. "Sasha, let's sit down at that table over there and write our poems."

We sat down at a separate little table and set out the caricatures in front of us. We looked at them for a while, hoping for inspiration. Then Stella said, "Watch out for folks like Khoma Brut, they'll soon relieve you of your loot!"

"Loot?" I asked. "Did he snatch some money, then?"

"No," said Stella. "He created a disturbance and got into a fight. I was just rhyming."

We waited for a while again, but I still couldn't come up with anything but "Khoma Brut will filch your loot."

"Let's think about this logically," I said. "We have Khoma Brut. He got drunk. Got into a fight. What else did he do?"

"Pestered some girls," said Stella. "Broke a window."

"OK," I said. "What else?"

"Used bad language."

"That's odd," Sasha Drozd piped up. "I used to work with this guy Brut in the cinema club. Just an ordinary guy. Perfectly normal."

"And?" I said.

"That's it."

"Can you give us a rhyme for Brut?" I asked.

"*Loot.*"

"We've got that already," I said.

"OK, then try *boot.*"

Stella declaimed, "Comrades, you see before you Khoma Brut. Let's flog him hard and then put in the boot."

"That's no good," said Drozd. "That's incitement to physical violence."

"*Hoot,*" I said.

"Comrades, you see before you Khoma Brut," said Stella. "His pranks would make a jackass honk and hoot."

"Your words are enough to make anyone hoot," said Drozd.

"Have you done that masthead yet?" I asked.

"No," said Drozd capriciously.

"Get on with it, then."

"They'll shame our glorious Institute," said Stella. "These drunken hooligans like Brut."

"That's good," I said. "We'll put that at the end. Make a note of it. That'll be the moral, fresh and original."

"What's original about it?" Drozd asked simplemindedly. I didn't bother to answer him.

"And now," I said, "We have to describe what he got up to. How about 'Drank himself drunk, stank like a skunk, then did a bunk, the great lousy lunk'?"

"That's terrible," said Stella, sounding disgusted.

I propped my head up on my hands and began peering at the caricature. Drozd ran his brush across the Whatman paper, with his backside sticking up into the air. Encased in their super-tight jeans his legs were curved into an arc. I had a flash of inspiration.

"Knees backward bent!" I said. "The song."

"'The little cricket sat there with its sharp knees backward bent,'" said Stella.

"That's right," said Drozd, without turning around. "Even I know that one. 'And all the guests go crawling home, their weak knees backward bent.'"

"Hang on, hang on," I said. I was feeling inspired. "He fights and curses black as hell, but see where he is sent; they take him downtown to a cell, his drunk knees backward bent."

"That's not too bad," said Stella.

"Get the idea?" I asked. "Another couple of stanzas, and we put in the refrain 'Knees backward bent' everywhere. 'His drunken head was in a whirl . . . He chased after a pretty girl . . .' That kind of thing."

"His head is spinning more and more, but he will not relent," said Stella. "He tried to break down someone's door with his knees backward bent."

"Brilliant!" I said. "Write it down. Did he really try to break down a door?"

"He did, he did."

"Excellent!" I said. "Right, just one more verse."

"He chased after the pretty girls with his knees backward bent," said Stella thoughtfully. "We need the first line."

"*Swirls*," I said. "*Twirls. Hurls. Furls.*"

"*Curls*," said Stella. "No blade has ever touched his curls."

"True enough," put in Drozd. "That's right. You've hit on an artistic truth there. He's never shaved or washed in his life."

"Maybe we should think up the second line first?" suggested Stella. "*Bent. Element. Increment . . .*"

"*Tent*," I said, "*Spent.*"

"*Vent,*" said Drozd.

We sat there in silence again for a long time, gazing stupidly at each other and moving our lips silently. Drozd tapped his brush against the edge of a cup filled with water.

"'No blade has ever touched his curls,'" I said at last. "'His words are an affront. He chased after the pretty girls with his knees backward bent.'"

"*Affront* doesn't really rhyme," said Stella.

"'But he will not relent,' then."

"We already did that."

"Where? Ah yes, we did that."

"As stripy as a tent," suggested Drozd.

At this point we heard a light scratching sound and turned around to look. The door to Janus Polyeuctovich's laboratory was slowly opening.

"Just look at that!" Drozd exclaimed in astonishment, freezing with his brush in his hand.

A small green parrot with a bright red crest on its head came creeping out through the crack.

"A parrot!" exclaimed Drozd. "It's a parrot! *Here, chick, chick, chick!*"

He started making movements with his fingers as if he were crumbling bread onto the floor. The parrot looked at him with one eye. Then it opened its black beak, as hooked as Roman's nose, and cried hoarsely: "*Rrreactor! Rrreactor! Derrritrinitation! Rrresist!*"

"He's really lovely!" exclaimed Stella. "Catch him, Sasha."

Drozd started moving toward the parrot, then stopped. "He probably bites," he said warily. "Look at that beak on him."

The parrot pushed off from the floor, flapped its wings, and started fluttering rather awkwardly around the room. I watched it in astonishment. It looked very much like the one I'd seen the day before. Its twin brother, in fact. But parrots are a dime a dozen, I thought.

Drozd waved it away with his brush.

The parrot landed on the balance beam of the laboratory scales, shuddered as it settled down, and called out quite clearly, *"Prrroxima Centaurrri! Rrrubidium! Rrrubidium!"*

Then it ruffled up its feathers, pulled its head back into its shoulders, and veiled its eyes with a white film. I think it was trembling. Stella quickly created a piece of bread and jam, pinched off the crust,

and held it under its beak. The parrot didn't react. It was obviously feverish, and the pans of the scales were shuddering and jangling against the upright.

"I think it's ill," said Drozd. He absentmindedly took the sandwich out of Stella's hand and started eating it.

"Guys," I said, "has anyone ever seen any parrots in the Institute before?"

Stella shook her head. Drozd shrugged.

"There are too many parrots around all of a sudden," I said. "There was that one yesterday too."

"Janus must be experimenting with parrots," said Stella. "Antigravity or something like that."

The door to the corridor swung open and Roman Oira-Oira, Vitka Korneev, Edik Amperian, and Volodya Pochkin crowded in. The room got noisy. Korneev had slept well and was feeling very cheerful; he started looking through the copy and insulting the authors' style in a loud voice. The mighty Volodya Pochkin, as deputy editor with primary responsibility for policing and law enforcement, grabbed hold of the thick back of Drozd's neck, doubled him over, and began jabbing his nose at the wall newspaper, chanting, "Where's the masthead? Where's the masthead, Drozdyllo?" Roman demanded to see our finished poems. And Edik, who had nothing to do with the newspaper, went across to the cupboard and starting rattling various pieces of equipment around inside it. Suddenly the parrot screeched: *Solarrr jump! Solarrr jump!* and everybody froze.

Roman stared hard at the parrot. The same expression I'd already seen appeared on his face, as though he'd been struck by an unusual idea. Volodya Pochkin let go of Drozd and said, "Hey, look at that, it's a parrot!" The crude Korneev slowly reached out his hand to grab the parrot around the body, but the bird slipped through his fingers and Korneev only caught its tail.

"Leave it alone, Vitka," Stella shouted angrily. "What do you think you're doing, tormenting a dumb animal like that?"

The parrot began to roar. Everyone crowded around it. Korneev held it like a pigeon. Stella stroked its little crest, and Drozd gently fingered the feathers on its tail. Roman looked at me. "Curious," he said. "Isn't it?"

"Where did it come from, Sasha?" Edik asked politely.

I nodded briefly in the direction of Janus's lab.

"What would Janus want with a parrot?" asked Edik.

"Are you asking me?" I said.

"No, it was a rhetorical question," Edik said seriously.

"What would Janus want with two parrots?" I asked.

"Or three," Roman added quietly.

Korneev turned toward us. "Where are the others?" he asked, looking around curiously.

The parrot in his hand fluttered its wings feebly, trying to peck at his finger.

"Let it go," I said. "You can see it's not well."

Korneev shoved Drozd out of the way and sat the parrot back on the balance. The parrot bristled its feathers and stretched out its wings.

"Never mind the bird for now," said Roman. "We'll sort that out later. Where's the poem?"

Stella quickly rattled off everything we'd written so far. Roman scratched his chin, Volodya Pochkin began snorting unnaturally, and Korneev rapped out a command: "Execution. With a large-caliber machine gun. When will you ever learn how to write poems?"

"Write them yourself," I said angrily.

"I can't write poems," said Korneev. "I wasn't born a Pushkin. I'm more of a natural Belinsky."

"You're more of a natural cadaver," said Stella.

"I beg your pardon!" said Vitka insistently. "I want a literary criticism section in this paper. And I want to write the critical articles. I'll demolish the lot of you! I'll remind you what you wrote about the dachas!"

"What was that?" asked Edik.

Korneev quoted verbatim, speaking slowly:

> *A summer dacha is my aspiration.*
> *But where to build? Although I try and try,*

Our own trade union administration
Still has not given any clear reply.

"That's right, isn't it? Confess!"

"What of it," I said. "Pushkin had some poor poems too. They don't even print them in full in the school anthologies."

"I know them, though," said Drozd.

Roman turned toward him. "Are we going to have a masthead today or not?"

"We are," said Drozd. "I've already done the letter *T*."

"What letter *T*? What do we want a *T* for?"

"You mean I shouldn't have?"

"You'll be the death of me," said Roman. "The newspaper's title is *For Progressive Magic*. Can you show me any letter *T* in that?"

Drozd stared at the wall, moving his lips silently. "How did that happen?" he said at last. "Where did I get the letter *T* from? There was a letter *T*!"

Roman became furious and ordered Pochkin to sit everyone back down in their right places. Stella and I were put under the command of Korneev. Drozd feverishly set about transforming the *T* into a stylized letter *F*. Edik Amperian tried to slip out with a psychoelectrometer, but he was set upon and coerced into mending the airbrush that was needed to paint the starry sky. Then it was Pochkin's own turn. Roman instructed him to type out the copy again, correcting the style and spelling as he went along. Roman himself began pacing around the laboratory, looking over everybody's shoulders.

For a while the work fairly raced along. We managed to write and reject several versions of the bathhouse theme: "Our bathhouse must be getting old, / The water there is always cold"; "If cleanness is your cherished dream, / Beware this dismal, icy stream"; "Two hundred colleagues—that's a lot / Demand a shower that's steaming hot."

Korneev swore outrageously, like a genuine literary critic. "Learn from Pushkin!" he dinned into our heads. "Or at least from

Pochkin. You have a genius sitting beside you and you're not even capable of imitating him! 'Down the road there comes a ZIM, and that'll be the end of him.' What sheer physical power those lines possess! What clarity of feeling!"

We made clumsy attempts to return the abuse. Sasha Drozd got as far as the letter A in the word *Progressive*. Edik mended the airbrush and tested it on Roman's research notes. Volodya Pochkin spewed out curses as he tried to find the letter T on the typewriter. Everything was going quite normally.

Then Roman suddenly said, "Sasha, take a look over here."

I looked. The parrot was lying under the balance with its legs drawn in. Its eyes were covered with a whitish film and its crest was drooping limply.

"It's dead," Drozd said in a sad voice.

We crowded around the parrot again. I had no particular ideas in my head, or if I did, they were somewhere deep in my subconscious, but I reached out a hand, picked up the parrot, and looked at its legs.

Immediately Roman asked me, "Is it there?"

"Yes," I said.

There was a white metal ring on the black folded leg, and engraved on the ring was the word "Photon" and the figures "190573." I gave Roman a bewildered glance. We must have looked a bit odd, because Vitka Korneev said, "Right, then, tell us everything you know."

"Shall we?" asked Roman.

"This is crazy," I said. "It must be some kind of trick. They're doubles of some kind."

Roman inspected the little corpse closely again. "No," he said. "That's just it. This is no double. It's the absolutely genuine original article."

"Let me take a look," said Korneev.

Korneev, Volodya Pochkin, and Edik gave the parrot a thoroughgoing examination and declared unanimously that it wasn't a double and they couldn't understand why that bothered us so much.

"Take me, for instance," said Korneev. "I'm not a double either. Why aren't you amazed by that?"

Roman looked around at Stella, who was just dying of curiosity, Volodya Pochkin, standing there with his mouth wide open, and Vitka, with a mocking grin on his face. Then he told them everything—how the day before yesterday he'd found a green feather in the electric furnace and thrown it into the wastepaper basket; how yesterday the feather wasn't in the basket, but on the table (this very same table) there was a dead parrot, a perfect copy of this one, and also not a double; how Janus had recognized the dead parrot, been upset, and burned it in the aforementioned electric furnace, and then for some reason had thrown the ashes out of the window.

For a while no one said a word. Drozd, who hadn't paid much attention to Roman's story, shrugged. It was clear from his face that he didn't understand what all the fuss was about, and that in his opinion there were much weirder things going on at the Institute. Stella too seemed disappointed. But the trio of masters had understood everything perfectly, and their faces clearly expressed protest.

Korneev said firmly, "You're lying. And clumsily at that."

"It's still not the same parrot," said the polite Edik. "You must be mistaken."

"It's the same one," I said. "Green, with a ring."

"Photon?" asked Volodya Pochkin in a public prosecutor's voice.

"Photon. Janus called it his little Photon."

"And the numbers?" asked Volodya.

"The numbers too."

"Are the digits the same?" Korneev asked menacingly.

"I think they are," I replied uncertainly, glancing in Roman's direction.

"Can you be more precise?" demanded Korneev. He put his big red hand over the parrot. "So tell me what these numbers here are."

"One nine . . ." I said. "Uh, uh . . . zero two, isn't it? Six three." Korneev glanced under his hand. "Wrong," he said. "And you?" he asked Roman.

"I don't remember," Roman said calmly. "I think it was zero five, not zero three."

"No, I said, "it was zero six. I remember, there was a little flourish on it."

"A flourish," said Pochkin derisively. "You Sherlock Holmeses and Nat Pinkertons! Now you're fed up with the law of causality."

Korneev put his hands in his pockets. "That's a different matter," he said. "I don't insist that you're lying. You've just got things confused. Parrots are all green, many of them are ringed, this pair came from the 'Photon' series. And you've got memories like sieves. Like all cheap versifiers and editors of wall newspapers."

"Like sieves?" Roman asked.

"Like a grater."

"Like a grater?" Roman queried, with a strange smile.

"Like an old grater," Korneev explained. "Rusty. Like a net. With wide mesh."

Still smiling his strange smile, Roman took a notebook out of his breast pocket and started turning the pages.

"All right," he said, "rusty, with wide mesh. Let's see now . . . One nine zero five seven three," he read out.

The three masters dashed toward the parrot, and their foreheads clashed together with a dry crunch.

"One nine zero five seven three," Korneev read out from the ring in a crestfallen voice. The effect was very impressive. Stella squealed out loud in delight.

"So what?" said Drozd, still working on his masthead. "I once had a lottery ticket with a number that matched and I went dashing to the savings bank to claim my car. But then it turned out—"

"Why did you write down the number?" asked Korneev, peering at Roman. "Is that a habit of yours? Do you write down all the numbers you see? Maybe you've got the number of your watch written down too?"

"Brilliant!" said Pochkin. "Well done, Vitka. You've hit the bull's-eye. Shame on you, Roman! Why did you poison the parrot? That was very cruel!"

"Idiots!" said Roman. "Who do you think I am, Vybegallo?" Korneev skipped across to him and inspected his ears.

"Go to hell!" said Roman. "Sasha, just look at these fools!"

"Guys," I said reproachfully, "what kind of joke is this? Who do you take us for?"

"What else can we do?" asked Korneev. "Someone's lying here. It's either you or all the laws of nature. I believe in the laws of nature. Everything else changes."

But he soon gave up arguing, sat down at one side, and started thinking. Sasha Drozd calmly carried on painting his masthead. Stella looked at them by turns with frightened eyes. Volodya Pochkin was rapidly scribbling down formulas and crossing them out.

Edik was the first to speak. "Even if there are no laws being broken," he said in a reasonable tone, "it's still very strange for a large number of parrots to appear unexpectedly in the same room, and their death rate is highly suspicious. But I can't say I'm very surprised, bearing in mind that we're dealing with Janus Polyeuctovich here. Does it not seem to you that Janus Polyeuctovich himself is an extremely curious individual?"

"It does," I said.

"I think so too," said Edik. "What's he actually working on, Roman?"

"That depends which Janus you mean. S-Janus is working on contact with parallel spatial dimensions."

"Hmm," said Edik. "That's not likely to help us much."

"Unfortunately not," said Roman. "I keep wondering how to connect the parrots with Janus too, but I can't come up with anything."

"But he is a strange person, isn't he?" asked Edik.

"Yes, no doubt about it. Starting with the fact that there are two of them but only one of him. We've gotten so used to the idea we don't even bother to think about it."

"That's what I was trying to say. We hardly ever talk about Janus—we respect him too much. But I'm sure every one of us must have noticed at least one strange thing about him."

"Strange thing number one," I said, "a love of dying parrots."

"OK," said Edik. "Next?"

"You petty gossips," said Drozd with dignity. "I asked him to lend me some money once."

"And?" said Edik.

"He gave it to me," said Drozd, "But I forgot how much he gave me and now I don't know what to do."

He stopped. Edik waited for a while for him to continue, then said, "Do you know, for instance, that every time I've worked with him at night he's gone off somewhere at exactly midnight and come back five minutes later, and every time I've had the impression he was trying to get me to tell him what we'd been doing before he left?"

"That's exactly right," said Roman. "I know all about that. I noticed a long time ago that at precisely midnight his memory is simply wiped clean. And he's perfectly aware of this defect of his. He's apologized to me several times and told me it's a reflex reaction caused by a serious concussion."

"His memory's absolutely useless," said Volodya Pochkin, crumpling up the piece of paper with his calculations and tossing it under the table. "He's always asking if he saw you yesterday or not."

"And what you spoke about if he did see you," I added.

"Memory, memory," Korneev muttered impatiently. "What's his memory got to do with it? That's not the problem. What's this work he's doing on parallel spatial dimensions?"

"First we have to collect the facts," said Edik.

"Parrots, parrots, parrots," Vitka continued. "Could they really be doubles after all?"

"No," said Volodya Pochkin. "I did all the calculations. They don't match any of the criteria for doubles."

"Every night at midnight," said Roman, "he goes into that laboratory of his and locks himself in for literally just a few minutes. One time he was in such a hurry to get in there, he didn't even close the door."

"And what happened?" asked Stella in a hushed voice.

"Nothing. He sat down in an armchair for a while and came back out. And he immediately asked if we'd been talking about anything important."

"I'm off," said Korneev, getting up.

"Me too," said Edik. "We've got a seminar."

"Me too," said Volodya Pochkin.

"No," said Roman. "You sit there and type. I'm leaving you in charge. Stella, you take Sasha and write your poems. I'm going out. I'll be back in the evening, and the newspaper had better be ready."

They went out, leaving us there to work on the newspaper. At first we tried to think up ideas, but pretty soon we wore ourselves out and realized we couldn't do it. So we wrote a short poem about a dying parrot.

When Roman got back the newspaper was ready. Drozd was lying on the table scarfing down sandwiches and Pochkin was explaining to Stella and me why what had happened with the parrot was absolutely impossible.

"Well done, all of you," said Roman. "An excellent wall newspaper. And what a masthead! Such a fathomless starry sky! And so few typing errors! Where's the parrot?"

The parrot was lying in a petri dish, the very same dish in the very same place where Roman and I had seen it the day before. I even gasped in surprise.

"Who put it here?" asked Roman.

"I did," said Drozd. "Why?"

"Never mind," said Roman. "It can stay there. OK, Sasha?"

I nodded.

"Let's see what happens to it tomorrow," said Roman.

4

Here's this poor old innocent bird o' mine swearing blue fire, and none the wiser, you may lay to that.

—Robert Louis Stevenson

But next morning I had my own responsibilities to attend to. The Aldan was fixed and ready to do battle, and when I arrived in the computer room after breakfast there was already a short line of doubles standing at the door with lists of jobs for it to tackle. I began by vengefully banishing Cristóbal Junta's double after writing on its sheet of paper that I couldn't read the writing. (Cristóbal Joséevich's handwriting really was hard to read, because he wrote in Gothic letters.) Fyodor Simeonovich's double had brought a program written personally by Fyodor Simeonovich. It was the first one that he had written without any advice, prompting, or instructions from me. I read it through carefully and was pleased to discover that it had been written competently, economically, and even with a certain originality. After correcting a few minor errors I passed the program on to my girls. Then I noticed the pale-faced bookkeeper from the fish processing plant languishing in the line. He looked rather frightened and uncomfortable, so I spotted him straightaway.

"It doesn't seem right, though," he mumbled, squinting warily at the doubles. "The comrades are waiting—they were here before me."

"Don't worry, they're not comrades," I reassured him.

"Well, citizens—"

"They're not citizens either."

The accountant turned absolutely white and, leaning down toward me, said in a faltering whisper, "You know, I noticed they weren't blinking . . . And that one in blue—I don't think he's breathing either."

230

I'd already dealt with half the line when Roman phoned. "Sasha?"

"Yes?"

"The parrot's gone."

"What do you mean, gone?"

"Just gone."

"Maybe the cleaning woman threw it out?"

"I asked her. She didn't. She never even saw it."

"So maybe the brownies are up to their silly tricks?"

"Right outside the director's laboratory? Hardly."

"True enough," I said. "What about Janus himself?"

"Janus hasn't come in yet. I don't think he's even back from Moscow."

"Then what are we supposed to make of all this?" I asked.

"I don't know. We'll have to wait and see."

Neither of us said anything.

"Will you call me?" I asked. "If anything interesting comes up?"

"Of course. Absolutely. Cheers, old buddy."

I forced myself not to think about the parrot, which in the final analysis was none of my business. I dealt with all the doubles, checked all the programs, and started work on a certain lousy job that had been hanging over me for ages. This lousy job had been given to me by the Absolutists. At first I'd told them it didn't make any sense and it had no solution, like all the rest of their problems. But then I'd consulted Junta, who had a very subtle understanding of these things, and he'd given me a few pieces of encouraging advice. I'd made a start on the job many times already and then set it aside, but this time I saw it through. It came out very elegantly. But at the very moment when I finished it and leaned back in my chair to survey the solution from a distance, Junta arrived in a dark fury. Looking down at my feet, he inquired in a chilly, unpleasant voice exactly when I'd stopped being able to read his handwriting. He informed me that it sounded very much like sabotage to him, and in Madrid in 1936 he used to have people put up against the wall for doing things like that.

I looked at him fondly. "Cristóbal Joséevich," I said. "I did solve it after all. You were absolutely right. Incantational space really can be convoluted according to any four variables."

He finally raised his eyes and looked at me. I must have looked really pleased, because he relented and growled, "May I please take a look?"

I gave him the sheets of paper, he sat down beside me, and we worked through the problem together from beginning to end, savoring with great delight two extremely elegant transformations, one of which he had suggested to me and the other of which I had found for myself.

"Our heads seem to work quite well, Alejandro," Junta said at last. "We possess an artistic quality of thought. What do you think?"

"I think we did very well," I said sincerely.

"I think so too," he said. "We'll publish this. No one would be ashamed to publish it. This is not hitchhiking galoshes or pants of darkness."

In an excellent mood now, we began analyzing Junta's new problem, and he soon got around to saying that even before then he sometimes used to think he was *pobrecito*, and he could tell I was a mathematical ignoramus the very first moment he laid eyes on me. I agreed with him fervently and suggested it was probably time for him to retire and I ought to be thrown out of the Institute on my backside and put to work as a lumberjack, because I was no good for anything else. He protested. He said a pension was out of the question for him, he ought to be made into fertilizer, and I shouldn't be allowed within a kilometer of a logging camp—where, after all, a certain intellectual ability was required—I ought to be placed as an apprentice to a junior ladler in the sewage brigade of a cholera ward. We were sitting there with our heads propped in our hands, indulging in self-abasement, when Fyodor Simeonovich glanced into the room. As far as I could make out, he was impatient to find out what I thought of the program he'd written.

"Program!" said Junta with a bilious laugh. "I haven't seen your program, Teodoro, but I'm sure it's brilliant in comparison to this."

He handed Fyodor Simeonovich the sheet of paper with his problem, grasping it squeamishly between his finger and thumb. "Feast your eyes on that squalid specimen of wretched mediocrity."

"*My* dear fellows," said Fyodor Simeonovich, perplexed, once he'd puzzled out the handwriting. "This is one of *Bezalel's* problems. *Cagliostro* proved that it has no solution."

"We know it doesn't have a solution," said Junta, instantly bristling. "What we want to know is how to go about solving it."

"Your reasoning is rather *strange*, Cristó . . . *How* can you look for a solution when there *isn't* one? It doesn't make much *sense*."

"I beg your pardon, Teodoro, but it is your reasoning that's rather strange. What does not make sense is searching for a solution when there already is one. What we're talking about here is how to deal with a problem that has no solution. This is a matter of fundamental principle, which I can see is unfortunately beyond your grasp as a mere practitioner without theoretical grounding. I believe I was mistaken to enter into discussion of this subject with you."

Cristóbal Joséevich's tone was highly insulting, and Fyodor Simeonovich got very angry. "I *tell* you what, my *dear* fellow," he said. "I can't discuss the matter with you in this tone in *front* of this young man. You *surprise* me, it's *pedagogically incorrect*. If you wish to *continue*, please step out into the *corridor* with me."

"At your service," replied Junta, straightening up like a spring and snatching at a nonexistent sword hilt on his hip.

They walked out ceremoniously, proudly holding their heads up high and not looking at each other. The girls started giggling. I wasn't particularly frightened either. I sat down in front of the sheet of paper that had been left with me, taking my head in my hands, and for a while I was vaguely aware of Fyodor Simeonovich's deep bass rumbling in the corridor, punctuated by Cristóbal Joséevich's chilly but furious interjections.

Then Fyodor Simeonovich roared, "Be so good as to step into my office!"

"By all means," rasped Junta. They were speaking very formally by this time. The voices faded into the distance.

"A duel! A duel!" the girls twittered. Junta had the dashing reputation of a swashbuckling duelist and quarrel-monger. They said
he used to take his opponent to his laboratory, offer him a choice
of rapiers, swords, or battle-axes, and then start jumping around
on the tables like Jean Marais, overturning all the cupboards. But
there was no reason to be afraid for Fyodor Simeonovich. It was
perfectly obvious that they would spend half an hour in his office
staring at each other across the desk in gloomy silence, then Fyodor
Simeonovich would heave a sigh, open up his traveling chest, and
fill two glasses with the Elixir of Bliss. Junta would flare his nostrils,
twirl his metaphorical mustache, and drink it. Fyodor Simeonovich
would promptly fill the glasses again and shout for some fresh
cucumbers from the laboratory.

Just then Roman called and asked me in a strange voice to come
up to his lab straightaway. I ran up the stairs.

Roman, Vitka, and Edik were already in the lab. And there was a
green parrot there too. Alive. He was sitting on the beam of the balance, as he had the day before, surveying everyone in turn, first with
one eye and then with the other, rummaging in his feathers with his
beak and evidently feeling just fine. By contrast, the scientists weren't
looking too good. Roman was stooped dejectedly over the parrot,
sighing fitfully every now and then. Pale-faced Edik was gently mas-
saging his temples with an expression of acute distress on his face,
as if he were racked by migraine. And Vitka was sitting backward
on a chair, swaying to and fro like a little boy playing at horses and
muttering something unintelligible with his eyes rolling insanely.

"The same one?" I asked in a low voice.

"The very same," said Roman.

"Photon?" Suddenly I wasn't feeling too good either.

"Yep."

"And the number matches?"

Roman didn't answer.

Edik said in a pained voice, "If we knew how many feathers the
parrot has in its tail, we could have counted them again and taken
into account the feather that was lost the day before yesterday."

"Maybe I should send for Brehm?" I suggested.

"Where's the corpse?" asked Roman. "That's what we have to start with! Tell me, detectives, where's the corpse?"

"*Corrrpse,*" screeched the parrot. "*Cerrremony! Corrrpse overboarrrd! Rrrubidium!*"

"What the hell is he saying?" Roman asked angrily.

"'Corpse overboard' sounds like a typical pirate expression," Edik explained.

"And rubidium?"

"*Rrrubidium! Rrreserves! Verrry grrreat!*" said the parrot.

"There are very great reserves of rubidium," Edik translated. "I wonder where, though."

I leaned down and started studying the ring. "Perhaps it isn't really the same one?"

"Then where's the first one?" asked Roman.

"That's a different question," I said. "That's a bit easier to explain."

"Explain it then," said Edik.

"Hang on," I said. "First let's decide if it's the same one or not."

"I think it is," said Edik.

"I don't think it is," I said. "See, there's a scratch here on the ring, by the number three—"

"*Numberrr thrrree!*" said the parrot. "*Numberrr thrrree! Harrrd to starrrboard! Vorrrtex! Vorrrtex!*"

Vitka suddenly roused himself. "I've got an idea," he said.

"What is it?"

"Associative interrogation."

"How do you mean?"

"Hang on. Everybody sit down, keep quiet, and don't interrupt. Roman, do you have a tape recorder?"

"I've got a dictaphone."

"Give it to me. Only everybody keep quiet. I'll make him talk, the rotten swine. He'll tell me everything."

Vitka drew up a chair, sat down facing the parrot with the dictaphone in his hand, hunched over, looked at the parrot with one eye, and barked: "Rubidium!"

The parrot started and almost fell off the beam. It flapped its wings to regain its balance and responded, *"Rrreserves! Rrritchey Crrrater!"*

We looked at each other.

"Rrreserves!" Vitka barked.

"Verrry great! Verrry grrreat. Rrritchey's rrright! Rrritchey's rrright! Rrrobots! Rrrobots!"

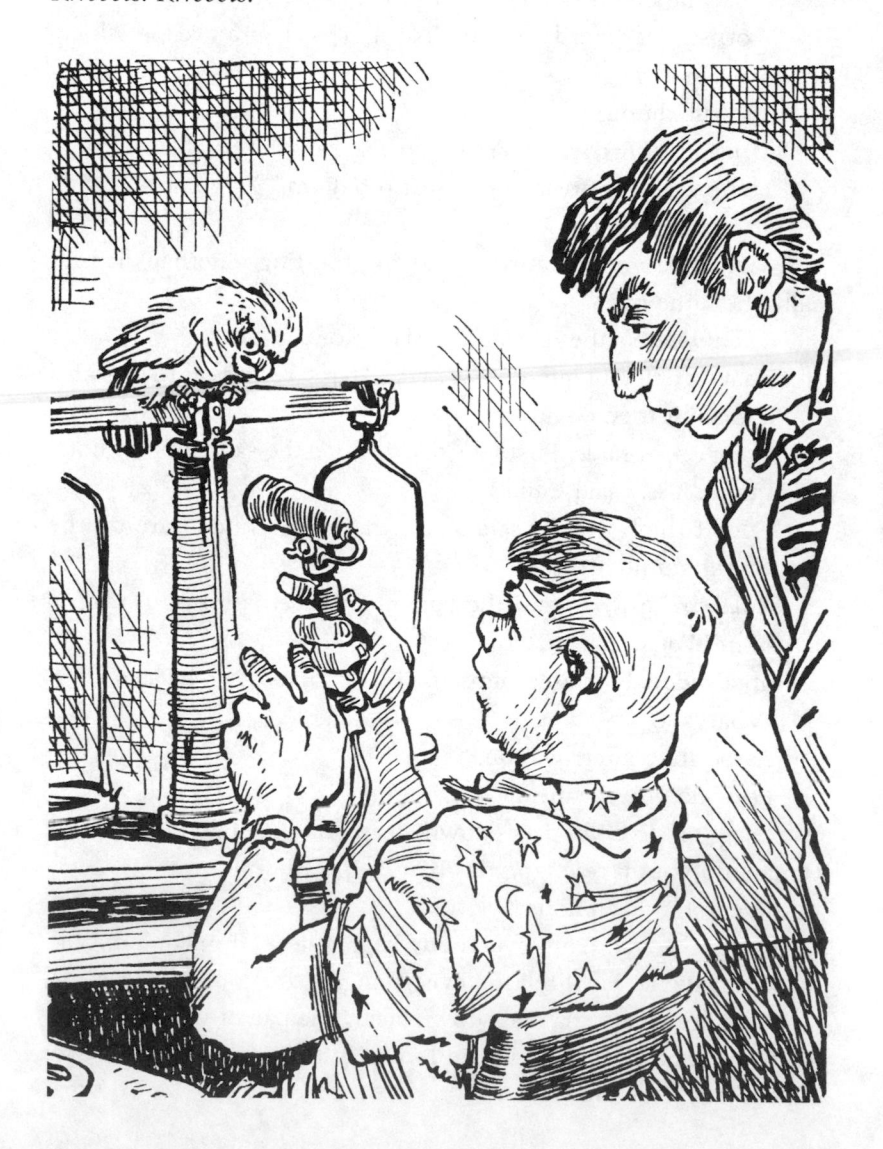

"Robots!"

"*Crrrash! Burrrning! Atmospherrre's burrrning! Withdrrraw! Drrramba! Withdrrraw!*"

"Dramba!"

"*Rrrubidium! Rrreserves!*"

"Rubidium!"

"*Rrreserves! Rrritchey Crrrater!*"

"Short circuit," said Roman. "A closed circle."

"Hang on, hang on," muttered Vitka. "Just a moment . . ."

"Try something to do with something else," Edik advised him.

"Janus!" said Vitka.

The parrot opened its beak and sneezed.

"*Jaaanus,*" Vitka repeated sternly.

The parrot stared thoughtfully at the ceiling.

"There's no letter *r*," I said.

"That's probably it," said Vitka. "OK then . . . *Nevstrrruev!*"

"*Overrr, overrr!*" said the parrot. "*Sorrrcerrror! Sorrrcerrror! Trrraveler herrre! Trrraveler herrre!*"

"That's no pirate's parrot," said Edik.

"Ask him about the corpse," I suggested.

"Corpse," Vitka said unwillingly.

"*Burrrial cerrremony! Hurrrry! Hurrrry! Addrrress! Addrrress! Verrrbiage! Worrrk! Worrrk!*"

"He must have had some interesting owners," said Roman. "What are we going to do?"

"Vitya," said Edik, "I think he's using spaceflight terminology. Try something simple, more commonplace."

"Hydrogen bomb," said Vitka.

The parrot lowered its head and cleaned its claw with its beak.

"Railroad! Train!" said Vitka.

The parrot said nothing.

"We're not getting anywhere," said Roman.

"Dammit," said Vitka, "I can't think of anything else commonplace with a letter *r* in it. Table, window, ceiling . . . Oh! *Trrranslator!*"

The parrot glanced at Vitka with one eye. *"Korrrneev, rrreally!"*

"What?" asked Vitka. It was the first time I'd ever seen Vitka disconcerted.

"Korrrneev's a boorrr! Rrrude. Superrrb rrresearcher! Rrridiculous jesterrr! Rrremarkable!"

We giggled. Vitka looked at us and said vengefully: *"Oirrra-Oirrra!"*

"Grrray-haired," the parrot responded promptly. *"Harrrd fought! Grrratifying!"*

"Something's not right here," said Roman.

"What isn't?" said Vitka. "That sounds spot on to me . . . *Prrrivalov!"*

"Prrrimitive prrroject! Prrrimitive! Harrrdworking!"

"He knows all of us, my friends," said Edik.

"Frrriends," the parrot echoed. *"Peppercorrrn! Zerrro! Zerrro! Grrravitation!"*

"Amperian," Vitka said hurriedly.

"Crrrematorium! Perrrished prrrematurely!" said the parrot, then it thought a bit and added, *"Amperrrmeter!"*

"It doesn't add up," said Edik.

"Everything always adds up," Roman said pensively.

Vitka clicked the catch and opened the dictaphone. "The tape's finished," he said. "Pity."

"Know what I think?" I said. "The simplest thing would be to ask Janus. Whose parrot is it, where is it from, and all the rest."

"But who's going to ask?" Roman inquired.

No one volunteered, Vitka suggested listening to the recording, and we agreed. It all sounded very strange. At the sound of the first words from the dictaphone the parrot flew onto Vitka's shoulder and began listening with obvious interest, interpolating occasional phrases like *"Drrramba ignorrring urrranium,"* *"Corrrrect,"* and *"Korrrneev's rrrude, rrrude, rrrude!"*

When the recording came to an end, Edik said, "In theory we could compile a lexical dictionary and analyze it on the computer. But even without that some things are already quite clear. First, it knows all of us. That's already amazing. Second, it knows about robots. And about rubidium. Where do they use rubidium, by the way?"

"It's not used anywhere in the Institute," said Roman.

"It's something like sodium," said Korneev.

"Rubidium's one thing," I said. "But how does it know about lunar craters?"

"Why do they have to be lunar?"

"Where on Earth do they call mountains craters?"

"Well, in the first place, there's an Arizona crater, and in the second place, it's not a mountain, it's more like a depression or a trough."

"*Temporral trrrough,*" declared the parrot.

"The terminology it uses is really extremely interesting," said Edik. "I would hardly call it common usage."

"That's right," said Vitka. "If the parrot spends all its time with Janus, then Janus is involved in some strange business."

"*Strrrange orrrbital trrransition,*" said the parrot.

"Janus doesn't work on space projects," said Roman. "I'd know about it."

"Maybe he used to, though?"

"No, he never used to either."

"Some kind of robots," said Vitka wearily. "Craters . . . Where did the craters come from?"

"Maybe Janus reads science fiction?" I suggested. "Out loud? To a parrot?"

"Yeah, OK . . ."

"Saturn," said Vitka to the parrot.

"*Dangerrrous attrrraction,*" said the parrot. It thought for a moment and explained, "*Crrrashed. Terrrible. Rrreckless.*"

Roman stood up and began walking around the laboratory. Edik laid his cheek on the tabletop and closed his eyes. "But how did it turn up here?"

"The same as yesterday," said Roman. "From Janus's lab."

"Did you see it happen?"

"Uh-huh."

"There's one thing I don't understand," I said. "Did it die or didn't it?"

"How do we know?" said Roman. "I'm no vet. And Vitka's no ornithologist. And maybe it isn't really a parrot after all."

"What, then?"

"How should I know?"

"It could be a complex induced hallucination," said Edik, without opening his eyes.

I pressed a finger against one eye and looked at the parrot. I saw two parrots.

"I see two of it," I said. "It's not a hallucination."

"I said a complex hallucination," Edik reminded me.

I pressed a finger against each eye and went blind for a while.

"You know what," said Korneev. "I declare that we are dealing with a violation of the law of cause and effect and therefore the only possible solution is that it's all a hallucination, so we should all stand up, get in line, and sing as we march off to see the psychiatrist. Everybody up!"

"I'm not going," said Edik. "I've got another idea."

"What is it?"

"I won't say."

"Why not?"

"You'll beat me up."

"We'll beat you up anyway."

"Go ahead."

"You don't have any idea," said Vitka. "You just imagine that you do. Off to the psychiatrist with you."

The door from the corridor squeaked open and Janus Polyeuctovich walked into the laboratory. "I see," he said. "Hello."

We stood up. He went around us all and shook our hands.

"Is Photon in here again?" he said, catching sight of the parrot. "He's not bothering you, is he, Roman Petrovich?"

"Bothering me?" said Roman. "Me? Why would he bother me? On the contrary."

"Well, it is every day—" Janus Polyeuctovich began, and suddenly broke off. "What was it we were talking about yesterday?" he asked, rubbing his forehead.

"You were in Moscow yesterday," said Roman in a respectful voice.

"Ah . . . yes, yes. Very well. Photon! Come here!"

The parrot soared across to Janus's shoulder and said in his ear, *"Grrrain! Grrrain! Sugarrr! Sugarrr!"*

Janus Polyeuctovich smiled gently and went through into his laboratory. We looked at each other, stunned.

"Let's get out of here," said Roman.

"Psychiatrrrist! Psychiatrrrist!" Korneev muttered ominously as we walked down the corridor on the way to the sofa in his office. *"Rrritchey Crrrater! Drrramba! Sugarrr!"*

5

There are always enough facts—it's imagination that's lacking.

—D. Blokhintsev

Vitka moved the canisters of living water down onto the floor, then we collapsed onto the sofa-translator and lit up. After a while Roman asked, "Vitka, did you switch off the sofa?"

"Yes."

"I've got this crazy nonsense running round my head."

"I turned it off and I blocked it," said Vitka.

"OK, guys," said Edik, "so why isn't it a hallucination then?"

"Who says it isn't?" asked Vitka. "I still suggest the psychiatrist."

"When I was courting Maya," said Edik, "I induced hallucinations that astounded even me."

"What for?" asked Vitka.

Edik thought about it. "I don't know," he said. "I suppose I must have gotten carried away."

"The question I'm asking is, why would anyone want to induce hallucinations in us?" said Vitka. "After all, we're not Maya, thank God. We're masters of magic. Who could overpower us? OK—Janus, Kivrin, Junta. Maybe Giacomo too."

"Our Sasha's a bit on the weak side," said Edik apologetically.

"So what?" I asked. "I'm not the only one seeing things, am I?"

"We could check that out," Vitka said pensively. "If we . . . well, you know . . ."

"Oh no," I said. "That's enough of that from you. There must be other ways, surely? Press on your eyeballs. Or give the dictaphone to an outsider. He can listen to it and say if there's anything recorded on it or not."

The masters of magic smiled pityingly. "You're a good programmer, Sasha," said Edik.

"But a maggot," said Korneev. "Still a little larva."

"Yes, Sashenka," Roman sighed. "You can't even imagine what a genuine, detailed, consistently induced hallucination is like."

A dreamy expression appeared on the masters' faces—they were obviously recalling sweet memories. I looked at them enviously. They smiled and screwed up their eyes. They winked at someone. Then Edik suddenly said, "Her orchids bloomed all winter long. Their scent was the very loveliest that I could invent . . ."

Vitka came to his senses. "Berkeleians," he said. "Pitiful solipsists. 'I dislike what I fancy I feel!'"

"Yes," said Roman. "Hallucinations are not something we should be talking about. That's too simpleminded altogether. We're not children and we're not old women. I don't want to be an agnostic. What was that idea you had, Edik?"

"Me? Oh yes, I did have one. But it's pretty primitive too. Matricates."

"Hmm," said Roman doubtfully.

"What are they?" I asked.

Edik reluctantly explained that in addition to the doubles I was so familiar with, there are also matricates—precise, perfect copies of objects or beings. Unlike doubles, matricates match their originals precisely, right down to their atomic structure. They can't be told apart by the usual methods. You need special equipment, and it's a very complicated and labor-intensive business. Balsamo had been awarded his master's degree for proving that Philippe Bourbon, popularly known by the sobriquet "the Man in the Iron Mask," was a matricate of Louis XIV created by Jesuits in secret laboratories in order to seize the throne of France. Nowadays matricates are produced using Richard Cirugue's biostereographical method.

I didn't have a clue who Richard Cirugue was, but I said straightaway that the idea of matricates could only explain the unusual similarity of the parrots. And nothing else. For instance, it still didn't explain where yesterday's dead parrot had gone to.

"Yes, that's true," said Edik. "I don't insist on it. Especially since Janus has absolutely no connection with biostereography."

"Exactly," I said, growing bolder. "Then it would make better sense to hypothesize a journey into the described future. You know, like Louis Sedlovoi."

"How's that?" Korneev asked, not sounding particularly interested.

"Janus simply flies into some science fiction novel, collects the parrot out of it, and brings it back here. When the parrot dies, he goes flying off again to the same page and then . . . That explains why the parrots are so similar. It's one and the same parrot, and it explains why it has that science fiction vocabulary. And apart from that," I went on, feeling that all this really didn't sound too stupid after all, "it might even explain why Janus keeps asking questions: every time he's afraid he might not have come back to the right day . . . I reckon I've explained it all pretty neatly, don't you?"

"And is there a science fiction novel like that?" Edik asked curiously. "With a parrot?"

"I don't know," I said honestly. "But they have all sorts of animals in those starships of theirs. Cats and monkeys and children . . . And in the West they have an absolutely vast amount of science fiction, more than you could ever read."

"Well, in the first case, a parrot out of Western science fiction is hardly likely to start talking Russian," said Roman. "But the biggest problem is, we've got absolutely no idea how these space parrots, even if they're out of Soviet science fiction, could know Korneev, Privalov, and Oira-Oira."

"Not to mention," Vitka drawled, "that it's one thing to transfer a material body into an ideal world and quite another to transfer an ideal body into the real world. I doubt if you could find a writer who's created an image of a parrot capable of independent survival in the real world."

When I remembered the semitransparent inventors I couldn't think of any objection to that.

"But anyway," Vitka continued benevolently, "our wee Sasha is showing definite signs of promise. His idea has a certain noble insanity about it."

"Janus wouldn't have burned an ideal parrot," Edik said with conviction. "An ideal parrot can't even rot."

"But why?" Roman suddenly said. "Why are we being so inconsistent here? Why Sedlovoi? Why would Janus copy Louis Sedlovoi? Janus has his own subject. Janus has his own research problems. Janus studies parallel spatial dimensions. Let's make that our starting point!"

"Yes, let's," I said.

"Do you think Janus has managed to establish contact with some parallel spatial dimension?" asked Edik.

"He must have established contact a long time ago. Why don't we assume that he's gone further than that? Why don't we assume that he's working on the transfer of material bodies? Edik's right: they're matricates, they have to be matricates, because there has to be a guarantee that the transferred object is absolutely identical. He selects the transfer mode on an experimental basis. The first two transfers were unsuccessful— the parrots died. Today's experiment seems to have succeeded."

"Why do they speak Russian?" asked Edik. "And why would the parrots have the kind of vocabulary they do?"

"It means there's a Russia there too," said Roman. "But there they already mine rubidium in the Ritchey Crater."

"The whole thing's far too forced," said Vitka. "Why parrots and not something else? Why not dogs or guinea pigs? Why not simply tape recorders, if it comes to that? And then again, how do these parrots know that Oira-Oira's old and Korneev's a superb researcher?"

"But rude," I put in.

"Rude, but superb. And anyway, where did the dead parrot get to?"

"Listen to me," said Edik. "This is no good. We're going at it like dilettantes. Like those amateurs who write letters to magazines: 'Dear scientists! This is the nth year I've heard a tapping under the ground in my basement. Can you please explain what causes it?' We've got to be systematic. Where's your piece of paper, Vitka? Let's get it all down in writing."

So we wrote everything down in Edik's lovely handwriting.

First we accepted the postulate that what was happening wasn't a hallucination, otherwise there simply wouldn't have been any point. Then we formulated the questions to which the hypothesis we were seeking ought to provide the answers. We divided these questions into two groups, the "parrot" group and the "Janus" group. The "Janus" group was introduced on the insistence of Roman and Edik, who claimed they had a definite gut feeling that there was a connection between Janus's oddities and the oddities of the parrot. They were unable to provide an answer to Korneev's question about the precise physical meaning of the words *gut* and *feeling*, but they emphasised the point that in himself Janus represented an extremely curious subject for investigation—and so, like father, like parrot. Since I had no particular opinion about this, they were in a majority, and the final list of questions was as follows:

Why are parrots numbers 1, 2, and 3, observed respectively on the tenth, eleventh and twelfth days of the month, so similar to each other that at first we took them for one and the same bird?

Why did Janus cremate bird number 1 and probably also the bird that came before number 1 (number 0), from which only one feather remained?

Where did the feather go?

Where did parrot number 2 (the one that died) go?

How can we explain the strange vocabulary used by parrots numbers 2 and 3?

How can we explain that number 3 knows all of us, even though we had not seen it before?

(I wanted to add "Why did the parrots die and what caused it?" but Korneev growled, "Why is the first sign of poisoning that the corpse turns blue, and what causes it?" and they didn't write down my question.)

What is the connection between Janus and the parrots?

Why does Janus never remember who he was talking to yesterday and what about?

What happens to Janus at midnight?

Why does S-Janus have a strange habit of talking in the future tense, while A-Janus has never been observed to do anything of the kind?

Why are there two of them, and what is the source of the story that Janus Polyeuctovich is one individual in two persons?

After that we thought very hard for a while, glancing constantly at the sheet of paper. I kept hoping for further inspiration from my noble insanity, but my thoughts simply evaporated into space, and the longer it went on, the more I inclined toward Sasha Drozd's point of view that there were weirder things going on in the Institute. I realized that this cheap skepticism was simply the product of my own ignorance and lack of experience in conceptualizing the world in terms of different categories, but there was nothing I could do about it. Everything that was happening, so my reasoning ran, was only really amazing if we believed that the three or four parrots were all the same parrot. They really were so similar to each other that at first I'd been misled. It was quite natural. I'm a mathematician—I respect numbers, and when numbers match, especially six-digit numbers, I automatically assume that the numbered items match as well. But it was quite clear that they couldn't all be the same parrot—that would violate the law of cause and effect, a law that I had no intention of abandoning because of a couple of lousy parrots, and dead ones at that. But if they weren't all the same parrot, that reduced the scale of the entire problem.

So what if the numbers matched? So what if someone had thrown out the parrot when we weren't looking? And what else was there? The vocabulary? What did a few words mean? There had to be some very simple explanation for that. I was just about to pronounce on the subject when Vitka said, "Guys, I think I'm onto something."

None of us said a word. We just turned to look at him—all at the same time, in noisy agitation. Vitka stood up.

"It's as simple as a pancake," he said. "Flat, trivial, and banal. It's hardly even worth telling you about it."

We slowly stood up. I felt as if I was reading the final pages of a gripping detective novel. Somehow all my skepticism had completely evaporated.

"Countermotion!" Vitka declared.

Edik lay down. "Excellent!" he said. "Well done!"

"Countermotion?" said Roman. "I suppose . . . Aha . . ." he twiddled his fingers. "OK . . . Uh-huh . . . But what if . . . ? Yes, that explains why it knows all of us." Roman made a sweeping gesture of invitation. "So they're coming from that direction."

"And that's why he asks what he was talking about yesterday," put in Vitka. "And the science fiction terminology . . ."

"Wait, will you!" I howled. The final page of the detective story had turned out to be written in Arabic. "Hang on! What countermotion?"

"No," said Roman regretfully, and I could see straightaway from Vitka's face that he'd also realized countermotion wouldn't do it. "It doesn't work," said Roman. "It's like a film . . . Imagine a film—"

"What film?" I yelled. "Help me!"

"A film running backward," Roman explained. "Get it? Countermotion."

"Damn and blast," Vitka said disappointedly, and lay down on the sofa with his hands clasped over his nose.

"No, it doesn't work," said Edik, also sounding regretful. "Don't worry about it, Sasha, it doesn't work anyway. Countermotion is defined as movement through time in reverse. Like a neutrino. But the problem is that if the parrot were a countermover, it would fly back to front and it wouldn't die in front of our eyes but come to life . . . But it's a good idea all the same. A countermoving parrot really could know something about outer space. It would live from the future into the past. And a countermoving Janus really couldn't know what happened to him yesterday. Because our 'yesterday' would be his 'tomorrow.'"

"That's the point," said Vitka. "I just wondered why the parrot described Oira-Oira as 'gray-haired.' And why Janus sometimes predicts what will happen the next day so cleverly and in such detail. Remember what happened at the firing range, Roman? It just seemed like they simply had to be from the future."

"But tell me," I said, "is countermotion really possible?"

"In theory it is," said Edik. "After all, half the matter in the universe is moving through time in the opposite direction. But nobody's ever dealt with it on a practical level."

"Who needs it, and who could survive it?" Vitka asked morosely.

"But you must admit it would be a remarkable experiment," observed Roman.

"Not an experiment, an act of self-sacrifice," growled Vitka. "Say what you will, but countermotion's mixed up in all this somehow . . . I've got a feeling in my gut."

"Ah, the gut!" said Roman, and nobody else said anything.

While they were all keeping quiet, I was feverishly running over in my mind what we actually had. If countermotion was possible in theory, then in theory it was possible to violate the law of cause and effect. But not really violate it, because the law would remain valid separately for the normal world and for the countermover's world . . . Which meant it was possible after all to assume that there weren't three or four parrots but only one, always the same one. What did that give us? On the tenth it's lying dead in a petri dish. Then they cremate it, convert it into ashes, and scatter them to the wind. But then on the morning of the eleventh it's alive again. Not reduced to ashes at all, but quite unhurt. True, by the middle of the day it's back in the petri dish again. That was awfully important. I could feel it was awfully important, that petri dish . . . The unity of place! . . . On the twelfth the parrot was alive again and asking for sugar . . . It wasn't countermotion, it wasn't a film shown backward, but there was more than a touch of countermotion about it all the same . . .

Vitka was right. For a countermover the sequence of events was as follows: the parrot is alive, the parrot dies, the parrot is cremated. From our viewpoint, leaving the details out of consideration, it was exactly the opposite: the parrot is cremated, the parrot dies, the parrot is alive . . . As if the film had been cut into three pieces and first they showed the third piece, then the second, and then the first . . . Like fractures in a continuum . . . Fractures in a continuum . . . Points of fracture . . .

"Guys," I said in a faltering voice, "does countermotion definitely have to be continuous?"

It took them a while to react. Edik smoked his cigarette, blowing smoke up at the ceiling. Vitka lay on his stomach without moving, and Roman stared vacantly at me. Then his eyes opened wide.

"Midnight!" he said in a terrible whisper. Everybody jumped to their feet.

It was as if I'd scored the winning goal in the cup final. They threw themselves on me, slavered on my cheeks, thumped me on the back and the neck, tumbled me onto the sofa, and then tumbled onto it themselves.

"Well done!" shrieked Edik.

"That's real brains for you!" roared Roman.

"And I had you down as a fool!" said the rude Korneev.

Then they settled down and after that everything went as smooth as grease.

First Roman announced out of the blue that now he knew the secret of the Tunguska meteorite. He wanted to tell us all straightaway, and we were delighted to agree, paradoxical as that might

sound. We were in no hurry to move on to what interested us most of all! We felt like gourmets. We didn't throw ourselves on our food. We breathed in the aromas; we rolled our eyes and smacked our lips; we walked around, rubbing our hands in anticipation . . .

"So, let us finally clear up the confused problem of the Tunguska marvel," Roman said in a stealthy voice. "The people who have tackled this problem before us were absolutely devoid of imagination. All those comets, antimatter meteorites, spontaneously exploding nuclear-powered spaceships, all those cosmic clouds and quantum generators—they're all just too banal, which means they don't even come close to the truth. I always thought the Tunguska meteorite was an alien ship, and I always believed they couldn't find the ship at the site of the explosion because it had long since left. Until today I used to think that the fall of the Tunguska meteorite was the ship's takeoff, not its landing. And that rough hypothesis explained a great deal. The idea of discrete countermotion makes it possible to wrap up this problem once and for all . . .

"What happened on June 30, 1908, in the region of Podkamennaya Tunguska? In about the middle of July that year an alien ship entered the space of the solar system. But these were not the simple, artless aliens of science fiction novels. They were countermovers, comrades! People who had come to our world from a different universe in which time flows against ours. The interaction of the opposed timestreams transformed them from ordinary countermovers, who saw our universe like a film projected backward, into discrete countermovers. The precise nature of this discrete countermotion does not concern us here. The important thing is that their life in our universe became subject to a rhythmic cycle.

"If we assume for the sake of simplicity that their diurnal cycle was equal to the Earth day, then from our point of view their existence would appear as follows. During the first day, let's say July 1, they live, work, and eat exactly as we do. But at precisely, let's say, midnight, they and all their equipment move on, not into July 2 but back to the beginning of June 30—that is, not one moment forward but two days backward, as seen from our point of view. And in just the same way, at the end of June 30 they don't move into July 1 but back to the beginning of June 29. And so on. When they got close to the Earth, our countermovers were amazed to discover, if they hadn't discovered it earlier, that the Earth makes

extremely strange leaps in its orbit, leaps that render astral naviga-
tion very difficult. And in addition, as they hung above the Earth
on July 1 by our count of time, they discovered a mighty fire at
the very heart of the gigantic Eurasian continent. They had seen
its smoke in their telescopes already—on July 2, 3, and so forth as
we count time. The cataclysm interested them in its own right,
but their scientific curiosity was finally provoked when on the
morning of June 30 by our count, they saw that there was no
sign of any fire and the taiga lay stretched out below the ship like
a calm green sea. The intrigued captain ordered the ship to land
in the very spot where yesterday, by his count of time, he had
personally observed the epicenter of a raging inferno. After that
everything happened the way it was supposed to. The switches
clicked, the screens flickered, the planetary engines roared to life
as the k-gamma plasmoine was injected . . ."

"The what?" asked Vitka.

"K-gamma plasmoine. Or, let's say, mu-delta ionoplast. The
ship, engulfed in flame, plunged into the taiga and naturally set
it on fire. That was the scene observed by the peasants from the
village of Karelinskoye and other people who were later recorded
by history as eyewitnesses. The conflagration was appalling. The
countermovers glanced outside, shuddered, and decided to sit it
out inside the heat-resistant refractory hull of the spaceship. Until
midnight they listened anxiously to the roaring and crackling of
the flames, then precisely at midnight everything went quiet. Naturally. The countermovers had entered a new day, June 29 by our
reckoning of time. And when the brave captain, having taken massive precautions, finally decided to venture outside at about two in
the morning, by the light of the powerful searchlights he saw the
fir trees swaying calmly and was immediately attacked by clouds
of the small bloodsucking insects known in our terminology as
gnats or midges."

Roman paused for breath and looked around at the rest of us.
We were really enjoying this, and looking forward to dissecting the
mystery of the parrot in exactly the same way.

"The subsequent fate of the countermoving aliens," Roman continued, "need not interest us. Perhaps on about June 15 they quietly and unnoticeably lifted off from the strange planet without any fuss, this time using nonflammable alpha-beta-gamma antigravity, and went back home. Or perhaps every last one of them died from being poisoned by mosquito saliva, and their spaceship went on standing on our planet, sinking back into the abyss of time, and the trilobites crawled over it on the bottom of the Silurian sea. Maybe even sometime around the year 906 or 909 a hunter stumbled across it in the taiga and for a long time afterward kept telling his friends about it, but they quite naturally didn't believe a word he said. In concluding my brief address, I should like to express my sympathy for the renowned explorers who have striven in vain to discover anything in the area of the Podkamennaya Tunguska River. Mesmerized by the obvious, they have only investigated what happened in the taiga after the explosion, but none of them has tried to find out what happened before it. *Dixi*."

Roman cleared his throat and drank a mug of living water.

"Does anyone have any questions for the speaker?" Edik inquired. "No questions? Excellent. Let's get back to our parrots. Who would like the floor?"

Everybody wanted the floor. And everybody started speaking at once—even Roman, who was a little bit hoarse. We grabbed the list of questions out of each other's hands and crossed them out one after another, and after about half an hour we'd put together the following absolutely clear and comprehensively detailed picture of the observed phenomenon.

In 1841 a son was born to the family of the poor landowner and retired army ensign Polyeuctus Khrisanfovich Nevstruev. He was called Janus in honor of a distant relative, Janus Polyeuctovich Nevstruev, who had precisely foretold the day and even the hour at which the boy child would be born. This relative, a modest and retiring old man, had moved to the retired ensign's estate shortly after the Napoleonic invasion, living in an outbuilding and devoting himself to scholarly pursuits. He was a little strange, as men of science are supposed to be, with many eccentricities, but he was absolutely devoted to his godson, always staying close by his side and insistently instilling in him knowledge from the fields of mathematics, chemistry, and the other sciences. In effect Janus Jr. spent hardly a single day without Janus Sr., which was why he failed to notice something that amazed everybody else: as the years passed, instead of growing more decrepit the old man seemed to become stronger and more vigorous. By the turn of the century old Janus had initiated young Janus into the ultimate secrets of analytical, relativistic, and universal magic. They carried on living and working side by side, taking part in all the wars and revolutions, enduring all the vicissitudes of history more or less valiantly, until finally they ended up in the National Institute for the Technology of Witchcraft and Thaumaturgy . . .

To be perfectly honest, this entire introductory section was pure literary improvisation. The only fact we knew for certain about Janus's past was that J. P. Nevstruev was born March 7, 1841. We knew absolutely nothing about how and when J. P. Nevstruev had become the director of the Institute. We didn't even know who had been the first to guess that S-Janus and A-Janus were one individual in two persons and let the secret slip. I'd heard about it from Oira-Oira, and believed it because I couldn't understand it. Oira-Oira had heard about it from Giacomo, and he'd also believed it because he was young and the idea delighted him. Korneev had been told about it by a cleaning woman, and at the time he had decided that the fact in itself was so trivial it wasn't worth puzzling over. And Edik had heard Sabaoth Baalovich and Fyodor Simeonovich talking about it at a time when he was still a junior lab assistant and believed in absolutely everything except God.

So we only had the vaguest possible idea of the Januses' past. But we knew the future with absolute certainty. In the distant future A-Janus, who currently spent more time dealing with Institute affairs than with scientific research, would become absolutely fascinated by the idea of practical countermotion and devote his entire life to it. He would acquire a friend, a little green parrot called Photon who would be given to him by famous Russian space pilots. That would happen on May 19 in either 1973 or 2073—that was how Edik had deciphered the mysterious number 190573 on the ring. Probably soon after that A-Janus would finally be successful and transform himself into a countermover, along with the parrot Photon, who at the time of the experiment would naturally be sitting on his shoulder and begging for a lump of sugar. At that precise moment, if we had even the slightest understanding of countermotion, the human future would lose Janus Polyeuctovich Nevstruev, but the past of mankind would acquire two Januses, for A-Janus would be transformed into S-Janus and start slipping backward along the axis of time. They would meet every day, but not once in his life would it even enter A-Janus's head to suspect anything, because he had been used to seeing the kind, wrinkled face of S-Janus, his distant relative and teacher, since he was a baby. And every midnight, at precisely zero hours, zero minutes, zero seconds, and zero tertia by the local time, A-Janus would move, like all of us, from one day's night into the next day's morning, while at the same moment, in an instant equal to a single microquantum of time, S-Janus and his parrot would skip from our present night to our yesterday morning.

That was why parrots numbers 1, 2, and 3, observed respectively on the tenth, eleventh and twelfth days of the month, had been so much alike: they were quite simply one and the same parrot. Poor old Photon! Perhaps he had simply succumbed to old age, or perhaps he'd caught a chill from a draft, but he'd fallen ill and come to die on his favorite balance in Roman's lab. He had died, and his grieving master had given him a ritual cremation and scattered his ashes, and he'd done it because he didn't know how dead countermovers behave. Or perhaps precisely because he did know.

We, of course, had observed this whole process like a film with its sequential parts transposed. On the ninth Roman finds Photon's surviving feather in the furnace. Photon's body no longer exists; he has already been burned tomorrow. The next day, the tenth, Roman finds it in a petri dish. S-Janus discovers the body in the same place at the same time and burns it in the furnace. The surviving feather remains in the furnace until the end of the day and at midnight it skips into the ninth. On the morning of the eleventh Photon is alive, although he is already ill. He dies before our very eyes under the same balance on which he will henceforth love to sit, and simple-minded Sasha puts him in the petri dish, where the dead bird will lie until midnight, when he'll make the transition to the morning of the tenth and be found by S-Janus, cremated, and scattered to the wind, but one of his feathers will survive and lie there until midnight, then skip to the morning of the ninth, where Roman will find it. On the morning of the twelfth Photon is fit and lively, he gives Korneev an interview and asks him for sugar, but at midnight he will skip to the morning of the eleventh, fall ill, die, be placed in the petri dish, at midnight skip to the morning of the tenth, be cremated and scattered, but the feather will be left, and at midnight it will skip to the morning of the ninth, be found by Roman, and be thrown into the wastepaper basket. On the thirteenth, fourteenth, fifteenth, and so on, Photon will delight all of us by being bright and talkative, and we'll pamper him and feed him sugar lumps and peppercorns, and S-Janus will come and ask if he's interfering with our work. By means of associative questioning we will be able to learn many interesting things from him about humanity's expansion into space and no doubt also something about our own personal future.

When we reached this point in our deliberations, Edik suddenly turned gloomy and declared that he didn't like Photon's remarks about his untimely death—to which the absolutely tactless Korneev remarked that the death of any magician is always untimely, but it comes to all of us anyway.

"But maybe," said Roman, "he'll love you more than the rest of us, so your death will be the only one he'll remember." Edik realized he still had a chance of outliving us all, and his mood improved.

However, the talk of death had set our thoughts running on melancholy lines. All of us, except Korneev of course, began feeling sorry for S-Janus. If you thought about it, his situation really was quite terrible. In the first place he was a model example of immense self-sacrifice in the name of science, because he was effectively deprived of any opportunity of benefiting from the fruits of his own ideas. And of course, he had no bright future to look forward to. We were moving toward a world of reason and brotherhood, but with every day that passed he moved further back toward the bloody Nicholas II, serfdom, the cannon fire in Senate Square, and—who could tell?—perhaps even Arakcheev, Biron, and the *oprichnina*.

And one awful day somewhere in the depths of time he would be met on the waxed floor of the Saint Petersburg Academy of Sciences by a colleague in a powdered wig—a colleague who had already been looking at him rather strangely for a week—who would gasp, throw his hands up in the air, and mumble with eyes full of terror, "Herr Nefstrueff! How can it be, ven only yesterday ze *Gazette* definitely wrote zat you had passed avay from a stroke . . ." And he would have to make excuses about a twin brother or false rumors, all the time knowing perfectly well what this conversation meant . . .

"Stop that," said Korneev. "Sloppy sentimentalists. He knows the future, doesn't he? He's already been in places we won't reach for ages and ages. And perhaps he knows exactly when we're all going to die."

"That's completely different," Edik said sadly.

"It's tough on the old man," said Roman. "Let's try to be a bit more gentle and kind with him. Especially you, Vitka. You're always so rude to him."

"Well, why does he have to keep pestering me?" Vitka growled. "What were we talking about, where did we see each other . . ."

"Now you know why he pesters you, so behave yourself."

Vitka scowled and began demonstratively perusing the list of questions.

"We have to explain everything to him in more detail," I said. "Everything that we know. We have to predict his immediate future for him."

"Yes, damn it!" said Roman. "This winter he broke his leg. On the black ice."

"We have to prevent it," I said firmly.

"What?" said Roman. "Do you realize what you're saying? His leg had mended ages before then."

"But he hasn't broken it yet," Edik objected.

We sat there for a few minutes trying to work it all out. Then Vitka suddenly said, "Hang on! What about this, guys? There's still one question we haven't crossed out."

"Which one?"

"What happened to the feather?"

"What happened to it?" said Roman. "It skipped to the eighth. And on the eighth I turned the furnace on and smelled something . . ."

"So what?"

"But I threw it in the wastepaper basket. On the eighth, the seventh, and the sixth I didn't see it . . . Hmm . . . Where did it get to?"

"The cleaning woman threw it out," I suggested.

"It's a very interesting problem though," said Edik. "Let's assume no one burned it. What's it going to look like in ages past?"

"There are even more interesting problems than that," said Vitka. "For instance, what happens to Janus's shoes when he wears them back to the day they were made at the Footman Factory? And what happens to the food he eats for supper? And in general . . ."

But we were already exhausted. We carried on arguing for a while, then Sasha Drozd arrived and shoved us, still arguing, off the sofa, switched on his Spidola, and started trying to borrow two rubles. "Oh, come on," he whined.

"We haven't got it," we told him.

"Come on, you must have a couple left . . . Let me have it!"

We couldn't carry on arguing like that, and we decided to go to lunch.

"In the final analysis," said Edik, "our hypothesis isn't really all that fantastic. Maybe S-Janus's true story is far more amazing."

Maybe it is, we thought, and went to the cafeteria.

I stopped by the computer room for a moment to let them know I was going to lunch. In the corridor I ran into S-Janus, who looked at me closely, smiled, and for some reason asked if we'd seen each other yesterday.

"No, Janus Polyeuctivich," I said. "We didn't see each other yesterday. You weren't in the Institute yesterday. Early yesterday morning you flew to Moscow."

"Ah yes," he said. "I'd forgotten."

He gave me such a kindly smile that I decided to do it. It was rather impertinent, of course, but I knew Janus Polyeuctovich had been well disposed toward me just recently, and that meant there couldn't be any serious kind of incident between us now. I asked in a low voice, looking around cautiously, "Janus Polyeuctovich, would it be all right if I asked you a question?"

He raised his eyebrows and looked at me intently for a while, then, evidently recalling something, he said, "By all means. Just one?"

I realized he was right. There was no way I could fit everything into a single question. Was there going to be a war? Would I turn out all right? Would they find the recipe for universal happiness? Would the last fool ever die?

I said, "May I stop in to see you tomorrow morning?"

He shook his head, and I thought I detected a slight note of mockery in his answer. "No, that's quite impossible. Tomorrow morning, Alexander Ivanovich, you will be summoned to the Kitezhgrad Plant, and I shall have to grant you a temporary reassignment."

I felt stupid. There was something humiliating about this determinism that condemned me, an independent human being with freedom of will, to absolutely fixed actions that no longer depended on me. It had nothing to do with whether I wanted to go to Kitezhgrad or not. The point was that now I couldn't die or fall ill or even turn testy and threaten to resign. I was foredoomed, and for the first time I understood the terrible meaning of that word. I had always known that it was bad to be foredoomed to be executed, for instance, or to go blind. But now it turned out that even to be foredoomed to the love of the most wonderful girl in all the world, or an absolutely fascinating voyage around the world, or a trip to Kitezhgrad (which I'd been wanting to visit for the last three months), could be extremely unpleasant too. I suddenly saw knowledge of the future in an entirely new light . . .

"It's a bad idea to start reading a good book from the end, don't you think?" said Janus Polyeuctovich, scrutinizing me quite openly. "And as far as your questions are concerned, Alexander Ivanovich, well . . . Try to understand, Alexander Ivanovich, that there's not just one single future for everybody. There are many futures, and every action you take creates one or another of them . . . But you'll come to understand that," he said earnestly. "You'll definitely come to understand it."

And later I really did come to understand it.

But, then, that's an entirely different story altogether.

equation has absolutely nothing to do with materialization, and at the moment described Saturn could not possibly have been in the constellation of Libra. (This last blunder is all the more unforgivable since, as I have learned, one of the authors is a professional astronomer.)

The list of inaccuracies and absurdities of this kind could easily have been extended, but I am not doing so here, because the authors have refused point-blank to make any corrections. They have also refused to remove terminology that they do not understand; one declared that the terminology was necessary to convey the ambience and the other said it created local color. In any case, I have been obliged to concur with their idea that the vast majority of readers will hardly be capable of distinguishing correct terminology from the erroneous variety and that no matter which kind of terminology is present, no sensible reader will ever believe it.

The attempt made to achieve the aforementioned artistic truth (according to one of the authors) and to create rounded characters (in the words of the other) has resulted in significant distortion of the images of real people involved in the narrative. The authors are in general inclined to oversimplify their characters, with the result that the only one who is more or less authentic is Vybegallo, and to some extent Cristóbal Joséevich Junta. (I do not include here the episodic image of the vampire Alfred, which has turned out better than any other.) For instance, the authors assert that Korneev is a coarse individual and imagine that the reader is capable of constructing for himself a correct impression of that coarseness. Yes, Korneev is indeed coarse. But for that very reason the Korneev described here appears like a "semitransparent inventor" (in the authors' own terminology) in comparison with the real Korneev. The same applies to the much vaunted politeness of E. Amperian. The R. P. Oira-Oira of these sketches appears entirely bloodless, although during the very period described he was in the process of divorcing his second wife and preparing to marry for the third time. The examples already adduced are probably sufficient to convince the reader not to place too much faith in the way that I myself am depicted in the sketches.

A few words concerning the illustrations. The artwork is extremely accurate and produces a highly convincing impression. (I might even have thought that the artist had some close connection with our sister institution, the National Institute for Cabalistics, Enchantment, Occultism, and Necromancy.) This serves to confirm yet again that even when genuine talent has been misinformed, it will still never completely lose sight of the genuine reality. Yet at the same time it is impossible not to note that the artist has had the misfortune of observing the world through the eyes of the authors, whose competence I have already discussed. However, I hope that the sense of humor typical of the team at NICEONe will restrain any urge they might feel to subject the authors to literary-critical persecution for libel, defamation of character, misinformation, and distortion of fact.

The authors have requested that I explain certain obscure terms and unfamiliar names that occur in the book. I have encountered some difficulty in my efforts to fulfill this request. Naturally, I have no intention of explaining terminology invented by the authors ("aquavitometer," "temporal transmission," and so forth). But I think that even an explanation of terms that are employed correctly will not be of any great benefit, if it requires fundamental, specialized knowledge to be understood. It is impossible, for instance, to explain the term "hyperfield" to a person who has a poor understanding of the theory of physical vacuum. The term "transgression" is even more expansive, and furthermore, different schools of thought employ it with different meanings. In short, I have limited my commentary to certain names, terms, and concepts that are, on the one hand, in sufficiently common usage and, on the other, employed in a specific context in our work. In addition, I have included commentaries on several words that have no direct connection with magic but which, it seems to me, the reader may find perplexing.

Gnome: In Western European traditions, an ugly little creature who protects underground treasure troves. I have spoken with several gnomes, who are genuinely little and ugly but know nothing about any treasure. In fact, most gnomes are long-forgotten and severely desiccated doubles.

Golem: One of the earliest cybernetic robots, made out of clay by Loew ben Bezalel. (See, for instance, the Czechoslovakian comedy film *The Emperor and the Golem,* in which the creature is very similar to the real one.)

Harpies: In ancient Greek mythology, the goddesses of the whirlwind; in reality, a variety of nonlife, a side product of experiments by early magicians in the area of selective breeding. In appearance they resemble large, reddish birds with the heads of old women. Extremely dirty, gluttonous, and quarrelsome.

Homunculus: As conceived by illiterate medieval alchemists, a humanlike being artificially created in a retort. In actual fact it is impossible to create an artificial being in a retort. Homunculi are synthesized in special autoclaves and used for biomechanical modeling.

Hydra: In ancient Greek belief, a fabulous, multiheaded water snake. In our Institute, a real multiheaded reptile, the daughter of Wyrm Gorynych and a female plesiosaur from Loch Ness.

Incubus: A variety of the living dead in the habit of entering into marriage with the living. Does not exist. In theoretical magic the term *incubus* is used with a quite different meaning, as a measure of the negative energy of a living organism.

Ifrit: A variety of genie. As a rule ifrits are well-preserved doubles of the greatest Arabic military leaders. In the Institute they are employed by M. M. Kamnoedov as armed guards, since they are distinguished from other genies by their high level of discipline. The ifrits' fire-throwing mechanism has been little researched and is unlikely to be subject to fundamental study, because it is of no use to anyone.

Incunabulum: A name given to the earliest printed books. Several of the incunabula are distinguished by their truly immense dimensions.

Jan ben Jan: Either an ancient inventor or an ancient warrior. His name is always associated with the concept of a shield and never encountered separately. (Mentioned, for instance, in Flaubert's novel *The Temptation of Saint Anthony.*)

Kitsune: See *shapeshifter.*

Levitation: A method of flying performed entirely without any technical apparatus. A well-known phenomenon practiced by birds, bats, and insects.

Malleus Maleficarum: An ancient handbook
for the conduct of third-degree interrogations.
Compiled and used by churchmen especially
for the identification of witches. In modern
times it has been abrogated as obsolete.

Maxwell's demon: An important element of
a thought experiment by the great English
physicist Maxwell, intended as an attack on the
second law of thermodynamics. In Maxwell's
thought experiment the demon is located
beside an aperture in a partition that divides a

vessel filled with molecules in motion. The demon's job is to let fast
molecules out of one half of the vessel into the other and close the
aperture in the face of slow molecules. In this way the ideal demon
is capable of generating a very high temperature in one half of the
vessel and a very low temperature in the other half, thereby produc-
ing a type-two *perpetuum mobile.* However, only relatively recently,
and only in our Institute, has it proved possible to find such demons
and train them for this job.

Oracle: As conceived by the ancients, a means
used by the gods to communicate with people:
the flight of birds (via augurs), the rustling of
trees, the ravings of a soothsayer, etc. *Oracle*
was also used as a name for a place where
prophecies were pronounced. The "Solovets
Oracle" is a small, dark room in which it has
been planned for many years to install a powerful computer for minor prophecies.

Phantom: A specter or ghost. In contemporary thought, a crystal-
lization of necrobiotic information. Phantoms inspire superstitious
horror, although they are entirely harmless. In the Institute they are

used for establishing precise historical truth, although they are not legally acceptable as witnesses.

Pythia: A priestess and prophetess in ancient Greece who prophesied after breathing in poisonous fumes. We have no Pythias practicing in the Institute, but many people smoke tobacco and study the general theory of prognostication.

Ramapithecus: In contemporary thought, the immediate predecessor of *Pithecanthropus* on the evolutionary ladder.

Shapeshifter: A person who can turn into one of various animals, e.g., into a wolf (werewolf), into a fox (kitsune), etc. Causes terror in superstitious individuals, but it is not clear why. For instance, when Korneev's wisdom tooth started causing him pain, he turned into a cock, and immediately felt better.

Star of Solomon: In international literature, a magic sign in the form of a six-pointed star possessing magical properties. At the present time, like the great majority of other geometrical spells, it has lost its power and is only good for frightening the ignorant.

Taxidermist: A maker of stuffed animals. This term is not in common usage in Russian, but I recommended it to the authors, because C. J. Junta flies into a fury when he is referred to as a mere animal stuffer.

Tertia: One-sixtieth of a second.

Upanishads: An ancient Indian commentary on four holy books.

Upyr: See *vampire*.

Vampire: A bloodsucking corpse in folktales. Does not exist. In reality vampires (also known as upyrs) are magicians who for some reason or other have chosen the path of abstract evil. From ancient times the means used to combat them have been a poplar-wood stake and bullets cast from native silver. In the text the word *vampire* is always used in the figurative sense.

Werewolf: See *shapeshifter*.

A. PRIVALOV

Afterword

by Boris Strugatsky

We came up with the idea of a story about wizards, witches, sorcerers, and magicians a long time ago, at the end of the 1950s. To begin with we had no idea of what might happen in it; all we knew was that the heroes would be characters from the fairy tales, legends, myths, and ghost stories of all cultures and times. And that their adventures would take place against the backdrop of a research institute with all its foibles, well known to one of us from his own personal experience, and to the other from the many stories recounted to him by his academic friends. We spent a long time gathering together jokes and nicknames and amusing characteristics for our future characters, and wrote them all down on separate scraps of paper (which, as always happens, were later lost). But no real advance took place; we were never able to think of a story or a plot for the adventure.

For all practical purposes, everything started on a rainy evening at the Kislovodsk high-altitude station, where two colleagues on loan from the Pulkovo Observatory were cordially dying of boredom: junior researcher B. N. Strugatsky and senior engineer Lidia Kamionko.

Outside, it was October 1960. I had just finished my task of finding a site for the Large Altazimuth Telescope in the damp and grassy slopes of the northern Caucasus and was waiting for the infinitely varied formalities involved in the transfer of the expedition's property, the write-off of unused surpluses, the completion of accounts forms, and other tedious activities to be completed. And L. Kamionko, who had come to the high-altitude station to make the final adjustments to some new item of equipment, was despairingly idle because of the emphatic absence of any weather that would allow her to make astronomical observations. And so, out of sheer boredom, we started to write a little story that evening, a tale with no beginning or end, with the same rain in it, the same dim bulb without a shade hanging from the ceiling by a cord, the same damp veranda filled with old furniture and boxes of equipment, the same melancholy boredom, but which was also a story in which the most ridiculous and entirely impossible things took place: strange, clumsy figures appeared out of thin air, making magical gestures, delivering absurd and ridiculous speeches, and the whole four-page surrealist abracadabra finished with the striking words "THE SOFA HAD DISAPPEARED!!!"

I went home via Moscow and stayed with my brother (and coauthor), and there, with his family, we read this sketch out loud, provoking friendly laughter and general approval. And everything stopped there; it never occurred to us that the mysteriously disappearing sofa was a magical sofa-translator, or that the strange people described in the story were wizards chasing said translator. Everything happened as it was supposed to: several years of reflection and adaptation lay ahead of us.

It may seem strange, but the story of how *Monday Starts on Saturday* came to be written has completely disappeared from my memory. It has vanished to such an extent that now, when I look back over the scattered lines of letters and diaries, I catch myself losing the thread of the conversation.

03/19/61—AS Letter: . . . You seem to have gone to the seventh heaven in vain . . . [Oddity number one. *Seventh Heaven* is one of the earliest possible titles we gave to *Monday Starts on Saturday*. But had I really "gone there" so soon, by March 1961? That seems to me entirely impossible.]

07/23/61—AS Letter: . . . What if we tried getting . . . *Wizards* finished? If it's no more than 4 printer's pages long, that would be great.*

08/04/61—AS Letter: Re: wizards. I don't know. It should be something short and cheerful. At most three printer's pages. Three parts. The first one's already written . . . [Oddities two and three. What does he mean, "getting *Wizards* finished"! Does this mean that there's already something done that we only need to "finish"? And what does he mean, "The first one's already written"? As far as I recall, we had nothing of the kind nearing completion, nor even drafted . . . Odd, it's very odd . . .]

Second part. The hero is sure that the wizards will leave him in peace now. But all day long, wherever he goes, the wizards follow him à la secretary Prysh. They lean mournfully out of walls and manholes, make incomprehensible gestures in his direction, annoy him when he meets his girlfriend, and sadly fly away when he starts to get angry. Their dullness and ignorance start to worry him. A wizard is easy to distinguish from other people: you just need to ask him to recite the seven times table. Wizards from all corners of the universe gather on Earth. They need the White Thesis, which has been lost since time immemorial: it was hidden in a tree, which was then taken to a workshop and turned into the sofa, which fell into our hero's hands . . .

And so on. Who is Prysh? What happens next? One thing is clear: whether we had something or nothing written by then, the

---

* Translator's Note: A printer's page would have constituted approximately forty thousand characters. The Strugatskys are envisioning a story about thirty-five to forty letter-size pages long.

enjoyment and rapture; no one is discussed so much and so passionately; no one's books are sought out with such fervor by every single
member of the reading public, from the high school student to the
college professor. And so once, while I was sitting in my office at the
Pulkovo Observatory, a call came through from the city from my old
friend Natasha Sventsintskaya, a woman who knew a great deal about,
and read a great deal of, Hemingway (at least she did in those days).
"Borya," she said with restrained excitement. "At Dom Knigi they've
just brought in a new book by Hem, called *Monday Starts on Saturday.*"
My heart leaped and then sweetly repined. It was such a perfect, such
an authentic Hemingway title: sad yet restrained, cruelly hopeless, cold,
and oh so human all at the same time . . . Monday starts on Saturday:
that means there is no rest in our life, our working days follow on one
from another without break, what is gray will remain gray, what is
dull will be forever dull . . . I did not hesitate for a second: "Buy it!" I
snapped. "Take as many as they've got. At any price!" Angelic laughter
down the phone line was the only reply.

It was a successful prank she played on me. And not in vain,
as so often happens with jokes. I immediately squirreled away this
wonderful invention, sure that it would be a perfect title for a future
novel about a love affair both wondrous and hopeless. That novel
was never written, nor was it ever even considered as it should
have been, but the squirreled-away title lived its own life in my
notebooks, waited for its opportunity, and when it came, a couple of
years later, took it. True, Arkady and I gave it a completely different,
one might almost say contradictory, profoundly optimistic meaning,
but we never regretted it for an instant. Natasha did not complain
either. In fact, I think she was even rather flattered.

And so historical justice demands that two wonderful women,
former colleagues at the Pulkovo Observatory, be given due recogni-
tion for their position at the sources of what is evidently the most
popular of Arkady and my stories. Stand forward, my dears: Lidia
Alexandrovna Kamionko, the coauthor of the famous, plot-creating
phrase "THE SOFA HAD DISAPPEARED," and Natalia Alexandrovna Sventsintskaya, the person who thought up that infinitely

sad, or perhaps joyfully optimistic, aphorism "Monday starts on Saturday"!

Overall, *Monday Starts on Saturday* is to a great extent a comic revue, the result of cheerful collective work.

DO WE REALLY NEED OURSELVES FOR ANYTHING? was a poster that actually did hang in one of the laboratories of, I think, the State Optical Institute.

"Down the road there comes a ZIM, and that'll be the end of him" is an inspired verse made up by my old friend Yuri Chistakov, a great expert in composing verses in the style of Captain Lebyadkin.

"A summer dacha is my aspiration. / But where to build? Although I try and try . . ." is a poem from the newspaper *For a New Pulkovo*.

And so on, and so forth . . .

To conclude, I cannot keep from mentioning that the censor did not assault this new story too much. It was a funny tale, and the cavils were funny as well. So the censor categorically demanded the excision of any mention of the Zavod imeni Molotova, or Molotov Auto Factory, from the text. ("Down the road there comes a ZIM, and that'll be the end of him.") The thing is, at this time Molotov was a marked man, condemned and excluded from the Party, and the auto factory that bore his name was rapidly transformed into the GAZ (Gorkovsky Avtomobilny Zavod, or Gorky Auto Factory), just as the ZIS (Zavod imeni Stalina, the Stalin Factory) had already been renamed as the ZIL (Zavod imeni Likhacheva, the Likhachev Factory). Laughing loudly, the two authors suggested that the poem should read, "Down the road there comes a ZIL, / And that'll be the end of him." And what do you think happened? To their great surprise, Glavlit* eagerly agreed to this ridiculous nonsense. And in this crude form the poem was printed and reprinted several times.

But there were lots of things we were unable to save. "The minister of state security, Malyuta Skuratov," for example. Or the

---

* TRANSLATOR'S NOTE: Glavlit is Glavnoe Upravlenie po Delam Literatury i Izdatelstv, the Central Directorate for Literary and Publishing Matters.

line from Merlin's story: "In the midst of the lake Arthur was ware of a hand hardened by toil . . ." And several other little trifles, which someone thought were harmful . . .

Everything (or almost everything) that was lost at that time is happily recovered in this present edition, thanks once again to the friendly and self-sacrificing efforts of the *ludens** who have gone through a heap of all kinds of earlier editions and drafts. Sveta Bondarenko, Volodya Borisov, Vadim Kazakov, Viktor Kurilsky, and Yuri Fleishman: thanks to you all!

---

* TRANSLATOR'S NOTE: The *ludens* are a humanoid race with superior mental powers that appear in the stories set in the Strugatskys' Noon Universe.